Claire pushed ⋯⋯ f
her mind, alo⋯

'I have a piece of advice,' said Ewan, 'that should help yer game.'

Something in his tone warned Claire it was likely to be an impudent suggestion. 'Indeed?' she rallied. 'And what might that be?'

'Don't wear a corset.' Suppressed laughter bubbled beneath his audacious suggestion. 'It makes it too hard for ye to bend over the table to make yer shot.'

He rattled on. 'It's only me to see ye, anyway, and I think ye've got a fine figure without squeezing it all out of shape. Ye're not wearing a corset now, are ye?'

'Ewan!' A furious blush tingled in Claire's cheeks. 'That is *not* a proper question for a gentleman to ask a lady!'

'Aye, well, I'm no gentleman, am I?'

In the process of tracing her Canadian family to their origins in eighteenth-century Britain, **Deborah Hale** learned a great deal about the period and uncovered plenty of true-life inspiration for her historical romance novels! Deborah lives with her very own hero and their four fast-growing children in Nova Scotia—a province steeped in history and romance!

Deborah invites you to become better acquainted with her by visiting her personal website, www.deborahhale.com, or chatting with her in the Harlequin/Mills & Boon online communities.

Novels by the same author:

A GENTLEMAN OF SUBSTANCE
THE WEDDING WAGER
MY LORD PROTECTOR
CARPETBAGGER'S WIFE
THE ELUSIVE BRIDE
BORDER BRIDE
LADY LYTE'S LITTLE SECRET
THE BRIDE SHIP
A WINTER NIGHT'S TALE
  (part of *A Regency Christmas*)
MARRIED: THE VIRGIN WIDOW*
BOUGHT: THE PENNILESS LADY*
WANTED: MAIL-ORDER MISTRESS*
HIS COMPROMISED COUNTESS

Gentlemen of Fortune

Did you know that some of these novels are also available as eBooks? Visit www.millsandboon.co.uk

HIGHLAND ROGUE

Deborah Hale

First published in Great Britain 2013
by Mills & Boon, an imprint of Harlequin (UK) Limited.
Paperback edition 2013
Harlequin (UK) Limited, Eton House, 18-24 Paradise Road,
Richmond, Surrey TW9 1SR

© Deborah M. Hale 2004

ISBN: 978 0 263 90661 5

Printed and bound in Spain
by Blackprint CPI, Barcelona

This book is lovingly dedicated to old friends and new.

To Diane Beaumont,
the person who taught me more about writing
than anyone...and more about generosity, too.
And to the Ladies of the Library: Shannon, Kari,
Laura Lee, Michelle, Anna, Alli, Doreen, Biddy, Christi,
Marcy, Kate, Karen, Susan, Linda, Tina, Angela and all
the gang. Thanks for giving me a special spot to hang my
bonnet in the eHarlequin community. I can't wait to see
Irving's Bookcase overflowing with all your titles!

Chapter One

London, 1875

"My stepmother? Oh, bother!" Claire Brancaster Talbot glanced up from her desk, where she sat reviewing some correspondence from the Admiralty.

To the best of her recollection, Lady Lydiard had never before set foot over the threshold of Brancasters' business office on the Strand. "Did she say what she wants to see me about, Catchpole?"

The sudden advent of Lady Lydiard appeared to have flustered the hitherto imperturbable Mr. Catchpole. Claire had long suspected her fussy, middle-aged secretary of entertaining a secret reverence for persons of title.

"Her ladyship did not vouch that information, miss." Catchpole removed his pince-nez, then immediately replaced it. "Should I have made so bold as to inquire?"

"I would scarcely call it *bold* to ask a caller's business." Claire stifled a sigh as she laid aside her paperwork. "However, I doubt her ladyship will keep me in suspense about what she wants. Show her in."

Rising from her seat, Claire smoothed down the skirt of her checked silk frock, hoping her stepmother would not fuss about the paucity of her crinolines or the complete absence of a corset. Not that Claire's angular figure truly required the latter to achieve a slender waist. Corsets did help create the illusion of bosoms, but she could happily do without those in the business world.

The door to her office opened and Lady Lydiard cruised in under full sail, her middle-aged waist cinched so tightly Claire marveled the woman could breathe, let alone sit or eat.

Mr. Catchpole trailed behind her ladyship with an unctuous smirk on his face that made Claire want to shake some sense into him. "Lady Lydiard to see you, Miss Brancaster Talbot. Shall I bring tea for you ladies?"

"One name will do, thank you, Catchpole," said Claire.

Adopting the name of her mother's family when she'd taken over Brancasters had been an edict of her grandfather's will. Though she signed both names on business correspondence, she found the pair too cumbersome for social use.

"And don't bother about tea," she added, without consulting her stepmother. "I doubt this is a social call."

Whatever the purpose of Lady Lydiard's visit, Claire had no wish to prolong it.

"Very good, miss." Catchpole made a deep bow and backed out of the office.

His obsequious withdrawal was lost on Lady Lydiard, who swept a glance around Claire's spartan but spacious office, her nose wrinkled slightly as though she could detect the unpleasant odor of *trade*. "So this is where you spend all your time?"

"Not all of it." Claire turned to look out her office window, onto the bustle of London's commercial district. "Just enough to keep your shares from losing their value, and to grow the fortune your grandchildren will inherit one day."

Lady Lydiard gave a choked little gasp that made Claire repent her veiled threat. For the sake of her dear half sister, she had resolved to improve the cool relations with her stepmother, at least until after Tessa's wedding.

When she turned back to offer some sort of apology, she found Lady Lydiard with a handkerchief pressed to her quivering lower lip. Claire's heart sank even as her exasperation rose. It was not fair that a woman she'd never cared pins about could provoke her emotions to such an unpleasant degree.

"Th-that's what I came to see you about!" Her ladyship promptly burst into tears, much to Claire's chagrin and impatience.

She had a wholesome horror of the tearful outbursts to which Lady Lydiard was prone.

"Why don't you...have a seat?" Claire struggled to think what she'd said that could be the reason for her stepmother's call...or her sudden fit of weeping.

Money trouble? It couldn't be. Whatever her differences with the woman, Claire had to admit Lady Lydiard lived comfortably within her generous allowance.

"Shall I summon Mr. Catchpole back and tell him we'll take tea, after all?" she asked, with a hint of desperation in her voice.

She found the ritual of tea drinking often provided a distraction in awkward social situations. This one certainly qualified.

"No tea." Lady Lydiard made a visible effort to collect herself as she settled onto the chair in front of Claire's desk. "I don't wish to keep you long from...whatever it is you do."

Claire bit back a sharp retort. The work she did for Brancasters Marine Works was at least as important as whatever most women of her class undertook to occupy their time.

"I need your help!" The words burst out of Lady Lydiard like a guilty confession. "It's Tessa. She's having second thoughts about marrying Spencer!"

Was *that* all? Claire gave a chuckle of relief as she resumed her seat behind the desk.

"Tessa is having *twenty-second* thoughts about marrying poor Spencer. It's apt to get worse as their wedding day approaches, I warn you. But she will go through with it, all the same. He's just the steady sort of fellow she needs, bless him. Beneath all her qualms, Tessa knows it, too, I suspect."

It didn't hurt matters a whit, in Claire's opinion, that the match made marvelous business sense, as well. Spencer Stanton's family owned a large shipping company that was one of Brancasters' best customers. Besides, Tessa had long passed her debutante days. Her "free-spirited" ways had frightened off less steadfast suitors years ago.

"This is different!" Lady Lydiard insisted. "There's another man she's taken a violent fancy to. From…*America*." She spoke the word as if it were some sort of profanity. "Gillis is his name…or is it Getty? No matter. I feel certain he's a fortune hunter of some kind."

The tension that had begun to ease out of Claire's body now made her muscles clench tighter than ever.

She would never forget her father's words to her one painful night, ten years ago. *My dear, you are too wealthy, too clever and too plain for any man to wed, except for your fortune.*

She hadn't wanted to believe him. What girl her age would? The suitors who'd pursued her over the years had convinced her that her father's harsh assessment was correct.

So she'd packed away her few, modest romantic illusions, along with the wistful yearning for a family. Over the years, she had given Brancasters all the time and devoted attention she might have lavished on a husband and children. In turn, the company had rewarded her dedication with growth and prosperity.

Damned if she would let it fall prey to that most loathsome of creatures—a fortune hunter! Especially one trying to sneak in the back door using her half sister.

"I'll talk to Tessa." Claire spoke in a tone of grave finality, as if her intervention was bound to settle everything.

This would not be the first time she'd provided the voice of calm reason to counter her sister's capricious impulses. Tessa was always grateful afterward. Sometimes she seemed strangely anxious for Claire to bring her back to earth, even while she was in the grip of some dizzying new enthusiasm.

"I *have* talked to her." Lady Lydiard wrung

her handkerchief. "It's no use. She won't listen. She's smitten with this creature, I tell you. Thank heaven Spencer is out of town on business. He's been terribly patient with her all these years, but I fear this might be the last straw."

Claire wasn't so sure. Tessa's fancies never lasted long. The hotter the flame, the more quickly it tended to burn itself out. Still, with so much at stake for Brancasters, she could not afford to take any chances.

Resting her forefinger against her lower lip for a moment, Claire pondered the most effective course of action.

"I should like to meet this man for myself," she said at last. "In the meantime I'll make some inquiries about him, and we can proceed from there."

Lady Lydiard gave a final sniff, but otherwise seemed to brighten considerably. "Thank you, Claire. You've always been such a sensible, detached sort of person. Almost as good as talking to a man, really."

"Thank you..." murmured Claire. "...I suppose."

"Lord and Lady Fortescue are hosting a ball this evening," Lady Lydiard said. "I feel certain *he* will be there. The scoundrel's gotten himself invited to every social event Tessa has attended for the past fortnight. And what with Sylvia Fortescue being an American..."

Claire nodded. Marriages of indebted British noblemen to American heiresses had become something of an epidemic of late.

She thought for a moment. "I do believe I received an invitation from Lady Fortescue. Since I didn't send my regrets, I suppose I am at liberty to attend if I wish, with a suitable escort."

"You *never* bother to send your regrets." Lady Lydiard clucked her tongue over such social negligence. "Then you fail to arrive, putting out the table of any hostess foolish enough to expect you. And what manner of *suitable escort* are you planning to bring?"

"A private agent, if you must know. I've used him before, to procure information. He's proven himself extremely discreet and reliable. I'd like him to get a close look at this new admirer of Tessa's."

Claire pulled open the top drawer of her desk and swept the Admiralty papers into it. There would be no more time for regular business today, if she was to contact Mr. Hutt and secure his services, then get herself suitably gowned and groomed for the Fortescues' ball.

There was no help for it, though. Thwarting the aims of this fortune hunter might prove as vital to the continued prosperity of Brancasters as any navy contract. Besides, Claire felt a duty to protect Tessa from her own foolishness.

* * *

Dancing had already begun by the time Claire and her escort arrived at the Fortescues' Grosvenor Square town house that evening.

"Miss Talbot, what a pleasant surprise." Lady Fortescue did not look or sound pleased. "Lady Lydiard sent word that you might be able to come tonight, after all."

"That was good of her." Claire returned her hostess's brittle, insincere smile with one of her own. "May I present my escort? Mr. Obadiah Hutt, a business associate of mine."

Lady Fortescue gave a cool but gracious welcome to Mr. Hutt, who looked surprisingly distinguished in evening clothes. Claire wondered if their hostess would have been quite as hospitable if she'd known the precise nature of their *association*.

Once they were out of earshot of Lady Fortescue, Mr. Hutt leaned toward Claire and murmured, "I'll just go have a look 'round, and a listen, if that suits you, miss?"

"By all means." Claire swept a quick glance around the ballroom, but saw no sign of Tessa or Lady Lydiard. "I always approve of people getting on with the job they're being paid to do."

Her agent cast a professional eye over the other guests. "If this fellow's been showing up frequently in society the past week or two, someone's bound to know something about him."

The more information Mr. Hutt could uncover, the better, even if it was not especially incriminating, thought Claire as he slipped away to begin his work. Tessa was apt to be attracted by a mystery.

"Why, Miss Talbot!" A familiar, velvety masculine voice rang out behind her. "Is that truly you, or have I had too much to drink already?"

She turned to find Major Maxwell Hamilton-Smythe watching her. As always, he looked impeccably tailored in his dress uniform. And as always, he had a glass in his hand and a roguish gleam in his eye.

In spite of herself, Claire returned his smile. "Nobody who knows you would discount the latter possibility, my dear Max."

The man was a snake. Claire had decided that long ago, when he'd pursued her so relentlessly. But he was the most handsome snake she'd ever set eyes on. There had been a time, when she was younger and not yet reconciled to a lifetime of spinsterhood, when Max Hamilton-Smythe had made her question whether buying a husband would be so terrible, provided she knew that's what she was doing, and she got good value for her money.

"As a matter of fact," she added with mock gravity, "I am a look-alike Miss Talbot has employed to stand in for her at dreary social gatherings she cannot otherwise avoid."

The wry jest had barely left Claire's lips when all thought of levity abruptly deserted her. What if Max was Tessa's fortune hunter?

With a giddy surge of relief, she remembered that Tessa's suitor was an American. Besides, Max had recently married some poor creature whose fortune exceeded both her beauty and her good sense.

Max bolted the last of his drink, then handed the empty glass to a passing footman. "Well, whoever you are, will you do me the honor of a dance?" He offered Claire his arm. "For old times' sake?"

"I'm not certain old times merit it." She took his arm just the same, and let him lead her to the dance floor. "Besides, shouldn't you be squiring your wife this evening?"

"She's not here." Max gave a cheerful shrug, as though her absence did not trouble him vastly. "Indisposed, the poor darling."

As Max whirled her around the ballroom, Claire tried to decide whether she pitied Mrs. Hamilton-Smythe her husband's callous neglect more than she envied the woman for being with child.

After two waltzes and a further exchange of good-natured barbs, Claire took her leave of the major, more convinced than ever that she'd been wise to keep out of his attractive clutches.

"It's been amusing to see you again, Max. But

I mustn't keep you from your mission to deplete Lord and Lady Fortescue's wine cellar. Do tell your wife I hope she's feeling better soon."

"About my wife…" Max maneuvred Claire into a corner near the musicians' dias and lowered his voice. "Just because I'm married now doesn't mean you and I couldn't—"

"It most certainly does, Max, you reptile."

He gazed at her as if the word were some kind of endearment, and added in a coaxing murmur, "Barbara and I have an understanding."

"Ah." Claire fought the urge to slap his face. "Then perhaps you and I should have one, as well."

Max's sea-green eyes glittered with lust…or perhaps it was avarice. Claire had never succeeded in telling the two apart.

"I understand that you are as monstrous a cad as ever." By the tone of her voice, anyone overhearing them might have thought she was paying him a compliment. "And you understand that I would not dally with you if you were the last man on earth. *Now,* do we understand one another?"

If she'd hoped to goad the major into losing his temper, Claire would have been disappointed.

Instead, he clucked his tongue at her while looking intolerably smug. "I promise, you don't know what you're missing. If you ever change your mind, you know where to find me."

On the underside of a rock!

Claire turned away from Max, intending to toss the insult over her shoulder.

Instead, she found her slippers glued to the floor as she watched Tessa waltz past in the arms of a man.

Tessa's partner was not quite as tall as the major, and most women might have deemed him not half so handsome. But Claire could not take her eyes off him, for he danced the way he walked, with a jaunty, athletic grace that made people turn and stare whenever he passed.

His hair, a rich dark brown, clung to his head in crisp, close-cropped locks. He had a high-bridged, aquiline nose and a wide, bowed mouth that managed to suggest both good humor and unswerving determination. Alert, roving gray eyes nestled beneath forceful dark brows. For the moment, they fastened on Tessa with an intensity that took Claire's breath away.

"Miss Talbot?"

"Go away, Max!" she snapped. "I don't want you for a lover any more than I wanted you for a husband."

"Begging your pardon, Miss Talbot, it's only me—Hutt."

A searing blush suffused Claire's face as she turned toward the agent. For an instant, she forgot about Tessa and her partner. "I'm sorry, Mr. Hutt! I thought you were…someone else."

"No harm done, miss." Not even the faintest suggestion of a smirk twitched at the corner of the agent's thin lips.

Once again, Claire congratulated herself on having secured his services.

"My inquiries have yielded some information about the gentleman, Miss Talbot." Though he'd succeeded in hiding his amusement over her gaffe, Mr. Hutt could not conceal his satisfaction over his own quick work. "I thought you'd want to know straightaway."

Tessa's fortune hunter!

Claire spun around again, her gaze combing the room in search of him.

Behind her, Obadiah Hutt began to rattle off his report in an eager voice. "I have discovered the gentleman's name, miss. And I've discovered he is *not* an American, as Lady Lydiard supposed."

Not an American. No.

From across the ballroom his voice drifted, mellow and musical, with the distinctive lilting burr of the Highland glens. Claire steeled herself to resist its enchantment, but failed.

When Mr. Hutt began to speak again, she held up her hand for silence.

"But, miss, don't you want to hear the gentleman's name?"

Across the ballroom, Ewan Geddes glanced

up and caught her watching him. For an instant, puzzlement knit his full dark brows together.

Then it cleared.

His bow mouth stretched into a wide, devilish grin, and he winked at her.

"I *know* his name, Mr. Hutt." The hand Claire had held aloft balled into a tight fist, as did the one by her side. "Furthermore, I know he is no gentleman."

Chapter Two

A good job he was at a ball with an orchestra playing, Ewan Geddes thought. It gave him an excuse for dancing around the room without looking like a daft fool!

For ten years he'd worked and struggled to get where he was now—with Miss Tessa Talbot in his arms and no man having the power to take her away from him. Surely Fate had wanted them together, no matter how unlikely a match they once might have seemed. Considering how far he'd risen in the world, Ewan knew nothing was impossible for a man who had faith in himself, and the boldness to act decisively when an opportunity arose.

The music stopped, but he continued to twirl Tessa around the floor, narrowly avoiding several other couples who had paused to wait for the orchestra to begin again.

"Ewan!" Tessa squealed. "What are you doing? We can't dance without music!"

"Ah, but there's music in my heart, lass." As he gazed down into her enormous turquoise eyes, the years fell away and he was eighteen again—an ardent lad in love for the first and only time. "Can ye not hear it? It's been playing a wild, sweet melody ever since I laid eyes on ye again."

Tessa lowered her gaze demurely, catching her full lower lip between her teeth.

That look made Ewan ache to kiss her, but he would not do it until she had promised to be his wife. And she could not make that promise until she'd withdrawn from her present betrothal.

She glanced back up at him suddenly, her eyes brimming with a reflection of his own giddy delight. "Ever since I saw you again, I've found myself humming a little tune day and night."

"Ye hum in yer sleep?" Ewan teased, holding her closer and slowing their music-less waltz until it was little more than an excuse to embrace in public.

"Of course not, silly!" Her laughter set the cluster of golden ringlets piled high on her head into a quivering dance of their own. "But the melody runs through my dreams."

"I know what ye mean." Ewan caressed her

face with his gaze. "The sound of yer voice
and yer laugh have run through my dreams for
years."

And the way she'd felt in his arms that last
night.

Fortunately for Ewan, the dance music began
again—a lush Strauss waltz that perfectly expressed the buoyant, heady feelings within him.
Otherwise, he might have broken his promise to
himself and caused a twittering scandal among
London society, by kissing another man's fiancée in the middle of the Fortescues' ballroom.

Tessa gave a breathless sigh. "It's so romantic
that you thought of me all those years you were
off in America, working so hard to make something of yourself."

It hadn't seemed very romantic when he'd
first arrived in Pennsylvania, a lad of eighteen,
raw from the Highlands, without a penny in his
pocket. But he'd had a fire in his belly, stoked
by injustice and true love denied. That fire had
fueled his rapid rise in the world.

"It was all for ye, Tessa Talbot. To make myself worthy of yer notice and yer company."

Well, almost all, Ewan insisted to his both-
ersome conscience. True, in those early years
he'd been at least as eager to take some revenge
against her father, who had sacked him without a
character reference. In time, however, he'd come
to enjoy the challenge of making his fortune for

its own sake. Once he'd had the resources to carry out his original plan, he'd assumed Tessa must have been long since married to someone else.

Then a copy of the *London Times* had fallen into his hands. Ewan vowed to have that blessed paper gilded and mounted. For it had informed him that the Honorable Miss Tessa Talbot, daughter of Lady Lydiard and her late husband, was engaged to be married.

Only engaged!

All his old fallow feelings for her had burst back into bloom, and Ewan had booked passage on the fastest steamer that would get him across the Atlantic.

"Worthy? What nonsense!" Tessa gave him a token slap with the hand that rested on his shoulder. "You know I've always thought more of *real* people who work for a living than I ever have of useless aristocrats."

Her fervent declaration should have pleased him no end, but for reasons that eluded Ewan, it made him strangely uneasy. He told himself not to be so foolish. He had everything he'd ever wanted within his grasp. Nothing and no one would stop him now. Least of all some vague foreboding he could not even put into words.

It was like the feeling he used to get when stalking game in the hills above Strathandrew. When he'd slowly turn, to discover a pair of wild, wary eyes fixed on him. Try as he might, Ewan could not shake it.

When the final notes of the waltz died away, he bowed to Tessa. "Shall we get something to drink, then find a quiet spot where we can sit and talk?"

While he waited for her answer, his gaze roved over the Fortescues' ballroom.

There! Near the orchestra dais. A tall, elegant-looking woman was watching him.

The color of her hair, her willowy grace of figure and her long, delicate features all put him in mind of a doe. But the relentless intensity of her gaze better suited a wildcat defending her young.

Did he know the woman? Ewan reckoned he might. But from where?

Then it came to him.

The elder Miss Talbot. What was her name? Catherine? Charlotte?

Whatever she called herself, no wonder she was looking daggers at him. The lady had always twitted and found fault with him during the summers when Lord Lydiard had brought his family north to their Scottish hunting estate.

She'd especially disapproved of his obvious fancy for her half sister. Ewan wondered if she might have been the one who'd tattled to old Lord Lydiard about his midnight meeting with

Tessa, on the Talbots' last night in Scotland, ten years ago.

Well, she'd get her comeuppance when he made Tessa his bride!

Long ago, Ewan had discovered that nothing vexed the elder Miss Talbot so much as when he pretended her slights had no power to vex *him*. Now, he shot her a wide grin of friendly recognition, with the faintest suggestion of mockery twinkling in his eyes. He knew it was bound to send her into a sputter of indignation. After all these years, he still relished the prospect of getting a rise out of her.

Miss Talbot crossed the ballroom floor with a brisk, purposeful stride. A man followed her.

"Claire!" Tessa cried when she spotted her sister. "What are you doing here? You never go out in the evenings."

The two women clasped hands and touched cheeks with unfeigned affection.

Ewan had often wondered at their closeness. They were only half sisters, after all, and as opposite in temperament as any two women could be. Each had ample cause to envy the other, too. Tessa, her elder sister's fortune and consequence in the family. Claire, her younger sister's beauty and charm.

Claire Talbot smoothed a stray curl off Tessa's forehead in a gesture that looked almost motherly. "I gather it's high time I ventured out in society more often. To keep an eye on what you've been getting up to while poor Spencer is away. After all, we wouldn't want any silly gossip to spoil your wedding plans, would we?"

Though she spoke to Tessa, Ewan could tell Miss Talbot's warning was aimed at him. Did she think him too stupid to know about her sister's betrothal?

Claire's mild rebuke appeared to fluster Tessa, which Ewan added to his growing list of grudges against the woman.

"We'll talk about all that another time, Claire." Tessa glanced at Ewan and immediately recovered her usual sparkle. "You'll never guess who's come to London after all these years!"

"My powers of deduction are better than you may imagine, dearest." Claire turned to Ewan and thrust out her hand. "Mr. Geddes, isn't it?"

Ignoring her intention to shake his hand, Ewan caught her long slender fingers in his and raised them to his lips instead. "I'm flattered ye remember me, Miss Talbot."

As he'd hoped, the gesture and the pretended warmth of his greeting succeeded in provoking her.

She pulled her hand away with the barest pretense of civility. "Pray, don't flatter yourself too much, sir. I take care to remember a good many people. Not always for the most pleasant of reasons."

Tessa must have sensed the tension between them, for her voice rang with forced brightness as she asked her sister, "Who is your escort tonight? I don't believe we've been introduced."

For a moment, Claire Talbot gave her sister a blank stare, then she turned to the man behind her. "Oh! Pardon my manners. This is Mr. Obadiah Hutt, a business associate of mine. Mr. Hutt, allow me to introduce my sister, Tessa, and Mr. Ewan Geddes...an old friend of the family."

Ewan bridled. Did she think he was ashamed of who he'd been or where he'd come from? Was her introduction a veiled threat to expose his past?

And who was this Hutt fellow, anyway? He lacked the languid ease of a gentleman, and he shook Ewan's hand with a firm grip, meeting his eye with a direct gaze...almost too direct.

"What Miss Talbot means, sir—" Ewan tried to stare her down, but she did not flinch "—is that I used to be a gillie on her father's estate in Scotland."

When a look of puzzlement wrinkled the other man's brow, Ewan explained, "A gillie's a sort of guide for hunting and fishing. Totes gear, loads guns, dresses the kill. That sort of thing."

Tessa clasped his arm in a show of support that touched Ewan. "He was perfectly marvelous at it, too! Why, I can still picture him striding off to the hills in his kilt, with a gun slung over his shoulder. Like a hero of Sir Walter Scott's, I always used to think."

Miss Talbot's business associate nodded at the explanation. "And what brings you down from Scotland, Mr. Geddes?"

"I didn't come from Scotland, sir." Hard as he tried to sound matter-of-fact, Ewan couldn't manage it. "I left my home ten years ago, and I've never been back since."

Thanks to Lord Lydiard. With a little help, perhaps, from the woman who now stood before Ewan, eyeing him with barely disguised hostility.

His old plans for revenge tempted Ewan sorely. Perhaps he should make a few discreet inquiries about Brancasters, after all.

I left my home ten years ago.

Ewan Geddes's words, and the glint of outrage beneath his facade of casual charm, made Claire's stomach constrict and her breath catch, as if strong hands had suddenly pulled the stays of her corset even tighter.

She'd come tonight expecting to do battle with a simple fortune hunter, like Major Hamilton-Smythe. Instead, she'd found an old adversary who might have far darker motives and a far greater capacity for mischief. One who might wish to harm the only two things in the world she cared about—her sister and Brancasters.

As the orchestra struck up a new tune, Claire turned to Obadiah Hutt. Behind the cover of her gloved hand, she whispered, "Ask her to dance."

When he seemed not to hear, or perhaps not to understand, she hissed, "My sister! Invite her to dance."

"Miss Tessa?" Mr. Hutt extended his arm, as Claire had bidden him. "May I have the honor?"

When Tessa cast a doubtful glance at Ewan Geddes, Claire urged, "Go ahead, dearest. There's apt to be less talk if you're seen dancing with a number of different gentlemen while Spencer is out of town."

"Very well, then." Tessa shot her sister a look as she took to the floor with Mr. Hutt— half warning, half pleading with Claire not to make a scene.

Claire and Ewan stood for a moment in awkward silence, watching Tessa and Mr. Hutt ease their way into the swirl of dancers.

"Well?" she challenged, when it became obvious he meant to ignore the opportunity. "Aren't you going to invite *me* to dance?"

She quashed a foolish flicker of eagerness to feel his arms about her once again. Hadn't ten years and a succession of men like Max Hamilton-Smythe taught her anything?

The Scotsman raised his dark, emphatic

brows and thrust out his lower lip in a doubtful expression. "Ye wouldn't think it too forward— a former servant taking liberties with the laird's daughter?"

Claire skewered him with an icy glare, but she kept her tone and smile impeccably polite. "That would not be a first for you, would it?"

That wasn't fair, her conscience protested. Ten years ago, she'd craved every liberty Ewan Geddes had been prepared to take with her. The trouble was, he'd only ever wanted to take them with her beautiful, vivacious younger sister.

For a moment, his gray eyes darkened like thunderheads over Ben Blane. Then, just as quickly, they cleared like the morning mist off Loch Liath. Both stirred something in Claire that she did not wish to have stirred. Heaven help her if she let this man gain any of his old power over her heart, or, worse yet, guess that he had.

He made a bow, so deep and sweeping it verged on mockery. "In that case, Miss Talbot, as my folks say, I might as well be hanged for a sheep as a lamb. Will ye do me the honor of a dance?"

No one had ever roused her usually temperate emotions the way he did. Claire struggled to subdue them.

"Did your people steal a great many sheep?"

she inquired with arch civility, as she took
Ewan's arm and let him lead her to the floor.

"Only as many as they needed to keep from
starving after they were driven from their land."
He spoke in a tone of cheerful banter quite at
odds with his words. But when he took Claire's
hand in his and slipped his arm around her waist,
she could feel the taut clench of his muscles.

Perhaps she provoked a more intense reaction
in him than he had ever permitted her to see.
The possibility restored a bit of her self-respect.

Remembering the reason she had lured him
to the dance floor in the first place, she ignored
his bait about starving Highlanders. "You look
very prosperous now. You've done well for yourself in America?"

Not so well, surely, that the Brancaster fortune would fail to tempt him?

"Well enough." His reply confirmed Claire's
suspicion. "There's no limit, in the New World,
to how far a man's brains and hard work will
take him."

And if that wasn't far enough, thought Claire,
he could always cross the Atlantic to see how
far hollow charm and a total lack of scruples
would take him.

"I believe a truly determined man will suc-
ceed anywhere, Mr. Geddes. My grandfather,
for instance. He built Brancasters from nothing,

and he didn't have to go all the way to America to do it."

Ewan acknowledged her point with a nod. "A great achievement, to be sure. Then he was able to marry his daughter off to a laird."

That stung. Had her father's hurtful warning about fortune hunters been the voice of experience speaking? Claire refused to let Ewan see her flinch. One needed a tough hide to trade barbs with the man these days.

"If you think that gives you leave to pursue my sister, Mr. Geddes, I beg to differ. Poaching a few sheep is one thing. Poaching another man's fiancée is quite another. Exactly what are your intentions toward Tessa?"

"Only the most honorable, I can assure you." The hand that held hers tightened, as did the one around her waist. "I agree, Miss Talbot, there is a difference between sheep thieving and courting a lady. Sheep, curse their stupid heads, don't give a hang who shears them. But a lady may have a strong preference about who she weds. If she changes her affections from one man to another before she gets to the altar, I'd hardly call that poaching."

Heavens! This dance had become more like a fencing match set to music. For all that, some traitorous part of Claire *enjoyed* their thinly veiled cut and thrust. She had not felt so alive in years.

"My sister may have a strong, even passionate preference for one man this week, sir, then be quite as smitten with another fellow the next. Did it never occur to you why a lady of her beauty and charm should still be unwed at the age of twenty-six?"

Ewan's roving gaze flitted to Tessa as she danced by in the arms of Obadiah Hutt.

"A bit fickle in her favors, is she?" He did not sound as troubled by the possibility as he should be. "What about ye, Miss Talbot? Why is an attractive lady of fortune like yerself still single at the age of...?"

"Twenty-eight." Claire rapped out the words with perverse pride. "As well you know, Mr. Geddes, since my sister was sixteen and I eighteen during your last summer at Strathandrew."

She let her reply sink in for a moment before she added, "I have not remained unmarried for lack of opportunity. Of that you may be sure. No woman with my size fortune has the luxury of going unpursued, no matter how great her deficiencies of beauty, wit or temperament."

For the first time since they had been reintroduced, Claire sensed a change in Ewan Geddes's manner. Gone was the antagonism disguised as affable banter. Something she'd said must have struck a nerve with him.

But what? And why?

* * *

For the first time since he'd met Claire Talbot, more than twenty years ago, Ewan felt a glimmer of sympathy for the woman.

In the past year or two, she'd been the target of several fortune hunters. It was not an experience he'd have wished on his worst enemy, let alone the sister of the woman he loved.

Around them, the music swelled to its dazzling conclusion. The dancers came to a stop and applauded politely. Some withdrew from the floor to rest or seek refreshment, while others lingered for the start of the next number.

Though he'd had every intention of escaping Miss Talbot's company at the earliest opportunity, Ewan heard himself ask, "Shall we have another go, then?"

She seemed as surprised by the invitation as he. "Y-yes. I suppose. Thank you."

Over her shoulder he could see Tessa staring his way with a look of puzzled annoyance. He tossed her a reassuring wink, hoping she'd understand that he was trying to jolly her sister around.

He was confident Tessa would break her engagement to marry him. But whether she'd stay the course against the disapproval of both her mother and her sister, Ewan wasn't so certain. Some intuition warned him that he could never win favor with Lady Lydiard. But Claire

Talbot might just learn to like him, if she'd let herself.

Perhaps he needed to take a different tack with the lady. Remember that he was no longer a nineteen-year-old gillie with a chip on his shoulder the size of a full-grown Scotch pine, and stop letting her gibes get under his skin. Lavish on her a little of the charm with which he'd won her sister's heart.

"Only a rank fool would claim ye lack for wit, Miss Talbot." He held her out at arm's length and pretended to scrutinize her from head to heels. "And I can't say I see any deficiency in yer looks, either."

Nor did he.

Oh, she might not have the breath-catching beauty of his Tessa, but Claire Talbot was a bonny woman all the same. What her distinct, regular features lacked in softness, they made up for in character. Her eyes were not the warm blue-green of some southern sea, but the bracing blue-gray of a Highland loch. If he had not known her age, he would have guessed her to be several years younger.

His modest compliment seemed to fluster her more than any of his subtle digs. "You needn't take pity on me, sir. I've lived with my sister long enough to recognize female beauty. And to know that I do not find it in my own looking glass."

The music began again, this time a gentler

melody that put Ewan in mind of a spring breeze whispering through the trees around Loch Liath.

He drew Miss Talbot toward him.

"Pity?" He stared at her as if he'd never heard anything so outrageous. "Ye'll get none of that here, lass. For ye never had a drop to spare for me in the old days."

And that, Ewan realized, was one thing he'd always liked about her. Oh, she'd taunted him, outright insulted him at times. Yet somehow she'd made him feel it was because she considered him an equal in character—a worthy opponent, not some poor soul she ought to patronize with gracious platitudes.

"I reckon there's more than one kind of beauty, don't ye?" he asked.

"What other kinds can there be?" She sounded dubious.

"Well…" Ewan scrambled for an example that would prove his point. "Plenty of folks think Surrey's a beautiful place."

"I am one of them."

"Does that mean the Highlands aren't beautiful, then?" He twirled her about so fast it made him a trifle dizzy. "Just because they don't look like Surrey?"

"Well, of course not!"

The sincerity of her outrage touched him.

"There ye go, then. Perhaps Miss Tessa's got

a Surrey kind of beauty and ye've a Highland kind."

"Harsh, rugged and cold?" Her eyes sparkled with triumph at having cornered him into a slight he hadn't meant.

"If I didn't know better, Miss Talbot, I'd swear ye were fishing for flattery."

"You were once a gillie. Tell me, am I using the right bait?"

If he hadn't known better, Ewan might have supposed she was trying to flirt with him. But Claire Talbot flirting? No, that was too outrageous.

"Ye shouldn't have to speak ill of yerself to get folks to praise ye. I expect ye know yer own worth well enough, and I think ye know what I meant about Highland beauty, too."

"Perhaps I do, Mr. Geddes." She spoke in a soft voice, and for a moment, her face took on a pensive look. Then her guard went up again. "You're a more skillful flatterer than most men of my acquaintance. You don't make the mistake of laying it on too thick."

Ewan laughed. "I think ye've given me an indirect answer to my question, Miss Talbot."

"Pray, what question might that be?"

"The impertinent one about why ye hadn't found a husband."

"Ah." She nodded. "With the equally impertinent reference to my advanced age?"

"Guilty as charged." Ewan flashed her a rueful grin. "Dare I offer a humble apology and throw myself on the mercy of the court?"

"Anything is possible, though I doubt you have a humble bone in your body." Her expression softened. "Very well, then, I accept your apology. I am not ashamed of my age, nor of being unwed."

"No reason ye should be. I'd say ye're not married because ye haven't yet found a man who can give ye a good run for yer money."

She considered his suggestion. "If one did present himself, I expect he'd be lost in the scrum of those anxious to *chase* my money."

Again Ewan found himself laughing at one of her wry quips. He'd often thought something like that of himself.

That was why he'd decided not to reveal the full extent of his wealth until Tessa had formally accepted his proposal. Not that he had any fear she'd wed him for his fortune. How much sweeter his victory would be, though, if she had no idea how far he'd risen in the world, but agreed to wed him just the same.

The thought made Ewan anxious to get back to her as soon as this waltz ended. He nearly missed the words Claire Talbot murmured. Ones she might not have meant to speak aloud.

"I once thought I'd met a man who could

give me a run for my money. It turned out I was wrong."

Ewan forgot about not feeling sorry for her.

Little wonder she mistrusted his feelings for Tessa if she'd been sought after by fortune hunters and let down by the one man she'd cared for.

The music ended and once again the dancers applauded.

"Thank you, Mr. Geddes." Claire Talbot backed away from him. "You're a fine dancer."

He bowed to acknowledge the compliment. "I've learned a thing or two in the past ten years. Including that I'm the one who should thank ye for the honor of yer company."

When she started to turn away, Ewan caught her hand. "I expect we've both changed a good deal in the past ten years, Miss Talbot. Maybe we should stop treating each other as though we're the same folk we were then, and make a new start. What do ye say?"

Her gaze seemed to search his face, weighing his sincerity.

Ewan found himself hanging on her reply with far more suspense than it merited.

Then her face blossomed into a smile as sudden and unexpectedly bonny as the blooming of the heather. "Very well, Mr. Geddes. What you say makes a great deal of sense."

Her agreement and the modest compliment elated Ewan far more than they ought to have.

"But," she added in a tone that brooked no contradiction, "that does not mean I will surrender my sister to you without a fight."

Ewan considered for a moment. "It doesn't mean I'll give her up without a fight, either."

Strangely, the prospect of such a battle of wits and wills with Claire Talbot fired his blood.

Chapter Three

"Come now, Tessa, be sensible, dearest," Claire begged her sister. "You can't mean to jilt poor Spencer over a man you barely know."

A few days after the Fortescues' ball, they sat in the morning room of Lydiard House. Claire occupied an armchair opposite a matching settee that held Tessa and her mother. A tea tray rested on the low table between them.

This was the first time in the three years since her father's death that Claire had paid a call on Lydiard House.

"I wish you wouldn't use an awful word like *jilt!*" Tessa thrust out her full lower lip in a pretty pout. "It sounds perfectly heartless!"

Lady Lydiard set down her cup of tea, for once in complete agreement with her stepdaughter. "It is a rather heartless thing to do, dear, no matter what you call it. Especially considering how long poor Spencer has waited for you."

"That's part of the problem, isn't it?" Tessa's splendid eyes flashed with more green than blue, a sure sign of rough sailing for anyone foolish enough to oppose her. "If Spencer had been truly eager to marry me, I cannot believe he would have stood for so many delays."

After the forbearance he'd shown her sister, Claire would not tolerate hearing Spencer Stanton abused. Not even by his own fiancée.

"Delays that were your idea, may I remind you! Spencer has only wanted to give you time to be certain of your feelings. Would you rather he'd blustered and bullied you to get his own way, like some men?"

"Of course not." Tessa sighed. "Spencer's been perfectly sensible and selfless, as always, and I feel ghastly about—" she hesitated over the word, then steeled herself and spat it out "—jilting the dear fellow. But I cannot go through with the wedding when I'm head over heels in love with another man, now, can I?"

It made a sort of topsy-turvy sense, though not a kind Claire could have much sympathy with. If she had given her word, and the gentleman in question had done nothing to make her change her mind, she could not have brought herself to break her promise.

"If you ask me, head over heels does not

sound like a very balanced frame of mind in which to make such an important decision." Claire reached across the low tea table to rest her hand on top of her sister's. "For Spencer's sake and especially for your own, please do not act in haste. How much do you really know about Ewan Geddes, after all?"

His name came far too readily to her tongue, curse him! It gave her a ridiculous little rush of pleasure to wrap her lips around it. And to hear it spoken by her own voice…as if that granted her some secret sense of ownership.

Worse yet, the sound of it conjured up a vivid image of the man, and a disturbingly intense memory of how it had felt to whirl around the dance floor in his arms, his voice beguiling her more deeply with every word. It was bad enough she hadn't been able to get him out of her thoughts last night. If he was going to plague her during the day, as well, how would she get anything done?

"Claire's right, dear," Lady Lydiard chimed in, speaking those words for the first time her stepdaughter could recall. "I disapproved of this man when I believed he was simply a stranger from America. But when Claire informed me he was one of our servants… Such an alliance would be out of the question, even if you weren't already engaged! Really, you might have told me."

"I didn't tell you because I knew you'd fuss. And why should it be out of the question, Mama? You always say what marvelous servants we have."

Lady Lydiard's patrician countenance took on a look of horror, like a fastidious clergyman listening to heresy. "Marvelous *in their proper places,* dear."

"Proper places—tush!" Tessa sprang from her spot on the settee and began to pace the morning room, her delicate hands gesturing wildly as she spoke. "You know I have no patience with that kind of thinking. People are people."

Where had Tessa picked up her egalitarian notions? Claire wondered. From reading Mrs. Trollope's novels at an impressionable age? From the handsome but radical-minded tutor their father had dismissed after discovering just how revolutionary some of the young man's views were? Or was it a natural expression of the rebellious streak her younger sister had displayed as far back as their nursery days?

"Besides…" Tessa made a dramatic sweeping gesture that almost spelled disaster for an Oriental vase perched too close to the edge of the mantelpiece. "Ewan Geddes is nobody's servant anymore. He is a perfectly respectable man of business in a place called Pittsburgh. And quite prosperous, I dare say. He was able to afford a holiday in London, after all, and his clothes are very well tailored."

The exchange between her sister and stepmother had given Claire a chance to rally her composure. Now Tessa's words reminded her of something else.

"I've made inquiries about Mr. Geddes, as it happens."

Tessa's mouth fell open. "What gives you the right to pry—"

Lady Lydiard interrupted her daughter. "Do be quiet, dear, and listen to what your sister has to say. What did you find out, Claire?"

For the first time in her life, Claire wavered a little under her sister's indignant glare. It was for Tessa's good, she reminded herself, and Brancasters'. Yet, somehow, her own foolish partiality for the man tainted her sisterly concern.

"He's staying at the Carleton, for one thing. A rather expensive hotel for a man who lists his occupation as 'marine engineer,' wouldn't you say?"

Her sister did not seem to draw the same conclusions as Claire had. Perhaps because Tessa had not been forced to guard herself against fortune hunters for so many years.

"How dare you set spies on Mr. Geddes, just because he and I are friends?"

"I'd call it a good deal more than friends," Claire snapped back, "if you are thinking of jilt-

ing your fiancé for the man. I've also discovered
that he is employed by the firm Liberty Marine
Works."

The significance of her sister's words seemed
lost on Tessa. She lifted her gracefully arched
brows in an unspoken question.

"Liberty Marine Works is a shipbuilding
firm." A sinking sensation had gripped Claire
when she'd first heard this incriminating piece
of information from Mr. Hutt. Now it returned.
"Like Brancasters."

Leaning on one arm of the settee, Tessa
brought her face close to Claire's. "Then you
and Ewan should have plenty to talk about at
dinner parties, after he and I are married."

"Teresa Veronica Talbot!" her mother thun-
dered. "Don't be impertinent!"

"Impertinent?" Tessa pointed an accusing finger at Claire. "Why don't you lecture *her* about
the impertinence of spying on a man who's committed no crime other than once having been in
our employ?"

Claire rose from the chair, gathering her self-
control around her as a buffer against her sister's
passionate outrage.

She was not proud of what she'd done, but
she'd had no choice. Now her sister must face
the unpleasant truth about Ewan Geddes, just
as she had.

"Don't you see, dearest? A man who lives

beyond his means that way can't be up to any good. Has it never occurred to you that he may be after your fortune?"

"What fortune would that be?" Tessa crossed her arms over her shapely bosom. "A minor interest in Brancasters and part ownership of Strathandrew?"

Claire bit her tongue to keep from reminding her sister that the Scottish estate had cost more in upkeep over the years than it was worth—an expense she alone had borne.

Perhaps Tessa sensed what her sister was thinking, for her lip curled in an unattractive sneer. "I consider myself fortunate *not* to have been burdened with great wealth. I am not forced to suspect that any gentleman who admires me has mercenary motives."

"Well, I have." Claire forced herself to speak calmly as she struggled to hide the hurt her sister's words had inflicted. "So I must beg you to trust my judgment. Do you suppose there haven't been times when I was tempted to trust the flattery of an attractive man? When I wanted to believe he would love me just as well if I hadn't a farthing?"

The defiant glitter in Tessa's eyes dimmed, and her pretty features crumpled like a child's. "I'm sorry, darling!"

She dashed into Claire's arms. "I didn't mean

to be hateful, truly! I just can't understand why you're doing this to me."

Claire's eyes prickled with tears she had forgotten how to shed. She couldn't bear to push the matter so hard it caused an irreparable breach between her and Tessa.

She returned her sister's embrace, then drew back, taking Tessa's hands in hers. "I'm not doing this *to* you, dearest. I'm doing it *for* you. And for Brancasters. I truly believe Ewan Geddes means trouble for all of us."

"Brancasters!" Tessa spat the word out like some vile oath as she wrenched her fingers out of Claire's grasp. "I should have known. You're more concerned with protecting your grandfather's precious company than with my happiness."

"Now, Tessa, you know that's not true."

Lady Lydiard could hold her tongue no longer. "Apologize to Claire, at once, Tessa." She rose from the settee. "Your sister would never have involved herself in this unsavory business if I had not appealed to her for help. If you must be angry with someone, let it be me."

Claire wasn't certain which of them her stepmother's words surprised more—her, Tessa, or Lady Lydiard herself.

Surprised or not, Tessa made no effort to apologize. "This is worse than I thought, if both of you are allied against me. I don't care, though. I will *not* let you spoil my chance of happiness!"

With that, she spun away and ran out of the morning room, slamming the door behind her.

Claire and Lady Lydiard stood frozen for a moment, listening to the muted pounding of footsteps up the stairs. Then her ladyship wilted down onto the settee again.

"This is worse than I thought." She echoed her daughter's words. "Tessa has always been such a willful child. And I fear I've only made it worse by indulging her so often. What if she runs away to Scotland and marries the fellow, just to spite us?"

Runs away to Scotland. Those words stirred an idea in Claire's mind.

She sank back onto her chair and took a drink of her tea, only to find it had gone cold. "I'm afraid that's just what might happen if we push her too far. We need to let her feelings cool to the point where she can be reasoned with."

"What are you suggesting?" In spite of the early hour, Lady Lydiard appeared in need of a stronger drink than tea. "That we should look the other way while this fellow continues to pursue my daughter all over London in such a scandalous fashion?"

"Not quite." Suddenly Claire's plan took shape with brilliant clarity. For only the second time in her cautious life, she tasted the heady draft of reckless zeal. "We need to keep them apart long enough for Tessa to come to her senses. In the meantime, we must force Ewan Geddes to tip his hand, so she can see him for the fortune-hunting troublemaker he is."

"And how are we to accomplish that?"

A tiny secretive smile tugged at a corner of Claire's mouth. The more details she added to her plan, the better she liked it.

"We must present Mr. Geddes with an even more tempting target for his schemes."

Her ladyship's eyes widened. "You?"

Claire nodded. Then she remembered another bold plan of hers that had involved Ewan Geddes, and how disastrously it had gone awry.

"This is a pleasant surprise, I must say." Two evenings later, Ewan looked around the table at the three Talbot ladies, his eyes coming to rest upon Tessa, seated opposite him.

Ten years ago, if anyone had told him the day would come when he'd be sitting down to dine at Lydiard House, he wouldn't have believed them. It felt as though he was in sight of the crest of a tall peak he'd been scaling for as long as he could remember.

"I was afraid ye ladies might not take kindly to my renewing Miss Tessa's acquaintance after all these years."

Lady Lydiard *didn't* take kindly to it. Ewan

could feel her critical gaze trained upon him, as if she was just waiting for him to fumble his forks or drink the contents of his finger bowl.

He would not be sorry to disappoint her.

From the foot of the table, Claire Talbot spoke up. "I won't attempt to deceive you, Mr. Geddes. Tessa's mother and I are concerned about the... haste with which she is making important decisions concerning her future."

"Claire..." murmured her sister, a distinct note of warning in her voice.

Ewan caught Tessa's eye, then gave a subtle shake of his head. A great family row wasn't likely to win him sympathy from her mother and sister. "It's fine. Honestly. I have no objection to hearing the truth."

They ate their soup in awkward silence for a while before Claire Talbot spoke again.

"As you may recall from our younger years, my sister has a strong will and knows her own mind. Since her mother and I both love her very much, we do not wish to cause an unfortunate breach in our family, as can sometimes occur under these circumstances."

"A wise and compassionate course, Miss Talbot." Ewan found himself warming to Claire in spite of himself.

It couldn't have been easy for a woman of her spirit to back down from the defiant challenge she'd flung at him on the night of the Fortescues' ball. But she recognized that opposing him too forcefully might push her sister straight into his arms. And she cared too much about Tessa to risk estranging her.

"A practical course, sir." Miss Talbot seemed pleased by his praise. "My years in the world of commerce have taught me to be practical, even when it comes to matters of the heart."

A serving maid stepped forward to collect their soup bowls. Ewan murmured a word of thanks when she took his. Was it his imagination, or did she look a bit familiar? Could she be one of the wee lasses from Strathandrew, brought south to serve in the family's London home?

Claire Talbot spoke again, distracting Ewan from his thoughts. "The reason we invited you here this evening was so we might begin to get better acquainted with you. Of course, we remember you from our summers in Strathandrew, but that was quite some time ago. Tell me, do you get much opportunity to hunt and fish over in America?"

"Not as much as I'd like," Ewan admitted, as the serving maid placed the fish course before him—poached Highland salmon.

A gillie on the estate must have caught it and sent it south by train, packed in ice.

"My work has kept me pretty busy, ye know.

It's only in the past year or two that I've been able to take my nose from the grindstone."

He took a bite of the salmon. The soft pink flesh melted on his tongue with a familiar salty-sweet flavor so delicious Ewan closed his eyes, the better to savor it. If Lady Lydiard hadn't been watching him so closely, he might have let out a faint groan of pleasure.

"I know what you mean," said Claire. "Since taking over at Brancasters, I have not had much opportunity for leisure, myself. Why, just this morning, I realized that it has been fully three years since I last spent any time at Strathandrew. It used to be the highlight of the year, when Tessa and I were children."

Her gaze took on a far-off look, and Ewan thought he detected a hint of wistful softness in her eyes.

He remembered the Talbots' summer visits, too. The flurry of anticipation as the great house was opened up and cleaned from cellar to attic. The larder stocked with all sorts of delicacies brought from the south. Fishing tackle sorted and line mended. Guns hauled out and cleaned in preparation for lots of hunting parties.

Then, on the day the Talbots' yacht moored in the firth, he would steal down to watch the family and their guests disembark. And to take his first, private look at Tessa, to see how much taller she'd grown. How her figure was beginning to fill out in just the right places. If she was wearing her hair in a new style. Whether she was still as bonny as he'd remembered her.

Now he had only to glance across the table... which he did.

The lass was as much a feast for his eyes as the salmon was for his palate—so dainty, soft and golden. She looked almost as though time had stood still for her during the years they'd been apart. For some reason he couldn't quite puzzle out, that notion troubled him vaguely.

Again Claire Talbot's voice broke in on his thoughts. "I've just had a grand idea. Why don't we all go up to Strathandrew for a few weeks? Mr. Geddes can come as our guest. It will give us an opportunity to get better acquainted, away from the formality of London. What do you think?"

She glanced around the table at the others, her eyes finally coming to rest upon Ewan.

Tessa slammed down her fork with a force that threatened the delicate china of her plate. "If you must know, I think you're far more interested in spiriting Ewan and me away from all the tattling tongues in London than you are about getting reacquainted."

Before Claire could reply to her sister's charge, Lady Lydiard spoke. "Please excuse my daughter's ill manners, Mr. Geddes. I can't think where she's picked them up."

Her ladyship's cool stare told Ewan she need look no further than him.

To Tessa she added, "I believe you owe Claire an apology. Thank heaven there is *someone* in the family who considers propriety."

"No apologies necessary," said Claire, though her face had gone a bit pale during her sister's rebuke. "Tessa is correct, in part, about my motive for suggesting a holiday in Scotland. I fail to see what harm it will do to exercise a little discretion. There is bound to be a good deal of gossip, in any case, dearest, if you break your engagement. Why add to it?"

"*When* I break my engagement."

The lass had spirit, that was certain. Ewan knew he should be grateful that she wasn't ashamed of her feelings for him, and that she was willing to defy her family on his account, if necessary. All the same, her sharp tone and quarrelsome air set his teeth on edge.

Beneath the table, he gave her foot a gentle nudge. "Well, I think a holiday at good old Strathandrew is a capital idea, Miss Talbot. I was hoping to make a wee visit home, anyway. It'll be almost like old times, eh?"

Tessa's features softened. Perhaps she was picturing the two of them riding through the hills, sharing a picnic lunch of Rosie McMurdo's fine cooking, or walking together by the burn in the late summer gloaming. Those thoughts certainly brought a smile to Ewan's lips.

Of course, that wouldn't be like *old times,* he reminded himself. During the summers of their youth, the thought of wooing Lord Lydiard's daughter was one he'd reserved for his hopeless dreams. Being able to court her in the familiar splendor of the Highlands, away from prying eyes and tattling tongues, would be like a dream come true.

A dream he'd cherished so long and so desperately, he doubted he could let go of it now, even if he'd wanted to.

Chapter Four

The faintly bilious sensation in the pit of Claire's stomach had nothing to do with the gentle rocking of the yacht. Unlike her sister and stepmother, she seldom suffered a moment's seasickness, even in the roughest weather. During their annual voyages to Strathandrew, she had taken keen enjoyment in prowling the decks, questioning the crew about sails and rigging, her senses quickened by the rhythm of the waves and the tang of the sea breeze as it rippled through her hair.

Several years since their last such voyage, Claire now stood on the deck of the *Marlet,* awaiting Ewan Geddes's arrival. She reached up to make certain her becoming new hat was firmly secured atop her flattering new coiffure.

Lady Lydiard's hairdresser had assured her the lower, looser style made her look quite five years younger. Claire had tried to ignore the shallow compliment, but she had not been able to subdue a ridiculous flicker of pleasure…any more than she could subdue the nervous, expectant flutter in her stomach.

Perhaps it was the corset.

Claire suspected the blame for a vast percentage of feminine maladies lay with this unnatural binding of women's bodies. It was a measure of her regard for Tessa that she had submitted to its tyranny.

Rubbish! protested a voice from deep in her memory—the voice of her late father. *You'd never have a hope of winning that bounder away from your sister with your looks. And no amount of corsets, cunning hats or fussy hairstyles will alter that!*

Claire's insides clenched as if powerful hands had jerked the laces of her corset tighter still. Pulling herself to her full height, she thrust out her chin. When he'd been alive, she had never given her father the satisfaction of guessing how much his constant censure had stung. She was not about to let that change just because he was dead.

There was some truth in the notion, though, she admitted to herself as she opened her parasol against the cheerful glare of the sun. She did not expect to win Ewan Geddes with her looks, but with her money.

Once she took care to let him know how little fortune Tessa had in her own right, no doubt he would alter his course in favor of a more lucrative opportunity. Still, Claire did not wish to make him view the prospect as altogether odious.

What time had it gotten to be? She foraged in her reticule and brought out a large gold pocket watch that had once belonged to her grandfather. She consulted the heavy old timepiece, then searched the bustling quayside for a glimpse of Ewan Geddes.

There he was! A powerful wave of relief buffeted Claire.

He strode down the quay with a pair of baggage porters scurrying along in his wake. Then he paused for a moment, peering around at the diverse assemblage of vessels. Claire could tell the precise instant he spotted the *Marlet,* for he gave a visible start, then headed toward the yacht.

Claire's insides pitched and swayed worse than ever. She had been a fool to go to such lengths to beautify herself for Ewan Geddes. No doubt he would see through her pitiful plan and laugh at her for even trying to win him away from Tessa. For an instant she considered going below decks and hiding out there with the excuse of some feigned indisposition.

Then she remembered everything at stake—

Tessa's happiness and Spencer's, as well as the fortunes of the company her grandfather had entrusted to her. She mustn't give up without a fight.

Resisting the urge to adjust her hat one last time, she approached the gangway as Ewan Geddes sprinted up it.

"Welcome aboard!" Claire smiled, surprised to discover how little effort it required. "I hope you did not have too much difficulty finding us?"

"None at all." He doffed his hat and bowed over the hand she extended to him. "I apologize for being so late. I had a few pressing business matters to attend to. I hope I haven't kept everyone waiting."

"Quite the contrary." Claire managed to withdraw her hand from his, with considerable reluctance. "I only arrived a short while ago myself, and there has been no sign of Tessa and her mother. I expect they'll be here soon."

She directed a member of the crew to show the porters where to stow Ewan's trunk. When she glanced back, she found him staring at her with an intense and somewhat puzzled look.

Immediately, she raised her hand to her hair. "I beg your pardon. Is something the matter?"

Ewan answered with a decisive shake of his head and a slow blossoming smile that might have made Claire's knees grow weak if she'd let them. "Quite the opposite, Miss Talbot. I was only thinking it's a lucky woman who can claim the passage of ten years has made her more bonny, not less."

Powerful, contrary feelings collided within Claire. Sweet dizzy delight at finally receiving the kind of compliment she'd waited a decade to hear. A flicker of triumph that all her ridiculous preparations had not been in vain.

Poisoning both of those was the bitter certainty that Ewan Geddes only flattered her to further his own selfish ends, like so many unscrupulous men before him. *Unlike* those other men, he had one most distressing advantage—she wanted to believe him as she had never wanted to believe them.

That sense of vulnerability brought a sharp reply to the tip of her tongue, but Claire managed to imprison it behind a forced smile. It would not do to trade barbs with Ewan Geddes if she hoped to make him pursue her. But she had spent too many years fending off fortune hunters' compliments to begin lapping them up now.

She affected a tone of breezy banter. "If you believe the past ten years have improved my looks, then you must have thought me very ill-favored when we were young!"

Averting her face, so his sharp scrutiny would not catch a glimpse of the pain her eyes might betray, Claire set off on a leisurely turn around

the deck. She heard Ewan's brisk footsteps following her.

"I can't deny, Miss Talbot…" He gave a soft
chuckle. "In those days, I only had eyes for yer
sister."

"Whereas you now notice other women?"
Hard as she tried, Claire could not resist bait-
ing him.

She braced for a sharp retort or a mocking
return jab. His gust of laughter, as invigorating
as a sea breeze, took her by surprise. "You find
my remark amusing?" she asked.

"Aye, in a way." His eyes sparkled with impudent glee, much better suited to a young Highland gillie than to a mature man of business in
a well-tailored suit. "Ye took me back ten years,
is all. To a time when the pair of us liked nothing better than going at each other hammer and
tongs."

His infectious camaraderie could seduce her
more easily than other men's passionate or sentimental lovemaking…if she did not resist.

"Are you saying there was something you
liked better than making calves' eyes at my sister, Ewan Geddes?"

"I reckon ye have me there, lass." He gave a
bark of wry laughter at his own expense. "Likely
I'm counting myself too high in yer regard, as
well. There must have been plenty of other

things ye fancied more than trading friendly insults with a hired boy."

He was wrong about that. There'd been *nothing* she liked better. At least when he'd answered her thinly veiled insults with comical quips that skirted the edge of outright insolence, she'd been assured of his attention, however fleeting. And she'd had a safe outlet for the futile fury that built up inside her when she'd watched the handsome young gillie showing off for the benefit of her sister.

Claire ignored his question, in case her tone or expression somehow communicated the truth. "Dear me! I wonder where Tessa and her mother can have gotten to?"

Where had Lady Lydiard's *messenger* gotten to? Claire cast a nervous glance at the quayside. Someone should have been here by now. Timing was critical to her plan.

Ewan leaned against the deck railing, turning his top hat around and around by its brim. "Do ye reckon Lady Lydiard might be dragging her feet?"

His shrewd insight made Claire chuckle in spite of herself. "It *is* the sort of thing she might do to express her disapproval, I'll grant you. In this case, I doubt it, though."

"Why's that?"

"Well…" She chose her words with care, so as not to rouse his suspicion. "I cannot pretend her ladyship is delighted with the prospect of having you as our guest at Strathandrew."

"Now there's an understatement if ever I heard one!" Ewan twisted his features into an exaggerated look of disapproval that aped Lady Lydiard's to perfection.

Biting back a grin, Claire fought the false sense that he was on her side. "My stepmother may be toplofty, but she is no fool. The one thing she wants less than you wooing Tessa at Strathandrew is you wooing her here in London under the noses of all the gossips."

"So she'll be here, come what may, looking all grim and disapproving and barely speaking a word." Ewan tossed his hat in the air, then caught it again. "Would it be wicked of me to hope her ladyship might meet with a wee mishap that would prevent her from sailing with us?"

His suggestion so closely echoed her plan, it took Claire's breath away. She reached for the deck railing to steady herself. When Ewan's large brown hand closed over hers, she felt even less steady.

"Are ye all right, Miss Talbot?" The solicitous warmth of his voice and his touch wrapped around her. "I didn't really mean any harm to yer stepmother, I swear!"

"Of course not." Claire struggled to rally her composure—something Ewan Geddes had always taxed more than any other man. How would she ever explain her excessive reaction to his jest about Lady Lydiard?

Footsteps sounded behind her and a familiar masculine voice spoke. "Pardon me for interrupting, Miss Brancaster Talbot. I was told to bring you this."

Claire spun around, barely resisting the urge to throw her arms around her secretary. She was so grateful for his well-timed interruption that she did not even remind him to call her by a single surname.

"Mr. Catchpole, what brings you here?" She took the paper he held out to her, as if she had no idea what message it might contain. "Some problem at Brancasters?"

She handed Catchpole her parasol to hold, so she would have both hands free to open the letter. "I told you, while I am on holiday in Scotland, Mr. Adams and Mr. Monteith will be in charge. If you encounter any serious difficulty... oh, dear!"

"What's wrong, then?" Ewan leaned closer to read the note over Claire's shoulder. Whatever it was, he didn't much care for the sound of it.

When she glanced up at him, he backed away. "I'm sorry. I didn't mean to look at your note."

What must she think of him? First that thoughtless remark about her stepmother, now trying to read her private mail. In the past five minutes, he'd done precious little to dispel the doubts she must have about him as a potential member of her family. He must do better if he hoped to enlist her as an ally in his fight to wed Tessa.

To his surprise, she did not look the least offended. She held out the paper to him. "This concerns you, too. By all means read it."

If the note concerned him, it could only be about one thing. In his haste to read the message, Ewan fairly tore the paper out of Claire Talbot's hand. Manners and a good impression be hanged!

He scarcely needed to glance at the closing salutation to know the message had come from Tessa's mother. The florid, swooping script was everything he would have expected from Lady Lydiard.

"'My dear Claire…'" He muttered the words under his breath as he read, squinting to decipher the words. "'I fear Tessa and I will not be able to join you and Mr. Geddes on the voyage to Strathandrew, after all.'"

In his mind, he could hear her ladyship speaking those words in a tone of cool, malicious triumph. Gritting his teeth, Ewan struggled through the rest of the note.

"It says Tessa's ill." He crumpled the paper in his fist, no longer caring what sort of impression he made on Claire Talbot. "I have to go to her!"

For a moment, Miss Talbot looked as though she meant to prevent him. Something must have changed her mind, though.

"If you feel you must." She shrugged. "Then by all means, fly to her side."

For some reason, her willingness to let him go, and her tone of wry amusement, calmed his sense of urgency. "Ye think I shouldn't?"

"That is for you to decide, of course." Miss Talbot retrieved her parasol from the fussy-looking middle-aged man who had brought the note. "Thank you for delivering her ladyship's message, Mr. Catchpole. We will not detain you any longer."

"Always happy to oblige, miss." Catchpole regarded his employer with a look that bordered on reverence. "If I may be so bold, I do hope you will enjoy your holiday in the north. You have driven yourself so hard these past three years. It's about time you had a proper rest."

Ewan's clerk had said much the same thing to him on the day he'd made his whirlwind departure for London.

Claire Talbot acknowledged the good wishes with a warm smile. "I do feel the need for a change of scenery. I know I can count on you to keep Mr. Adams and Mr. Montieth up to scratch for me."

Her shoulders slumped, just a trifle. Beneath

her well turned out facade, Ewan thought he could make out subtle signs of fatigue.

Once Mr. Catchpole had departed, she turned to Ewan again. "The note does not say Tessa is deathly ill, only indisposed." She lowered her voice. "A *feminine* indisposition, perhaps. I fear you would only embarrass her by making a great to-do about it."

A scorching blush suffused Ewan's face, right to the roots of his hair. "Of course…I should have thought…"

"Men seldom need to consider such things, Mr. Geddes." Her brisk tone soothed his chagrin. "I often wish we women could be so fortunate."

She nodded toward the note Ewan still clenched in his fist. "Lady Lydiard says she and Tessa will come north by train in a few days' time. I can ask Captain MacLeod to delay our departure for them, but I doubt they would thank me for it, especially if the sea is rough at all."

"Not good sailors, are they?" Ewan liked nothing better than the sway of the deck beneath his feet. He'd never been able to work up proper sympathy for poor souls who got seasick.

"The worst." Claire pulled a face. "It was probably selfish of me not to arrange for us all to travel by rail in the first place. It wouldn't be the same for me, though, going to Strathandrew without a lovely sail on the *Marlet* to get there."

Ewan found himself nodding. He had been

looking forward to the voyage over the Irish Sea and through the southern isles. But Tessa…

"I quite understand," said Claire, "if you would prefer to wait and accompany Tessa and her mother."

The prospect of a long journey in a tiny railway carriage with Lady Lydiard made Ewan shudder.

Claire strolled back toward the gangway. "Given the circumstances between you and Tessa, I understand perfectly if you would like to keep as close to her as possible until you are safely wed."

Pride would not allow him to let that challenge pass. Hurrying to catch up with Claire Talbot, he stepped into her path. "Hold on a minute. Do ye think I'm afraid to let yer sister out of my sight for a few days in case she'll change her mind about me?"

"I don't know, Mr. Geddes." She looked him up and down with a shrewd gaze. "*Are* you afraid?"

"Not in the least." A faint qualm deep in his belly contradicted Ewan's emphatic words.

"Sometimes a little fear can be prudent, you know. After all, look what happened when Tessa's last beau had to be apart from her."

"That was different," Ewan insisted. "I came looking for her, to renew our…acquaintance. It wouldn't have mattered if that Stanton fellow had been stuck to her like wallpaper paste."

Claire Talbot arched one fine eyebrow. "Wouldn't it?"

"No!" He felt like a lad again, chafing under her gibes. Only now he couldn't make himself act as though it didn't matter. "She cared something for me long ago and I for her. That never went away through all the years since. A few days apart now isn't going to make any difference."

Miss Talbot did not look as though she believed him. Perhaps because she sensed the doubts he tried so hard to hide from himself.

"I can prove it!" Ewan regretted those desperate words the instant they left his mouth. But pride would not let him take them back.

For he'd glimpsed a flicker of triumph in Claire Talbot's cool eyes, mixed with vast relief. The kind he'd seen once or twice in the eyes of a gambler whose bluff had not been called. "You have nothing to prove to me, Mr. Geddes."

But he did, though. To her. To himself. To Tessa's mother. He had to prove the lass's love for him was more than some whim that would go away as quickly as it had come, if he were not constantly by her side to fan the flames.

"I don't want to impose upon yer sister while she's feeling poorly." Ewan dredged up every excuse he could think of to convince himself that Claire Talbot had not maneuvered him into doing what she wanted. "And I must admit, I was looking forward to sailing north on the *Marlet.* I've never much cared for trains."

Claire's lips twisted into a mocking grin. "Or the continuous society of Lady Lydiard in close quarters over several days?"

"Aye, perhaps." Another worthwhile reason for making the voyage occurred to him. He would never have a better opportunity to win Claire Talbot over to the notion of him marrying her sister. "Anyway, it's not fair ye should have to sail all the way up to Argyll without any company."

"You needn't feel sorry for me, Mr. Geddes." She collapsed her parasol with swift, fierce movements. "I have never been a social creature like my sister. I enjoy my own company very well."

"Strange, Miss Talbot. That's the second time ye've told me not to take pity on ye. Is there some reason I should?"

"Don't talk nonsense!" She looked half inclined to break her parasol over his head. "Of course there isn't. It's just that I get tired of hearing people say what a shame it is I've never found a husband. As if I couldn't have such useless incumbrances by the hundredweight if I wanted them!"

Her vehement tone rocked Ewan back on his

heels. And she wasn't finished yet. "I run one of the most prosperous commercial enterprises in the kingdom, yet there are people who persist in thinking me a failure because I have not snared a husband to sire half-a-dozen children on me!"

Put in those terms, marriage and motherhood did not sound very appealing. Why, then, did Claire Talbot's voice ache with longing?

Chapter Five

What had triggered that preposterous outburst? Claire would rather have sunk beneath the deck or dived into the foul waters of the Thames than continue to face Ewan Geddes. For someone who insisted she did not wish to be pitied, she certainly sounded pitiful.

Fortunately, the captain of the *Marlet* came to her rescue before she expired of humiliation.

"Begging yer pardon, Miss Talbot," he called, "but the tide's turning. Do we sit tight or do we sail?"

For a moment, Claire hesitated, stealing a fleeting glance at Ewan Geddes.

It had all been going so well. She'd taken a calculated risk in urging him to stick close to Tessa, rather than trying to entice him to come with her. From their younger years, she recalled that he had often been contrary, doing things he was forbidden, while resisting what he was urged or ordered to do.

Fortunately for her purposes, he appeared not to have changed in that regard. She had challenged his trust in Tessa's constancy and he had taken the bait. Or rather, he had been *about* to take the bait. Then her pride had reared up, putting her whole plan in jeopardy.

"We sail, Captain MacLeod." She gave the order in the decisive tone she had learned to use in business to win her way.

She had composed herself well enough by now to look Ewan Geddes in the face. "Will you sail with us, or will you disembark, sir? I beg your pardon for my outburst. It would be most kind of you to furnish me with company on the voyage. I would welcome the opportunity to observe your character at close quarters, to judge whether you might make a suitable husband for my sister, after all."

There, she had swallowed her pride, and given Ewan Geddes a further inducement to accompany her. Claire hoped it would be enough. She also hoped she had managed to conceal how desperately she wanted him to come…for Tessa's sake and Brancasters'.

Ewan gave a stiff bow. "I welcome the challenge of convincing ye of my worth, Miss Talbot. I always enjoyed the zest of yer company in the old days."

"Liar!" Claire struggled to subdue the intoxicating sensation that his cordial words set bubbling inside her. "I was horrible to you and you were horrible to me."

The captain must have been following their conversation, for he bellowed, "Raise the gangway! Weigh anchor!"

"Come." Claire beckoned Ewan toward the galley way. "I'll show you to your cabin. If you like, you can rest before you change for dinner."

He followed her down the steep, narrow stairs that led below deck.

"I apologize for going so slowly," she said. "These steps are quite treacherous to negotiate in full skirts and petticoats. I often envy men your attire. It is so practical and designed for ease of movement. Sometimes I think the design of ladies' fashions are contrived to hobble us."

Ewan laughed. "I wouldn't have agreed with ye when I first went to America and had to wear trousers. For the longest time, I felt like I'd been bound—" he stumbled over his words "—down below."

His indelicate confession sent a rush of heat through Claire even as it made her nearly double over with laughter. But corsets were not designed for doubling over.

To make matters worse, the *Marlet* gave a

sudden lurch as it slipped from the quay. Already unbalanced, Claire might have tumbled down the last few stairs had Ewan not brought his arm around in a swift, deft movement to catch her... just below the bosom.

As he pulled her toward him, the bracing masculine scent of his shaving soap enveloped her, making her light-headed.

The instant she was no longer in danger of pitching forward, Ewan slid his arm from around her. "I'm sorry! I didn't mean to take liberties with ye, Miss Talbot!"

Claire managed to right herself, though her limbs had never felt less steady.

"You have nothing to reproach yourself for." She hoped he would attribute her breathless tone to the shock of almost falling, and the pressure of his arm around her chest. "In such a situation, one must act decisively, not dither about propriety. You saved me from a nasty spill and I am grateful."

"Then ye have changed a good deal in ten years, Miss Talbot."

Claire fixed all her concentration on descending the rest of the stairs without another mishap. Once she had reached the bottom, she risked a glance back at Ewan. "I beg your pardon?"

His wide, mobile mouth crinkled at one corner and in the shaft of sunlight streaming down the galley way, his eyes twinkled. "I recollect one time I took yer arm when we were walking over some rough ground. Ye yanked it away as though ye'd touched a red-hot stove. Then ye said, 'Unhand me, lout! I'm quite capable of making my own way.'"

Her proud, foolish words, parroted back to her in his exaggerated falsetto, left Claire torn between laughter and cringing. How he must have detested her to have remembered the incident and her exact words after all these years!

She longed to offer him a belated apology and some excuse for her conduct. But what could she say? Admit she'd burned for him with the fierce desire of youth? Confess that the sudden touch of his hand had made her fear she would burst into flames?

Thank heaven she had outgrown such passionate nonsense!

"As I recall…" Claire savored the tart tone of her voice, which had always served to keep Ewan Geddes at arm's length and prevent him from guessing her true feelings. "…you came back with some sort of pithy reply to knock me flat. You always did."

"Me!" He affected a look of comic outrage. "Sass his lairdship's daughter? I'd have been skinned alive for it!"

Seen from his side, it must have felt like a very unfair fight. Claire had known the opposite was true. Her secret feelings for him had always given Ewan Geddes the advantage.

"Oh, you never did trespass into outright insolence," she reminded him. "But you always managed to get the upper hand, somehow. Your answer would have a double meaning, or it would sound so horribly polite, when all the time it was obvious you were mocking me."

Ewan mulled over what she had said for a moment. "Perhaps I did come off best now and then. I reckon ye put me in my place often enough, though. Ye had a tongue like a wasp in those days, lass."

"And you had a hide as thick as a Highland steer," Claire countered, "or pretended to."

Her words made her think of something she'd never considered before. Was it possible Ewan had only *pretended* not to care what she'd said to him back then? Might he have taken her barbs to heart, nursing a deep resentment over the years? Now he gave every appearance of looking back on their old squabbles with wry amusement. Could that be only a pretense, too?

"Do ye reckon we'll be able to get all the way to Scotland without tearing one another to pieces?" he asked.

Claire gave a little shrug. "Anything is possible. We aren't a pair of beastly youngsters anymore, though time has not blunted my waspish tongue as much as I would like."

Not that she had wished it to, especially. Her tart tongue and pose of cool indifference had been her only weapons against Max Hamilton-Smythe and men of his ilk.

Ewan did not look as though he grudged her that. His forceful features seemed to soften in a most appealing way. "Aye, well, I've been told I haven't lost the chip off my shoulder. So I reckon that sets us even."

Her hand prickled with the urge to rise and caress his rugged cheek. Suddenly, Claire realized how close they had been standing, and for how long, with their gazes locked. Had she already let this man charm her into forgetting who he was and what he wanted?

Heavens above, the *Marlet* had barely slipped its moorings! What state would she be in by the time they reached Strathandrew? Ready to stand as Tessa's bridesmaid, perhaps, and to hand over half her shares of Brancasters to the happy couple as a wedding present?

"I do beg your pardon." She hoped her tone would not betray the swift reversal of her feelings. "I fear I am neglecting my duties as a hostess. We have days ahead of us to talk over old times. For now, I must show you to your cabin as I promised."

What could he possibly have said or done to vex Claire Talbot? Ewan pondered the matter as he followed her a short distance down the narrow, wood-paneled corridor.

True, they'd been discussing the hostility that had once bristled between them. But they'd been doing it with tolerance and restraint born of maturity, each willing to own a share of the fault.

Then, in less than the flicker of an eye, a change had come over Miss Talbot. A very subtle one, to be sure, but unmistakable for all that. It was as if a balmy west wind had suddenly veered, to whistle down from the north. Or some invisible door, held invitingly ajar, had been slammed shut in his face.

If she'd been vexed with him for taking hold of her in such a bold way to keep her from pitching down those steep stairs, he could have understood it. She hadn't turned a hair over that, though.

Ewan wished *he* could forget the bewildering instant he'd pulled her close to him. The feather on her hat had tickled his nose, while the pressure of her bosom against his arm had tickled him…elsewhere. The notion that his old nemesis could affect him that way had staggered Ewan. Clearly, he'd been far too long without a woman.

A wee rest before dinner might do him good. Or a wash up with very cold water.

"These will be your quarters for the voyage." Claire stopped in front of a door.

Following so close on her heels, absorbed in

his own thoughts, Ewan almost bumped into her. Quick reflexes rescued him, but only just. When his hostess turned toward him, she started and gave a little gasp to find him hovering so near.

She took a step backward. "I hope the accommodations will suit you."

The unexplained stiffness of her manner rasped against his vague sense of confusion. "I made the long voyage to America in steerage, don't forget. I reckon a guest cabin on the laird's private yacht will do better than *suit* me."

Claire flinched at the gruffness of his tone, but otherwise ignored it.

"Dinner will be served at seven." She pointed down the corridor. "This opens into the dining room. In the meantime, if there is anything you need, do not hesitate to ring for one of the stewards."

Ewan struggled to recover his manners, for Tessa's sake and for his own pride. "I'm sure I'll be very comfortable, thank ye, Miss Talbot. I'll see ye at dinner."

With that, he ducked into his cabin and closed the door behind him.

He stood there for a moment, listening to her brisk footsteps continuing on down the corridor, wondering if this voyage to Scotland with her had been such a wise decision, after all. Whether it was or not, he concluded at last, there wasn't much he could do about it now except make the best of the opportunity it presented.

His gaze swept the generously proportioned cabin, which smelled of lemon oil. The highly polished wood and brass fittings gleamed softly in the light that filtered through a curtained porthole. The place had an air of understated masculine elegance. It would suit him very well.

His trunk had been safely stowed on a low platform, the rim of which would keep it from sliding in heavy weather. The bed, the dressing screen, a compact wardrobe and a small writing desk had all been bolted to the cabin floor for the same reason.

When Ewan pulled out the leather upholstered chair, he found it had been weighted in the legs. He glanced behind the screen to discover a washstand with a brass-framed shaving mirror mounted above it. Might this have been Lord Lydiard's cabin back when the family used to take their annual late summer holiday in the Highlands?

Tossing his top hat onto the bed, Ewan tugged off his coat and unbuttoned his high collar. He flashed a jaunty wink at the prosperous gentleman who stared out of the mirror at him. "A fancy billet for a humble gillie boy, eh? Not much question ye've risen in the world, laddie!"

Folk who knew him back in America likely

thought he took this kind of life for granted. They'd be wrong, though.

There'd been a short while, as he'd first begun to amass his fortune, when he'd been tempted to spend it on luxuries. But that had only made him feel wasteful. So he'd gone back to frugal living, and invested most of his earnings in the company, which had responded by becoming even more profitable.

That would all have to change once he married Tessa. He would buy her a fine house, or perhaps have one built, designed to accommodate her every fancy. He'd shower her with splendid clothes and jewels and every comfort she'd enjoyed in her life so far.

Would she be willing to return to America with him? he wondered. Or would she want to settle in England to remain near her family?

While he continued to plan his new life, he stowed his coat and hat in the wardrobe, then unpacked a few clothes from his trunk. For a while after that, he roamed the cabin, not certain what to do with himself.

It was too early yet to dress for dinner, and he saw no reason to wash or shave again, having made an adequate job of both earlier. Sleeping during the day went too much against the grain of a man used to working from dawn till dusk and often later.

He toyed with the notion of sitting down at

the writing desk and composing a letter to Tessa.
He could explain why he'd decided to go on to
Strathandrew ahead of her, then he could wish
her a swift recovery and safe journey on the
train. How would he ever post it, though, from
out at sea? And even if he managed that feat,
could he trust Lady Lydiard not to keep the message from her daughter?

Though he'd had a good solid education at
the village school, writing was still enough of a
chore for him that he didn't fancy going to the
trouble of it for nothing.

When a cautious knock sounded on the cabin
door, Ewan jumped to answer it, welcoming a
potential distraction, even for a few moments.
"Aye, what can I do for ye?"

"That's what I came to ask ye, sir," replied a
small wiry man a few years Ewan's junior. "Any
clothes ye need laundered or..."

The steward's gaze rose from Ewan's chin
to look him full in the face. "Hang me! Ewan
Geddes, is that ye in those toff clothes?" He
thrust out his hand. "Jock McMurdo. Rosie's
nephew from Strathandrew."

"Wee Jockie, aye!" Ewan grabbed his hand
and shook it vigorously. "How've ye been, man?
It does me good to see ye again!"

No word of a lie, that. His restlessness had
eased all at once, as if a fresh sea breeze had
just blown down the galley way.

Jockie stared at Ewan, shaking his head. "Auntie said ye'd made yer fortune in America. What brings ye back home again—as a guest of Miss Talbot, no less?"

What would Jock and the rest of the folk at Strathandrew say when they discovered he might soon be more to Miss Talbot than a guest?

"It's a bit of a long tale, but I promise ye'll hear it by and by. About what ye asked before, my gear's all still as clean as when I left the hotel. The only thing I need is a bit of something to do. I'm not used to hanging about idle. I don't suppose ye could put me to work?"

Jockie laughed until he saw Ewan meant it. "Peel taties in the galley, ye mean? The captain'd have me keelhauled!"

"Would he, now?" Ewan tried to hide his disappointment. "Well, we can't have that, can we?"

"Ye could come up and take a turn around the deck," Jockie suggested. "I could introduce ye to the rest of the crew. At least ye'd get a breath of air and have folks to talk to."

The notion tempted Ewan, but… "Miss Talbot said we should come below to get out from underfoot of the crew."

"The *Marlet*'s slipped her moorings now." Jockie shrugged. "It's pretty quiet on deck. Besides, ye look like a man who's sharp enough to get out of the way when he needs to."

Not always, Ewan admitted to himself, even

as he nodded to Jockie. He'd never been wise enough to keep out of Claire Talbot's way when she had her temper up.

Was it possible he hadn't wanted to?

"Mark me, the gentleman won't be able to take his eyes off you at dinner, miss." Claire's new maid, a bouncy little Welsh girl, brushed one last curl around her forefinger.

Claire did not need to stare at herself in the dressing table glass to know that a fierce blush burned her cheeks. "It is a matter of total indifference to me whether Mr. Geddes so much as glances in my direction."

"Just as you say, miss." The girl chuckled to herself as if she did not believe a word of it. "Though I think he'll be a fool if he doesn't. I suppose you don't care whether you look at him, either."

Before Claire could stammer an answer, Williams prattled on, "You'll be missing something if you don't. For I caught a glimpse of him and I wouldn't mind a few more. He's as fine looking a gentleman as ever I saw."

"I suppose he's well enough looking," said Claire, "if you like that type."

"And do you, miss?"

Far too much.

Claire shrugged. "I suppose."

If only she could make herself feel as calm

as she sounded! Now that she was about to put her plan into action, a host of misgivings assailed her, and she began to doubt her ability to carry it off.

Her brief encounter with Ewan in the galley way had opened her eyes to a difficulty she had not foreseen. If she hoped to lure the man to abandon Tessa in favor of her, she must pretend to put their contentious youth behind them and make a fresh, more amiable start. But she must not let herself truly fall under the spell of his charm, or he would break her heart all over again, the rogue!

Never, since she had come of age and taken the helm of Brancasters, had Claire faced such a challenge. At least then, despite her youth and her sex, and the prejudice of the commercial world toward both, she'd felt better equipped for the task she'd set herself.

After all she had strong organizational abilities and a head for business. Her father would have laughed himself ill at the thought of her as a seductress!

She forced herself to look at her reflection. "You've done a fine job, Williams. No wonder Lady Cunningham treasures you so. It was good of her to lend me your services, and most kind of you to oblige."

The way in which Williams had dressed her hair looked fussier than Claire liked, but it was probably the sort of thing men admired. The maid's artful use of cosmetics gave her face more color without looking painted.

"I was glad to, miss, for the chance of a holiday in Scotland. I've heard it's lovely this time of year, but her ladyship doesn't care to travel. It's no great chore to make you look beautiful. You have such a lovely complexion, and fine eyes." She hesitated. "Do you mind if I offer a suggestion, though, miss?"

"By all means. You are the expert."

"Perhaps I should just hold my tongue, but I did wonder, miss, whether you needed to wear quite so many jewels?"

Indeed she did, though Claire did not dare confess why. "Do you think they are unbecoming? There are some very valuable pieces here."

She had emptied her own jewelry box of many that had never been worn since her mother's death. Lady Lydiard had contributed several more of distinguished pedigree from the family collection. "Why, this sapphire necklace alone is worth thousands of pounds."

"And lovely it is, miss. It goes well with your eyes. But the earrings are a newer style. Do you think they go together? And the bracelets—do you need them on both wrists?"

Claire would have preferred none at all, and a plainer gown, come to that. Heavy with diamonds and pearls, the bracelets were awkward things. And the weight of the earrings was already challenging the tightness of her corset to see which could inflict the most discomfort upon her. She hoped one day Tessa would appreciate the sacrifices she had made!

She was not so far gone in taste as to dispute Williams's opinion about the necklace and the earrings, either. But the point of wearing these jewels was not to enhance her questionable beauty, but to advertise her unquestioned wealth.

"I appreciate your interest and your suggestions, Williams." Claire rose from the dressing table. "But I get so few opportunities to wear my jewels, I hate to forgo one when it arises."

"I understand, miss." The Welsh girl bobbed a curtsy. Servants knew better than to contradict their masters, no matter how foolish their actions.

Claire held out her hand. "Now, if I might have my fan, please?"

It was a costly item as well, each delicate slat of ivory elaborately carved in an identical pattern. And it might well prove useful for more than impressing the extent of her fortune upon Ewan Geddes.

"There you go, miss."

Claire snapped it open, then gave a practice flutter to cool the tingling warmth that swept through her whenever she contemplated what she was about to do.

Chapter Six

Blast it all, he was going to be late! And not just fashionably so.

Racing down the galley way steps at a dangerous speed, Ewan yanked out his pocket watch and peered at its bland, accusing face.

"Past seven already," he muttered, "and I still have to change clothes!"

At least Lady Lydiard was not on board. Claire Talbot had the look of a woman who prized punctuality, though. Was he a fool to believe he had any chance of making a good impression upon her, no matter how well he behaved himself on the voyage?

Remembering her sudden coolness toward him, and the fine time he'd been having up on deck with the crew of the *Marlet,* made him wonder if he would ever feel at ease in Miss Talbot's world. And did he want to?

He stumbled on the last couple of stairs, but managed to stagger the few steps to his cabin. He flung open the door and raced inside, stubbing his foot with violent force into one of the bedposts. With a bellow of pain and rage at himself for not watching his step, he commenced to jump around the room on his sound foot, growling a litany of foul Gaelic curses he'd learned in his youth from Fergus Gowrie, the gamekeeper at Strathandrew.

Ewan did not realize the cabin door was still open until he heard a high-pitched giggle. He glanced up to see a tiny dark-haired lass scooting by, one hand clamped over her mouth in a vain effort to stifle her mirth. Whoever she was, Ewan had no doubt she'd understood every coarse oath that had left his lips.

Would she repeat them to Claire Talbot? Ewan slammed the cabin door and began tearing off his shirt, popping a collar button in the process.

When someone knocked on the door, he barked, "What do ye want? Tell Miss Talbot I'll be along directly!"

The door eased open and Jock popped his head in. "It's only me with a kettle of hot water for ye, if ye fancy a washup?"

"I reckon I could stand one—" Ewan nod-

ded toward the washstand "—though it'll have
to be quick."

"Can I give ye a hand?" asked Jock as he
poured the steaming water into the basin.

Be waited on by one of his old mates? The
notion made Ewan squirm, though he probably
could get ready quicker with some help.

"Don't trouble yerself, laddie." He rummaged
in the wardrobe for a clean shirt, pulling on the
first one that came to hand. "I'm used to manag-
ing on my own. Thanks for the water, though."

"Just as ye like, then," said Jock. "If ye change
yer mind, ye've only to ring the bell."

Once Jock had closed the cabin door behind
him, Ewan glanced down at his shirt to find it
misbuttoned. He cursed again.

By the time he fumbled his way through a
quick wash, finished dressing and pulled a comb
through his hair, he was in a vile temper.

Miss Talbot's greeting, when he finally
reached the dining room, did not improve it.

"There you are." She fluttered a very elegant
fan in front of her face. "I was afraid you had
decided to jump ship."

Ewan almost wished he had. Late as he was,
he still had a long evening ahead of him. What
did he have to talk about with this woman, anyway, besides how much she used to vex him?
Despite his promise to make a fresh start, he

was beginning to remember why they'd never gotten on.

"I was busy with something," he muttered. "I didn't notice the time." Belatedly and grudgingly, he added, "I apologize for keeping ye waiting."

"Pray, what kept you so occupied?" Though Claire Talbot's tone sounded polite enough, a steely light in those blue-gray eyes of hers made him feel as if he were being interrogated. "I feared you might be restless and anxious for some diversion."

"I was at first." Ewan circled the dining table, eyeing the settings of china, crystal and silver even more elaborate than those at Lydiard House. "Then I met up with one of my old mates from Strathandrew who introduced me 'round to the crew. We got talking and the time just...went."

"Did it?" Her fingers appeared to clench the fan harder.

Perhaps she took it as an insult that a bunch of common sailors had made him late to dine with her. Ewan wondered what she would say if she knew he'd rather be eating in the crew's mess this very minute than in her too-quiet, too-lavish dining room.

She drew in a long, slow breath through her nose. "You're here now. That's the important thing. Would you care for a drink before dinner?"

A dram sounded like a fine idea, to settle him down after the fuss of being late. "Aye, I'll have a whiskey, thank ye."

Claire nodded to a young man in uniform stationed by a small sideboard.

He poured Ewan a liberal measure of amber liquid from a heavy, cut-glass decanter. "Water with that, sir?"

Ewan shook his head and reached for the glass. He considered it almost sacrilege to dilute good whiskey. The smooth single malt rolled over his tongue and down his throat, warming as it went.

"Anything for you, Miss Talbot?" asked the young steward.

Claire shook her head. "The dinner wines will be sufficient for me, thank you."

Was that her way of chiding him for accepting the drink *she'd* offered?

Ewan tossed the rest of his whiskey back in a single swig. "That was good! I believe I'll have another, if ye don't mind."

"By all means, Mr. Geddes. I am pleased our refreshments meet with your approval." She gave her wrist a little shake, showing off a bracelet heavy with precious gems.

How many years, or decades, of hard work would it have taken for him to afford such a bauble when he'd first started out in America? Was Miss Talbot trying to impress upon him what different worlds he and Tessa came from? Well, she needn't bother—he knew well enough.

"Are ye sure ye'll be able to handle yer knife and fork with all those rings getting in the way, Miss Talbot?" He bolted his second drink of whiskey, then handed his glass to the young steward for another refill. "Or do ye take some of them off when ye eat?"

Miss Talbot shot him an icy look, but answered in the tone of someone receiving a compliment. "Lovely, aren't they?"

She fluttered her fingers to show off the jewels. The hard surfaces of the gems glittered in the light from the oil lamps. They taunted Ewan, though he reminded himself he could buy such things by the barrowful now, if he wanted.

"This one was a favorite of my mother's, I'm told." Claire Talbot sauntered toward him and lifted her hand for him to admire the ring.

Then she rattled on about cuts and carats and mountings until his head spun. Though perhaps the three whiskeys in rapid succession contributed to his dizziness, as well. Ewan was grateful when she finally suggested they sit down to eat.

He had almost gotten himself seated when he realized she was still standing, with an awkward, expectant air.

"Pardon me!" He jumped up, catching the edge of the tabletop with his knee and making the glasses tinkle precariously. "I didn't think."

He hauled out Miss Talbot's chair with too much force and almost stumbled. "It's not often I have the pleasure of dining in the company of a lady."

If this evening was any example, it was a pleasure he could well do without.

"We must correct that, mustn't we?" As she stepped past him to take her seat, Miss Talbot's arm brushed lightly against his. The fleeting, casual contact sent a dark whisper of arousal through Ewan's flesh.

That would be the whiskey at work, too, he told himself. For years the only spirits to pass his lips had been a wee rum toddy now and then, to help ease him to sleep. In public, he preferred to keep his wits about him at all times. More than once he'd taken advantage of being the only sober man at a table of business acquaintances.

He could not deny Claire Talbot was a fine-looking lass, in spite of all the priceless gewgaws she'd decked herself out with. But she was not the woman he'd crossed the Atlantic for. Not the woman he meant to make his own.

He had no business responding to her this way!

Gingerly, Claire settled herself on the chair Ewan held out for her. She wrinkled her nose at the faint but pungent whiskey fumes she smelled on his breath when she passed him. Every fortune hunter she'd ever met had also been a prodigious drinker. Clearly this one was no exception.

"Yer sister doesn't deck herself with a load of jewelry," said Ewan. He shoved her chair into the table with such force Claire feared she would be sliced in two.

His tone had a subtly accusing edge, but she ignored it in her eagerness to exploit the opening he had provided her. "Tessa does not have a collection of pieces such as I inherited from my mother and grandmother."

Claire rested her arm on the table, so he might get a better look at her bracelet and rings. "Though we share an affection as close as any full sisters, you must remember Tessa and I have different mothers. It is from *my* Grandfather Brancaster that our fortune derives."

She hoped the implication of her words would soak into his whiskey-befuddled mind.

Apparently it did. For after a moment's pensive silence, while the waiter set shallow bowls of turtle soup before them, Ewan cast a speculative glance over her. "Ye mean yer worth a good deal more than yer sister, Miss Talbot?"

"I mean…" She struggled to produce an inviting smile, while her loathing for Ewan Geddes battled her vexing attraction to him. "…I have a great deal more capital and a far greater income. At present, Tessa has less than five hundred pounds a year from our father's estate. That will increase, of course, upon her mother's death. But Lady Lydiard is in good health and likely to live for many years."

Ewan made a wry face as he took a sip of his soup. Was the taste not to his liking, or could it be the news regarding Tessa's want of fortune that made him grimace?

Claire lifted a spoonful of soup to her lips. It tasted fine to her—neither too hot nor too salty. "By contrast, I have an income exceeding fifty *thousand* a year, and more in property, as well as my shares in Brancasters."

Once he got started on the soup, Ewan seemed to find it more to his taste. He cleaned the bowl with single-minded concentration while Claire listed more of her financial assets.

When she paused to finish her soup, he leaned back in his chair, staring at her in a way that made her most uncomfortable, yet strangely roused. "What a shame gold can't buy ye happiness, isn't it, Miss Talbot?"

Claire willed her features to freeze in an impassive mask so Ewan Geddes would not guess how much distress his casual comment had inflicted upon her. She had long since discovered that gold could not buy the kind of happiness to which she had once aspired. And the cut-glass imitation that was readily available for purchase came with a heavy surtax of heartbreak.

She reached for her wineglass, desperate for

anything that would delay the necessity of a reply. She took only a sip, though, determined to retain the advantage of sobriety over her adversary.

Then it occurred to her that he had given her another opening. She must not respond to him with her true feelings, but in the character of a lonely heiress who might be vulnerable to the charms of a skillful fortune hunter.

As she set down her wineglass, she heaved a sigh that was not wholly counterfeit. "Alas, you are correct. I have often thought how pleasant it might be to have an amiable companion in life and the joy of children."

Ugh! She could not mouth much more such stuff even if it brought Ewan Geddes running to court her. Such sentiments were simply too close to the true feelings she sought to hide from the rest of the world.

"If it's any comfort, I know how ye feel, Claire." He covered her beringed fingers with his large brown hand. "I know...better than ye might think."

The gall of him! Claire could scarcely resist the urge to wrench her hand away. What did he know about her or the things she wanted?

"I have no cause to complain," she insisted, as she often had to herself over the years. "Most women and a great many men would envy my worldly goods. A big house in Mayfair. A sporting estate in the Highlands. A private yacht at my disposal. The assets of a thriving company like Brancasters under my control."

There, she had waved the bait right under his nose. Now to see if the rat would nibble!

The return of the steward, bearing a course of oysters, made Ewan pull his hand back abruptly from where it had rested over hers. That did not bode well.

"More wine, Mr. Geddes?" Claire held up her own glass. "This is a particularly fine vintage. Terribly expensive, of course, but worth every penny."

"Not on top of the whiskey." He gave a lopsided grin. "Or I might only waste the precious stuff by heaving it all back up again."

He pushed away the plate of oysters, artistically arranged on a bed of ice with twists of lemon and a sprinkling of capers.

As they continued to dine, Claire faced the frustrating certainty that her brilliant plan was not working. Apart from that one touch of his hand, a gesture of pity rather than pursuit, Ewan Geddes had shown not the slightest interest in her fortune or in her as a woman. If anything, he seemed to grow more brusque and unsociable as the evening progressed.

If it had not been for Tessa and Brancasters, Claire would have dumped a plate of oysters over his head and been done with him!

A timid voice in the back of her mind had the effrontery to suggest that Ewan Geddes might not be a fortune hunter, after all. Perhaps he truly cared for Tessa and would not be lured away by the riches Claire dangled in front of him. She told that fool voice to keep quiet and let her get on with what she was trying to do.

"Ah, roast pheasant, done to a turn! Surely this will tempt your appetite, Mr. Geddes." Claire tried to keep her voice from betraying her mounting desperation. "My cook is a treasure—well worth the salary he commands."

How many more ways could she possibly steer the conversation back to the subject of her fortune? If Ewan Geddes didn't soon show a little interest, what would she do?

The pheasant did taste good. Or would have if it had not been poisoned by Claire Talbot's latest boast about her blasted fortune. The woman seemed bent on giving him an account of every guinea!

What was she trying to do by flaunting her wealth in front of him like this? Impress upon him the vast chasm that separated him from Tessa? Perhaps she'd pull out the family crest next, to remind him of the Talbots' noble lineage!

Ewan wished he hadn't tossed back that trio of whiskies so fast. He had hoped they would smooth the edge off his bad mood, but they had only made it darker. He found himself brooding on old grievances against the lairds, eager to take offense, galled by a sense of inferiority he'd battled his whole life to escape.

A moment of expectant silence roused him from his brooding thoughts. "Sorry, did ye say something, Miss Talbot?"

He forced himself to look at her, though he shrank from the sensations it was apt to provoke in him.

For all her effort to play the part of a diligent hostess, Claire Talbot looked so regal and haughty...yet so vexingly attractive. She made him want to grab hold of her and kiss her until that stiff highborn spine of hers loosened and she melted in his arms. Caress those stiff, sculpted ringlets into a wanton tumble.

"I was just observing that you seem rather preoccupied, sir." Her cool eyes seemed to divine his improper thoughts and scorn them.

He had better not stay around her much longer, or fatigue would join forces with the whiskey to sap his better judgment.

"I'll own I have a thing or two on my mind, Miss Talbot, and it's been a long day for me." Ewan pushed away from the table and rose from his chair, though not as steadily as he would have liked. "I trust ye'll excuse me if I go back to my cabin and turn in for the night."

"But Mr. Geddes, we have several more courses left!" Her words came out almost in a wail. "You must stay to try the fillets of veal, at least. The sauce is one of Monsieur Anton's specialties."

"Aye, no doubt it's made with rare spices that cost two guineas an ounce. Thank ye for yer splendid hospitality, Miss Talbot. I fear it's a mite too rich for the belly of a lad raised on mutton and oatmeal."

Claire Talbot leaped to her feet. "Are you implying that the servants at Strathandrew were not properly nourished?"

Ewan congratulated himself on shaking Miss Talbot out of her pose of polite contempt without resorting to behavior he would regret tomorrow morning.

"I'm not saying anything of the kind, if ye'd take a minute to listen. What I mean is I was raised on good, plain food, and I've never developed much of a taste for yer sort of delicacies. If ye find them so toothsome, go ahead and eat my share while ye're at it. Good night to ye, Miss Talbot."

With that he turned and marched toward the door, while behind him Claire Talbot cried, "You cannot just leave like that. Come back here at once!"

Ewan spun about on his heel and barely escaped tripping himself. "Is that an order, miss?"

"Yes! No! I mean, do you truly propose to make me dine alone for the rest of the evening?"

He nodded. "I reckon ye'll enjoy the company more that way."

"That's not true. I've been most grateful for your company." She looked as if she might choke on those words.

"If ye are, ye've got a queer way of showing it." Once again he turned and strode off.

This time Claire Talbot did not make the mistake of trying to summon him back.

Once he reached his luxuriously appointed cabin, Ewan took off his clothes, muttering under his breath all the things he should have said to Claire Talbot. Things he'd wanted to say ten years ago, but hadn't dared for fear of getting the sack. Discretion warned him that he should continue to hold his tongue, for Tessa's sake, but he wasn't so sure.

Claire Talbot's behavior this evening had convinced him she would never give her blessing to a match between her sister and their former gillie. He'd been a fool to think he had a chance of winning her over. And she'd been a heartless vixen for leading him to believe it, then rubbing his nose in the Talbot fortune.

It had been on the tip of his tongue to tell her how much *he* was worth these days—every penny of which he'd earned from his own hard work and ingenuity. It would almost be worth it to see the look on her face. But he would rather see a different sort of look on Tessa's face, when he surprised her with an account of his wealth once she'd agreed to be his wife.

Little by little, his stomach began to settle, the tightness in his chest began to ease and his breathing began to slow. The gentle movement of the *Marlet* lulled him to sleep.

Before he let it overcome him entirely, Ewan made a promise to himself. If Claire Talbot tried any more of her nonsense tomorrow, he would not stand for it.

Chapter Seven

Claire jolted awake the next morning, her breath coming in shallow spasms, her brow beaded with cold sweat. She must have tossed about or called out in her sleep before that, for Williams came rushing in from her small adjoining cabin.

"Is something wrong, miss? I was afraid you were being murdered in your bed!"

"Just a dream." Claire shook her head in an effort to banish it, but the memories clung stubbornly in her mind, as though everything she'd dreamed had truly happened.

She'd been walking up the aisle of the old kirk near Strathandrew. Walking toward Ewan Geddes, who stood at the foot of the altar wearing the kind of kilt and gillie vest he had worn in their youth. He'd looked so ruggedly handsome, she'd wanted to run down the aisle toward him, but her feet had felt heavy as bricks.

"A bad one, was it?" asked Williams. "Can I get you anything, miss? A glass of warm milk or a tipple of something stronger to soothe your nerves?"

"No." Claire rubbed her eyes. "I shall be fine once I can fully wake up."

Another part of the dream came back to her. When she'd finally reached the altar, Ewan had seized her in his arms and kissed her, the way he'd done one long-ago night in the darkness. That kiss had made her heart flutter and her knees tremble. Now, as she remembered it with such fierce clarity, her lips ached to feel it again.

"Shall I go fetch your breakfast, miss?" asked Williams. "Or would you like to see if you can go back to sleep for a while longer? It's early yet, and it isn't as though you have urgent business to attend, is it?"

She did have business to attend, Claire reminded herself. Though not the kind her maid meant. And that business was more urgent than ever.

"I should like breakfast, please." She reached for her dressing gown and pulled it on. "Once I wake I never can get back to sleep."

"Very well, miss." Williams headed back to her own cabin. "Would you like a tray, or—?"

"In the dining room, please," said Claire.

Though she quailed at the thought of another disaster like last night's dinner, eating in her cabin would provide no opportunity to socialize with Ewan Geddes. And she needed to take advantage of every remaining opportunity after having bungled last night's so badly.

While her maid scurried off to don her apron, Claire rose and slipped behind her dressing screen. Finding a small amount of cold water in the bottom of the ewer, she poured it in the basin, then splashed her face with it. The mild shock succeeded in helping her shake off the dream, but not fully.

It would take more than a little cold water to wash away the final image that had so distressed her. While Ewan Geddes had held her in his arms, kissing her with such raw ardor, Tessa had suddenly called his name from the back of the kirk. Claire had clung to him when he pulled away from her.

"It's not ye I want!" The contempt in his eyes had stung her heart. Like the way he'd looked at her last night when he'd left the dining room, but even more severe.

That was not what had woken her, though, the way she'd woken from other nightmares. What had shocked her awake had been watching Tessa dash up the aisle and fling herself into Ewan's arms—watching him kiss Tessa the way he'd kissed her, the way she longed for him to kiss her again.

When the scene flashed in her mind again, Claire clenched her eyes shut, though she knew it would not help. If anything, it only brought the painful image into sharper focus.

She dashed another palmful of water into her face.

Williams bustled back in, ready to face the day. Claire envied her maid's well-rested, cheerful countenance.

"I'll just go tell Monsieur Anton to prepare your breakfast, shall I, miss? Then come back to get you dressed?"

Claire peeked out from behind the dressing screen. "While you're about it, would you please check if Mr. Geddes is up yet?"

"Aye, miss, I won't be a moment."

Once the maid had left, Claire sat down on her bed, expelling a shaky breath. The dream made her realize that her long-ago feelings for Ewan Geddes were not entirely in the past.

After the way he'd treated her last night, she detested him more than she ever had. Yet the power he'd once exerted over her was still as potent as ever. Could there be anything worse for a woman, particularly one who prided herself on her sense and discretion, than to harbor passionate feelings for a man who despised her?

All the more reason she must get him out of her life…and Tessa's.

Perhaps she had not made herself plain enough last night. She had taken every opportunity to impress Ewan Geddes with the extent of her fortune. But had she done enough to hint that she might be ripe for seduction by a man like him?

Today she must take a new tack and pursue it with all her energy. She could not count on Lady Lydiard to keep Tessa away from Strathandrew for long. And she had not bargained on Ewan Geddes being so resistant to her plan.

The cabin door opened and Williams slipped back in. "Monsieur Anton says he'll have breakfast ready by the time you're dressed, miss. I'd be afraid to eat it, though, he's in such a temper."

Claire rose from the bed with an exasperated sigh. "What about this time?"

"On account of all the food that was sent back from dinner last night, miss. I hope you and Mr. Geddes are in better appetite today."

Men! If she could have managed to sail to Scotland without them, Claire would have pitched every male creature on the *Marlet* overboard!

"Speaking of Mr. Geddes—" she tried to sound only mildly interested "—did you inquire about him?"

"Didn't have to, miss." The maid threw open Claire's wardrobe, which contained gowns enough for a very long stay at Strathandrew. "Just as I was heading to the galley, I saw him come out of his cabin and go up on deck." She gestured toward the wardrobe. "Now, which of these do you fancy for this morning, miss?"

Anything that might tempt a man to try his luck with me. Claire bit her tongue to stifle those too-frank words. "Oh, something pretty." What did she know about dressing to attract a man?

"They're all pretty, miss."

"Something bright," said Claire, growing more flustered by the minute. "Something that... doesn't cover up too much of me."

"I see." The maid lifted out a rose-colored gown with a great quantity of lace about it. In an innocent tone she inquired, "And I suppose you don't care in the least whether the gentleman so much as glances at you?"

Claire peered at the gown. Under ordinary circumstances, she would have considered it too fussy for morning wear, and pink had never been her color. But certainly it was bright, with sleeves that ended at the elbow and a neckline that dipped quite low.

Desperate times, she told herself as she nodded her approval of Williams's choice, called for desperate measures.

This was desperate! Ewan squinted against the sun's brilliant glare as he stumbled up the stairs to the deck. Hungover from three wee drams of whiskey!

He'd known men who drank the stuff like mother's milk and never seemed a whit the worse for it. This morning he was almost ashamed to call himself a Highlander! His temples throbbed, his tongue felt as if it could use a shave, and his belly protested even the gentle rocking of the yacht. He hoped a dose of fresh, salty air would do him some good.

Leaning against the deck railing, he closed his eyes and drank in deep, cleansing drafts of it. The knotted flesh of his neck began to unclench…until he heard footsteps behind him.

To his relief, the captain's deep, resonant voice boomed forth. "A fine day, Mr. Geddes. I trust ye slept well?"

"Oh, aye," Ewan lied. He could not recall the last time he'd spent such a restless night.

Provocative images of Claire Talbot had tormented him through the endless dark hours. The sensuous roll and sway of the ship had only made it worse, until he ached with sensations he was ashamed to feel. If he dreamed of any woman that way, it should be Tessa—but he could not.

When he tried to substitute her for her sister, that felt wrong somehow, too. He kept picturing her as she'd been ten years ago, which made him feel like an old lecher…or would have if he'd been able to summon up any carnal desire.

What could be wrong with him? Had Claire Talbot laced that whiskey with some wicked potion?

"Whereabouts are we?" Eager for any distraction from such thoughts, Ewan nodded toward the white chalk coastline, which did not look too far distant.

Captain MacLeod pulled the pipe from his mouth and pointed the stem northward. "That'd be Sussex there, Mr. Geddes."

Ewan frowned. "Only Sussex. I thought surely we'd be off the coast of Devon by now."

He did not want this voyage to go on a minute longer than need be. After last night, an extended rail journey with Lady Lydiard seemed almost appealing. At least he would not need to fear entertaining improper thoughts about *her!*

"Not much of a wind, lad, in case ye hadn't noticed," the captain growled. "The *Marlet* ain't a paddle steamer that can just puff along without a care for wind or seas."

"Odd, isn't it?" Ewan cast a glance at the great canvas sails, trimmed to catch the fitful breezes. "Brancasters builds the most modern iron-clad steamships in the kingdom, yet its owners still travel by wood and sail."

Before the captain could offer his opinion, Claire Talbot spoke up from behind them.

"Not odd, surely?" She stepped up to the railing between the two men, but closer to Ewan.

Far closer than he would have liked.

"I believe it is all a question of function." Though she addressed her words to him, she fixed her gaze on the pale chalk cliffs of the coast. "Brancasters builds naval vessels and merchant ships that must be swift and reliable. The *Marlet* is a pleasure craft. The journey itself is at least as important as how quickly we reach our destination. I prefer to dispense with the noise and smoke of a steam engine, and the necessity of toting a load of filthy coal to fuel it."

Though Ewan felt a grudging agreement with those sentiments, something about Miss Talbot's tone and manner made him bristle. No doubt his presence on the *Marlet* was as welcome as a noisy, smoky steam engine or a filthy load of coal.

Without bothering to ask his opinion, she breezed on. "If it means we require an extra day or two to reach Strathandrew, that is no great hardship, in my opinion."

No great hardship for her, perhaps. For Ewan's part, he wondered how he would stand another day in her company, let alone several.

He tried to keep his gaze from straying toward her, but without much success. Why had she chosen to wear *that* dress for a morning aboard ship? If he hadn't known better, he would have sworn she meant to taunt him.

The ruches of lace softened the sharper angles

of her figure, while the warm color made her look younger than her years. She was no longer bristling with jewelry, apart from a modest gold locket that nestled in the slender hollow of her throat. Neither had her hair been tortured into an elaborate confection of kinks and curls. A few wisps fluttered in the gentle breeze, tempting Ewan to raise his hand and smooth them back from her face. Then if his knuckles happened to graze her cheek…

What was he thinking?

Ewan made himself take a step away from her.

"There's something aristocratic about a sailing ship, isn't there?" He addressed the question to no one in particular. "It glides along all quiet and stately, without seeming to make any effort about it. A bit capricious, but that's all part of the charm, eh?"

It all sounded quite innocent—even flattering. He did not mean it that way.

"I suppose so." Her reply had a guarded edge, as if she sensed a possible ambush, but could not tell what direction it might come from. "I had never thought of it quite that way."

Was it his fancy, or did she draw closer to him? Ewan might have backed off again, but that would have felt like a retreat.

"Aye." He rubbed his unshaven chin. "Steam packets are the working class of the sea these days—noisy, smelly and dirty, but they get the job done."

"Wind and sail have served mankind well for thousands of years, Mr. Geddes. It seems rather hard to abandon them altogether for the sake of progress and efficiency."

Captain MacLeod must have sensed the veiled hostility of their exchange and sought to avoid it, the way he would have steered the *Marlet* out of the path of an oncoming storm. "I should go relieve my first mate at the helm for a spell."

He strode off, puffing hard on his pipe and shaking his head. Ewan would have liked an excuse to get away, too, but he feared Claire Talbot would only follow him. He was trapped with the woman on this bloody slow boat to Scotland!

Claire let out a breath of relief as she watched the captain depart. She'd gone cold with dread when she'd overheard Ewan asking why a full night's sailing had not brought them farther on their voyage. What if Captain MacLeod had told him of her instructions?

Fortunately, the captain had provided a credible answer that did not betray her. Still, she had not wanted to give Ewan the opportunity to quiz him further. She had been obliged to thrust herself between them, though it threw her foolish senses all awry, standing so close to her guest.

They could not seem to focus on anything else

when he was nearby. Though she tried to keep her eyes fixed on the coastline, she could not stop herself from glancing at him far too often. A subtle tremor went through her whenever her errant gaze lingered over his chiseled jaw, shadowed with a dark stubble of whisker. Her ears seemed to shut out every sound but the mellow lilt of his voice, and her skin prickled with anticipation of his most casual touch.

To think her stepmother had recently praised her as a sensible, detached sort of person. Claire had never felt more foolish or fanciful in her life!

Before Ewan could further imply that she was a sentimental fool for keeping the *Marlet* in service, she swung about to face him. "Have you eaten breakfast yet?"

"I wasn't hungry."

Hard as she tried, Claire could not let it pass. "How curious. You were not hungry last night, either. I thought sea air was supposed to whet the appetite."

He scowled, yet still managed to look far too handsome for his own good...and hers.

Claire tamped down her exasperation. She had so little time. If the two of them kept antagonizing one another like this, the *Marlet* could sail around the world before she'd entice Ewan Geddes into wooing her.

"Seasick?" She tried to sound solicitous.

"From this, ye mean?" He gave a snort of contempt and gestured toward the gently undulating waves. "I've eaten like a horse on far worse seas."

It was her company, then, that took his appetite away? Had he been tempted by her wealth, as she'd intended, but shrank from what he must do to get it?

She made a stiff little bow, then turned to go. "As you wish. I could do with some breakfast."

In fact, it would be a miracle if she choked down more than a mouthful. But that was the most convenient excuse to get her away from Ewan Geddes before she burst into tears or pitched him overboard.

She had almost reached the galley way when Ewan called out, "What's yer grand cook serving up this morning? Poached peacocks' eggs and broiled goose liver?"

Vexing man! He had forced her into a humiliating retreat. Could he not be satisfied with that?

"Plain hens' eggs, I'm afraid." She tossed the retort back over her shoulder. "Fried ham and perhaps some kippered herring. Oh, and I instructed Monsieur Anton to prepare oatmeal porridge in case you hankered after it."

She had not gotten halfway down the stairs when she heard his voice behind her again. "Porridge, ye say?"

Would he plague her with his company at the moment she could not abide it? "I expect you would only find some fault with Monsieur Anton's preparation of the dish, Mr. Geddes. So it is probably just as well if you don't bother with breakfast, after all."

"Waste good oatmeal?" His footsteps followed her. "Granny Cameron would rise up from her grave and denounce me for a Sassenach."

That made her turn and confront him. "I know what that word means, sir. No doubt it is what all of you called me and my family."

She half expected him to acknowledge it with pride. Instead he cried, "Hang on to the railing, will ye? I'm not close enough to catch ye if ye take a fall."

"You heard Captain MacLeod. The sea is calm." All the same, she reached for the railing.

The last thing she wanted at that moment was for Ewan Geddes to lay hands on her, whatever the reason.

"Come or don't then, as you wish." She turned and headed for the dining room, taking care to watch her step. "I will not try to persuade you either way, for you will be bound to do quite the opposite, no doubt."

"Are ye saying I'm contrary, Miss Talbot?"

"If the shoe fits, Mr. Geddes…"

Claire thought she heard him chuckle. If she needed any further proof of his contrariness, there it was. When she tried to get close to him, he went out of his way to avoid her. When she tried to avoid him, he pursued her. Flatter him and he took offense. Insult him and he laughed. Perhaps if she tried to drown the man, he would take a violent fancy to her!

"Ye know, this oatmeal isn't bad," said Ewan a short while later, after he had eaten rather a large bowl of it. He sounded surprised, as though he'd expected it to be laced with poison. "This may be just what I needed after all that rich food last night."

"And the whiskey," Claire muttered under her breath.

"Aye, that, too," he admitted with irritating good cheer.

Then he glanced at her plate. "Where's your appetite gone all of a sudden?"

You took it away!

When she did not dignify his question with an answer, he provided one of his own. "Is this fare too simple for ye?"

This time she could not stifle a sharp retort. "Perhaps it's the company!"

"Now who's being contrary?" Ewan took a sip of his tea. "Last night, ye didn't want me to leave. Just a wee while ago ye invited me for breakfast, and yesterday ye pulled every string possible to make me come with ye on this damn slow boat."

Claire rose from her chair and threw down

her napkin. "I most certainly did not! That was your own decision entirely."

"Bollocks! Ye tricked me into it...ye dared me. Said ye wanted to get to know me better, to judge if I'd make a suitable husband for yer sister."

"And you claimed to welcome the challenge," Claire retorted. "Is this your idea of making an agreeable impression upon your future relations?"

She almost choked on those words. The prospect of attending Ewan and Tessa's wedding, celebrating holidays with them, perhaps being godmother to their children...

Ewan rose to his feet, but slowly. It had been most rude of him to remain seated after she'd stood up. "I was a fool for thinking ye meant to give me a fair chance! But then, ye're used to playing me for a fool, aren't ye, Miss Talbot?"

Did he know? Claire's stomach gave such an alarming lurch she feared she might retch up what little breakfast she'd eaten. She must get a breath of air!

"I have no idea what you are talking about, Ewan Geddes." She strode toward the door. "I doubt if you do, either!"

"Ye know well enough." He was following her—the rogue! "Don't try to pretend ye don't."

Claire considered ducking into her cabin. But in his present mood, she feared Ewan Geddes would have no scruples about pursuing her. If that happened, who knew what a pathetic fool she might make of herself? She still desired the man as much as she detested him. Laws, she must be mad!

Instead, she charged back up toward the deck, hoping he would not come after her. Or if he did, that the presence of the crew might shame him into minding his manners.

He quashed her first hope under his forceful tread as he followed her along the galley way. "Ye never had any intention of giving me a chance, did ye?"

The volume of his voice told Claire her second hope had also been in vain.

Once the deck was securely beneath her feet, she spun about to confront him. She had not dared risk being pitched into his arms again. "I beg your pardon?"

He had followed so close on her heels that when Claire turned, she found herself staring up into his blazing eyes, almost as close as they had been during their waltz at the Fortescues' ball. She tried to back away, only to find the unyielding barrier of the mainmast behind her.

"Ye can't have it." Ewan Geddes loomed over her, tall, menacing and devilishly attractive— damn him! In reply to her puzzled look he added, "My pardon—ye can't have it. It was a low trick, luring me aboard by acting sweet as pie. Then the minute we weighed anchor ye started goading me at every chance, so ye'd have plenty of tales to tell yer sister about what a lout I acted."

Claire would have laughed in his face if she hadn't feared he might strangle her in his present rage. Was *that* what he thought she'd been trying to do? If only he knew the truth!

"I made every effort to see to your comfort and offer you my best hospitality!" she protested, with a clear conscience.

"By talking on and on about yer blasted fortune? Rubbing it in my face? Well, let me tell ye something, Claire Talbot—"

She refused to let him bully her with his bluster or his magnetic presence. "I have no doubt you will tell me, sir, whether I give you leave or not."

To her surprise, that seemed to take the wind out of his sails. His mouth opened, then closed again. Fell open a second time, though no sound came out.

"Well?" she demanded. "Do you mean to tell me or not?"

"Aye." He seemed to force the word out, and Claire had a bewildering certainty that whatever he was about to say would not be what he'd originally intended. "I'm telling ye I've had enough and I want off."

"I beg your…" She stopped herself from

giving him another opportunity to insult her. "That's impossible. We cannot—"

He raised his hand and pointed. Claire glanced over her shoulder. The *Marlet* was passing very close to an island off the southern coast.

"Tell the captain to put in there," said Ewan, "and let me off."

So he could catch the first train to London and compare notes with Tessa? Her sister would elope with him on the spot and probably never speak to her again. And what might Ewan Geddes do to revenge himself upon her? The Brancaster shares Tessa had inherited from their father were few, but in the hands of a man more clever than scrupulous...

"No."

"What are ye saying, woman?"

"I believe my meaning is plain enough, sir. You will remain on the *Marlet* until we reach Scotland. After that, you may go where you wish."

Was she mad? her better judgment protested. What good would a few more days do? At this rate, it would be a wonder if they managed to reach Strathandrew without killing one another!

Indignation and desperation drowned out the quiet voice of reason. She would not allow Ewan Geddes to dictate to her. Without even trying, he made her say and do too many things against her will.

For a moment she feared he might strike her... or take some other equally shocking action. Then he appeared to master his passion by a fierce act of will.

"Fine, then." He strode past her. "I'll swim to shore."

"You wouldn't dare." The words had scarcely left her lips before Claire realized they were the worst possible ones she could have uttered.

Ewan pried off his boots and stockings, tossing them onto the deck. "Just ye watch me."

Suddenly she was aware of the unnatural hush on deck, and the crew of the *Marlet* watching them both.

"Are you just going to stand there?" she cried. "Someone stop him!"

No one moved, but from the helm Captain MacLeod called, "We can't hold the man against his will, miss. That'd be kidnapping."

Dear heaven! Might he have her charged with attempted abduction? Claire could just imagine the newspaper accounts.

"You could drown!" she warned him.

Ewan clawed at his neck linen and collar buttons as he struggled out of his coat, waistcoat and shirt. The sight of his broad, naked shoulders and muscular bare chest took Claire's breath away.

"I'd rather take my chances with the sea than with ye!"

He was bluffing. He must be.

"Please." She would have to order the captain to head for shore. "Don't be a fool."

"I'll be and do what I want, woman. I'm not yer servant anymore!"

Before she could relent, Ewan scrambled over the deck railing and dived into the ocean.

Chapter Eight

Had he lost his mind?

The question tumbled over and over in Ewan's thoughts as his body tumbled through the air on its plunge from the deck of the *Marlet*.

It was a far longer drop to the water than he'd realized. Or perhaps it just seemed that way.

He slammed into the waves, knocking the wind out of him. When he finally came up, sputtering, the *Marlet* had already moved some distance away. There could be no question of swimming back to it. Not that he'd give Claire Talbot the satisfaction, anyway.

So he struck out for shore, which looked much farther off than it had from the deck of the yacht. He swam hard for a while, propelled by the power of his outrage.

But outrage, he soon discovered, did not make

an ideal fuel. True, it blazed hot. But that only made it burn itself out faster. Soon cold ocean water quenched even the embers.

After swimming hard for what seemed like a long time, but coming only a little closer to shore, Ewan once again began asking himself if he'd lost his mind. A simple *yes* would have troubled him less than the answer he got from his conscience.

It informed him, in no uncertain terms, that he'd been an ass. And not just for diving off the ship just now.

He hadn't given Claire Talbot a fair chance. He'd wanted to and tried to for a while, but the first sign of coolness on her part had set him on the offensive again. Being late for dinner had soured his mood. He never should have downed that first whiskey so fast, let alone two more.

Perhaps the lady hadn't meant to offend him with all her glittering jewelry and rich food. In some awkward fashion, might she have been trying to do him an honor—showing him that he was worth dressing up and putting out the best victuals for? More than possible, Ewan acknowledged as a large wave broke over him, setting him coughing and struggling to stay afloat.

Things looked different depending on your vantage point. He'd learned that long ago during his gillie days. The water and shore had both looked closer from the deck of the *Marlet,* perhaps because he'd wanted them to. Claire Talbot's actions had appeared haughty and hostile because that was how he'd wanted to see them. And if his uncouth behavior had made her lash out at him, who could blame her?

His arms felt as weak and limp as two long bladders full of suet. But when he tried to rest, the water's coldness began to seep into his bones. Mustering his strength, he kept on swimming.

The chill of fear snaking through him made the Channel waves feel positively warm by comparison. What if he did not make it to shore? What if he had thrown his life away over foolish, misplaced pride? Considering his actions, what grounds did he have for pride, anyway? Damn few. But plenty of grounds for shame.

His bewildering feelings of lust for Claire Talbot foremost. She was not to blame for those, no matter how he'd tried to excuse himself by pretending so.

Would he ever get the chance to tell her he was sorry?

As she watched Ewan Geddes dive into the Channel, Claire feared *she* would drown…in guilt.

She had been wrong about him. The man was no fortune hunter. After she'd flaunted her wealth in front of him, he had jumped into the ocean to get away from her. What more compelling evidence did she need?

She should have seen the truth for herself, last night at dinner. Perhaps she would have seen it if she had not let her feelings toward him blind her.

"Man overboard!" She scarcely needed to add her cry to the others. The crew had been watching. They would be witnesses that she had all but pushed him into the water with her own two hands. "Captain, bring the ship around!"

"It's no good, miss." Captain MacLeod shook his grizzled head. "If we try to get any closer to shore, we'll founder on the shoals."

"The boats, then!" Claire jumped into the nearest one, a tiny affair that would not hold more than half a dozen people in a pinch. She and Tessa had often rowed around the shore of Loch Liath in it.

The captain bellowed a warning, but Claire ordered the two nearest crewmen, "Let it down, *now!*"

They were too well trained to hesitate, let alone refuse. Or perhaps they were anxious on Ewan's behalf and eager to do what they could. The little boat had barely hit the water when Claire realized she should have ordered one of the crew to jump in with her to man the oars.

"No help for it now," she muttered, taking them in her own hands and pulling for all she was worth. "Please…don't let him drown…before I get a chance…to tell him I'm sorry!"

It wasn't exactly a prayer. Her experience with earthly fathers had not predisposed her to put much trust in a heavenly one. At the moment, though, she felt a need to call on some source of strength beyond her own.

After several minutes of strenuous rowing, she rested at the oars and tried to take her bearings. Seeing no sign of Ewan, she grew anxious. Could he have drowned so quickly? Surely he would not have jumped overboard unless he'd been confident he could swim to shore.

Then she spotted a dark, round object low in the water. His head? As she peered closer, an arm rose out of the sea, pale against the murky waves.

Her own limbs went quite weak with relief for a moment, but she could not afford to let them stay that way. Keeping her left oar at rest, she rowed a few strokes with the right one to adjust her course. Then she struck out in his direction, silently begging him to stay afloat until she could reach him.

Her palms began to sting from rubbing against the wet wood. She would soon have a wicked crop of blisters, no doubt. How she wished she had put on a more serviceable dress this morning, rather than this bit of pink frippery that hampered her movements. It would be a wreck after this escapade, but that was the least of Claire's worries.

As she rowed toward Ewan, an appalling thought struck her. What if he refused her help once she reached him? After the way she'd treated him and the things she'd said, she could hardly blame him if he did.

Then she spotted him, only a little way off. The waves would soon bring the lifeboat abreast of him.

"Ewan!" She held one oar out to him. "Grab on to it! Please!"

He seemed dazed by the sight of her. For a moment, Claire feared the waves would sweep her past him before he understood what she wanted him to do.

"Here!" She bent as far out of the lifeboat as she dared. "Grab the oar...*now!*"

When his hands suddenly thrust out of the water to do so, a ragged sob escaped Claire's lips. With renewed strength, she pulled on the oar, towing Ewan closer to the boat, until at last he was able to throw an arm over the stern and hang there, gasping. She tossed the oar back into the boat, then bent to hoist him aboard.

She could feel the flush burning in her cheeks and the sweat prickling her brow. Rivulets of water trailed down Ewan's face from his sodden hair, but he looked too exhausted to wipe them away.

Though she had little spare breath for speech, there was something she must say now, before pride froze her tongue. "Ewan…?"

"Claire…"

In the same breath, they both gasped, "I'm sorry."

His words surprised her so, Claire nearly lost her grip on him. Ewan started, too, and almost let go of the boat.

The fear that he might fall back into the water roused them both to one final effort. Claire pulled with all her might at the same instant Ewan gathered the last of his strength and hauled himself up. For an instant, the bow of the lifeboat rose dangerously into the air. Then Claire tumbled backward, while Ewan fell on top, pinning her beneath him.

All the air gushed out of her lungs. As fast and hard as she gasped, she could not seem to recover it. Her head spun and her back protested painfully where she had slammed onto the bench. If not for the sturdy whalebone frame of her corset, she might have broken a rib.

Ewan sprawled on top of her, panting and shivering, his head resting against her bosom. With the tattered remnants of strength in her arms, Claire raised them to wrap around his bare shoulders. How often had she dreamed of lying beneath him, cradling him in her arms? She'd never imagined it quite like this, though.

And she must stop imagining such things! She was no longer a calf-eyed girl, hankering after a handsome young man who scarcely noticed her. She had responsibilities now, and obligations. Chief of which was the debt of affection she owed her sister.

If Ewan Geddes cared nothing for Tessa's fortune, but truly loved her, and she him, Claire owed it to her sister to promote the match. Especially after going to such unscrupulous lengths to prevent it. She owed it to Tessa and Ewan, and most of all to herself, to weed out the foolish infatuation that had begun to take root in her heart again after lying fallow for so many years.

Just for that moment, though, she forgot those obligations, and her discomfort, to soak up the satisfying sensation of Ewan's half-naked body pressed against hers. She would have given every penny of her fortune for him to raise his head and press his lips to hers.

He should get off the poor lass before he squashed her flat! If only he could get his stubborn body to cooperate.

Perhaps he could find the strength to roll off her if he really tried, but she wasn't complaining, and it felt so good to lie there pressed against her. It took all the willpower Ewan could muster to keep from lifting his head and kissing her.

Last night he had wanted to kiss her, too. For

the worst reasons a man could have. To shock her, to overpower her and to vent the primitive urges she provoked in him. He would have been ashamed to use his lips on any woman that way.

Now he wanted to kiss her in a far different way, for far different reasons. To say he was sorry. To say he was grateful. To acknowledge some bewildering bond that pulled them together no matter how hard they fought to deny it and keep their distance.

That kind of kiss was much harder to hold back.

Perhaps because he'd just escaped the cold, killing jaws of the sea, his veins pulsed with life and heat. He could not imagine a sweeter sensation than the slender softness of a woman beneath him.

He knew he must restrain himself, but at that moment, he could not remember why. He scavenged just enough energy to tilt his head. His gaze met hers and held for a long, breathless, searching moment.

"Hullo!" A distant, urgent cry shattered the wordless connection between them. "Miss Talbot, are you there? Are you all right?"

Claire stirred beneath him, and Ewan discovered he did have the strength to roll off her, after all.

She grabbed the edge of the boat and pulled herself upright. "We're here!" she called back, though Ewan doubted her breathless voice carried far. "And we're safe."

Wrapping his arms about his wet, bare chest, Ewan dragged himself onto the narrow bench in the bow of the lifeboat. From there, he could see a larger craft speeding toward them, three pairs of oars moving together in a swift rhythm. He knew he should welcome their arrival.

His thoughts grew muddled for a time, until he heard Claire's voice, as warm as the coarse wool blanket she wrapped around him. "We'll be back on the *Marlet* soon. I'll order Captain MacLeod to dock at Portsmouth."

Ewan opened his mouth to ask why, then he remembered. He shook his head. "N-n-not unless ye want to be rid of me, d-d-damn fool that I am."

He dragged his eyes open and forced them to focus. Their tiny lifeboat was being towed back toward the ship by the larger one. Claire sat on the middle bench, a gray wool blanket covering the wreck of her pretty gown. Her hair hung in wet, limp strands around her face and she looked altogether miserable.

But she answered him with a trace of her usual spark. "You were a damn fool to dive off that boat, but so was I for making you do it."

"*Ye* were a damn fool to come after me." Ewan wiped away a drop of water that had slid down to the tip of his nose. "But I thank ye just the same.

I don't know how much longer I could have kept afloat out there."

"Did you mean it?" Claire pulled the blanket tighter around her. "About staying aboard the *Marlet*? Are you willing to chance the rest of the voyage with me? I'm not keen to fish you out of the Irish Sea."

Ewan felt his lip curl into a grin. The lass had a lot of spirit, to poke fun after what had just happened.

"If I'm fool enough to jump into the Irish Sea," he advised her, not entirely in jest, "do us both a favor and let me drown."

For an instant, she looked a trifle shocked by his quip, but a hiccup of laughter gushed out of her, followed by another and another, in which Ewan joined. They were still laughing when they were pulled aboard the *Marlet*.

Captain MacLeod looked at them as if they were a pair of escaped lunatics. "See here, I'll have no more goings-on like that on my ship, do ye ken?"

Claire did not remind him that the *Marlet* belonged to her. Instead, like a naughty child being scolded, she stared at her feet and muttered something that sounded apologetic. Unfortunately, she ruined the penitent effect by bursting into another fit of giggles.

"Away with ye!" The captain scowled, though Ewan detected a twinkle in his deep-set eyes.

"Go get yerselves into dry gear before ye catch yer deaths."

As Ewan stumbled toward the galley way, he heard Claire's voice behind him. "Jock, will you tend to Mr. Geddes, like a good fellow. I'm not certain how much strength he has in his arms just now."

An hour ago, he would have resented such a gesture from her. Now he turned and offered her a warm smile. "Have ye got someone to tend to ye, lass? Rowing's as hard on the arms as swimming, I'll be bound."

His concern appeared to fluster her. She pushed the drooping strands of hair away from her face. "I'm certain my maid will take very good care of me, thank you."

"See that she does." Ewan watched Claire make her way below deck, then he turned to Jockie. "And why are ye grinning like a fool?"

"Don't ye mean grinning *at* a fool?"

"Aye," Ewan admitted. He'd called himself that and worse too often of late to take offense when somebody else did. "Why are ye grinning like a fool at a fool?"

Jockie winked. "Because I just won a fiver, mate. With a wee bit of help from ye and Miss Talbot."

"Always glad to oblige." Ewan headed below. "What did I do?"

"Ye didn't drown," said Jock, "but ye didn't

make it to shore, either. The crew had a bit of a wager on the whole thing, ye see."

"A wager? On whether I'd drown?"

"That was only part of it," explained Jock, as if that made it all right. "There were bets on ye drowning and some on ye getting to shore. I almost put my money on that, for the odds were long."

Ewan held tight to the rail as he staggered down the stairs. "I'm touched by yer faith in me."

Jock chuckled. "A lot of the crew bet on the other boat reaching ye first, but I put my money on Miss Talbot. If she set her mind to it, I knew there'd be no stopping her."

"She's quite a lass, isn't she?" Ewan murmured, more to himself than to Jock, as he entered his cabin, then slipped behind the dressing screen to peel off his wet trousers.

"To tell ye the truth..." Jock closed the cabin door behind him and lowered his voice. "I never had much use for the rest of the family. But Miss Talbot, she's a good sort. They say she has a lot of Old Man Brancaster in her. Tell me, did she make ye grovel very long before she let ye climb in that lifeboat?"

"Not as long as she should have." Ewan pitched his wet trousers over the screen at Jock. "And what do ye mean, ye haven't much use for the rest of the family? What about Miss Tessa? She's a bonny lass."

"Aye, to look at." Jock muttered, his words almost drowned out by the sounds of the wardrobe being opened.

"She's a lively wee thing." Ewan grabbed a towel from the washstand and began rubbing himself dry. His toes and fingertips were puckered like big pale raisins, but his arms were beginning to regain some of their strength.

"Aye," said Jock. "Used to getting her own way and all. His lairdship doted on her, while he hardly spared a thought for her sister." He hung articles of dry clothing over the edge of the dressing screen. "By the way, I rescued the clothes ye left lying on the deck when ye jumped overboard."

Ewan muttered his thanks, but his mind fixed on what Jockie had said about Claire. A qualm of guilt rolled through his belly, though he couldn't reck-on why.

Jock chuckled.

"What's so funny?" Ewan surged up on tiptoe, to peer over the screen.

"I was just thinking what would have happened if that had been Miss Tessa up on deck when ye jumped overboard, instead of Miss Claire."

"Aye?"

"With all the screaming and the swooning…" Jock could scarcely get the words out for laughing. "The crew would have been so busy tending to her, ye'd have drowned for sure."

A vivid image of the scene rose in Ewan's mind. It made him feel heartily disloyal. "If it had been Miss Tessa up there instead of Miss Claire, I never would have jumped in the first place!"

Jock headed out the cabin door with Ewan's wet trousers and drawers over his arm. Still chuckling, he shook his head. "Don't ye be too sure about that, mate."

Chapter Nine

After a thorough wash, a change of clothes, a hot toddy and a long nap, Claire felt sufficiently recovered to venture out to the dining room for tea. She was more than a little surprised to find Ewan already there, tucking into a hearty spread of sandwiches and cakes.

She hesitated on the threshold, overcome with awkwardness. When she'd looked upon the man as an enemy to thwart at all costs, it had been so much easier to approach him. Now she did not know how to proceed. She cringed, recalling what a fool she'd made of herself while trying to entice him.

Another memory hovered at the fringe of her thoughts, as well. That of Ewan sprawled on top of her in the lifeboat. It left her feeling roused and strangely vulnerable.

She tried to back out of the room without him noticing her, but he glanced up and caught her.

Dropping a half-eaten sandwich onto his plate, he jumped to his feet. "Please don't go away on my account, Miss Talbot."

"Are you sure?" Claire hated the note of uncertainty she heard in her voice. "I can come back later. I thought you must still be resting in your cabin."

Why hadn't she asked her maid to check first?

He took a step toward her. "I hope ye wouldn't have stayed away on my account. I promise I'll mind my manners at meals from now on." His self-deprecating smile was infectious. "Even if ye come to breakfast decked from head to toe in diamonds."

Claire gave an exaggerated shudder. "I fear that would not be very comfortable. Especially for sitting down."

"I don't reckon it would be." He offered her his arm to lead her to the table.

He looked so genuinely eager for her company, yet a tightness around his eyes betrayed a shadow of worry that she might refuse. Somehow, it eased Claire's embarrassment.

She let him escort her to the table and hold her chair.

"Anyway," said Ewan, passing her the tray of sandwiches, "I know why ye wore all yer jewels and had yer cook make all that rich food."

Claire fumbled the sandwich tray. "I'm sorry! How clumsy of me!"

"It's my fault." Ewan seized the dish and set it back down on the table where she could reach it. "I should have remembered...yer hands."

Before she realized what he meant to do, he reached for her nearest hand and peeled back the glove from her wrist, exposing her bandaged palm. "I wouldn't blame ye if ye didn't want to dine in the same room with such a lout."

But how could *he* stand to dine with *her* if he guessed what she'd been trying to do?

Discretion told her to avoid the subject and pray it never came up again. Yet she *had* to know—was it possible he did not despise her for trying to entrap him?

She reached for a walnut tea cake as an excuse to withdraw her hand. "You know why I wore so many jewels and served rich food?"

"Oh, aye." Ewan pulled a wry face. "No pleasing some folk, is there? If ye'd dressed plain and served simple food, I might have gotten all offended that ye didn't think I was worth making a fuss over."

So he didn't know the truth! A surge of relief weakened Claire's arms worse than rowing the lifeboat had.

Perhaps it showed on her face, too, for Ewan asked, "That *was* what ye were trying to do, wasn't it? Make me feel I was worth putting on a bit of a show for?"

"Something like that." The lie stuck in Claire's throat and threatened to choke her. "More tea?"

Ewan nodded. "Look, I know it's a lot to ask after the way I acted, but do ye think ye could give me another chance? Forget the last twenty-four hours ever happened and start over again with a clean slate?"

Yesterday he had asked her to do that, but she had not been sincere in accepting his offer. Now, though she wasn't sure she deserved another chance, she wanted one very much. Perhaps if she got to know him better—not the boy he'd once been, but the man he'd become—she could rid herself of any improper feelings toward him. Only then might she come to like and respect him as her future brother-in-law.

"I cannot let you take all the blame for what happened, but I would like us to start afresh. For Tessa's sake."

"That's settled, then." Ewan lifted his teacup as if in a toast. "Here's to new beginnings and second chances. Rare blessings, both."

"To new beginnings and second chances." Claire raised her own cup and gingerly clinked it against his.

As Ewan Geddes gazed at her for the first time in their lives with a soft glow of fondness and admiration in his eyes, Claire struggled to ignore the sweet, warm flutter in her heart.

For Tessa's sake. Those words did not sit well with Ewan, for reasons he could not work out.

Of course he wanted to get better acquainted with Claire Talbot for her sister's sake. If all went well, they would be family one day. That thought troubled him, too.

He wondered why.

Could it be on account of the very unbrotherly feelings she roused in him? Aye, perhaps. But those feelings weren't real, were they? Likely they were just some queer twist of the passionate hostility that had flared between them for as long as he could recall. Once they settled down and got to know each other, those yearnings would fade into something he could live with.

And if they didn't? Better to know that now, before he got himself in too deep.

Ewan stirred from his musings to find Claire watching him with a most intent expression. He had a guilty feeling that she could read his thoughts.

"Tell me about America, Ewan," she said. "Do you like it there? You've done well for yourself."

Better than she knew. Once again he was tempted to tell her the truth about his fortune— though for quite the opposite reasons from what had compelled him in the moments before he'd jumped overboard. Then, he had wanted to crow over her. Now he wanted to be honest with her. But he feared the effect it might have on their truce, so new and fragile, to discover he owned a rival company.

When he did not reply right away, she prompted him further. "It could not have been an easy task to establish yourself."

Ewan shrugged. "What *is* easy that's worth doing in life? It's as I told ye at the Fortescues' ball, America has plenty of opportunities for a man who's willing to work hard and take a few chances."

"And one who's clever?"

"Aye, well…" A blush prickled in his cheeks. "I had a decent education for a lad in my position."

He had the Talbots to thank for that, though he was not certain he had ever acknowledged it, even to himself.

"And over there—" he jerked his head in the direction he thought might be west "—they reckon every Scot's an engineer, or can be with a wee bit of training."

Claire smiled at his deliberate exaggeration. "And you have provided them with further proof for that assumption."

He didn't want to make his rise in the world sound too easy. "For all the folks who're willing to give a lad a chance, there are more who think every newcomer should be sent back where he came from. Especially if he gets too far above his station."

While they gorged themselves on cakes and sandwiches, Claire continued to prompt him with questions and comments until Ewan found himself telling her more about his business and his recent life than he'd ever intended. More than he'd told Tessa in all the time since he'd come to London.

"And what about ye?" he said at last, not daring to tell her too much more about his situation. "It can't have been easy for a woman to take the helm of a company like Brancasters, supposing ye did inherit it from yer grandfather."

"No indeed." Claire shook her head with a rueful look that told Ewan she was remembering battles she'd fought and wounds she'd sustained. "The same type of people who think immigrants have no right to make something of themselves are the ones who believe women have no place in the business world…or anywhere else outside the nursery."

For the next little while, he laughed and nodded over stories that sounded so familiar he could have told them himself, just by changing a few names and other particulars.

"Finally," said Claire, "I realized I was only beating my head on a wall trying to make our customers accept me as the working manager of

Brancasters. So I hired two gentlemen to repre-
sent me."

"Those chaps yer secretary spoke of—Adams
and Monteith?"

"That's right. They dress well and speak well
and they know enough about the business to give
our customers confidence. But I am still the one
who draws up the bids, seeks out suppliers and
oversees the profitable operation of the company."

"Does it not bother ye, though," asked Ewan,
"to have somebody else given credit for the work
ye do?"

At first it seemed as if Claire meant to answer
with an emphatic no. But after a moment's con-
sideration she said, "Sometimes. More so when
I first started. Now I have the gratification of
seeing Brancasters prosper, due to my efforts."

"As long as *ye* know ye've done a good job,
other folks and their opinions can go hang, eh?"
Ewan often wished he cared less about what others thought of him.

Claire's lips twisted in a sly grin. "I also have
the secret satisfaction of knowing I am playing
them all for fools. Someday, when the information can no longer do the company any harm, I
mean to make it public, so women who come
after me may encounter a little less prejudice in
the commercial world."

"Ha!" Ewan slapped his hand against the tabletop. "Good for ye, lass!"

He had always thought her as so privileged, with everything she wanted in life handed to her on a silver platter. It had never occurred to him that she might have had to strive as hard as he had for what she wanted. A spark of admiration for her kindled and took fire within him. She'd had the pluck to fight for what she desired, as well as the wit and grace to settle for the best she could get.

"Do ye reckon those two hirelings of yers will be able to keep Brancasters running for a few weeks without ye?"

Claire chuckled. "As long as dear Mr. Catchpole keeps a close eye on them, I think the firm may escape bankruptcy until I return!"

As her laughter subsided, a pensive look settled over her slender features. "Harry Adams intends to retire next year." She murmured the words more to herself than to Ewan.

"Have ye got somebody in mind to take his place? Yer Mr. Catchpole, maybe?"

That brought a ready smile to her lips, but the set of her brow gave her a troubled look. "I'm not certain Mr. Catchpole would make quite the proper impression on our customers. Like me, he is better suited to wielding real authority behind the scenes. I had thought Spencer Stanton might be an ideal choice."

"The man Tessa's going to marry...er, *was* going to marry?" Ewan corrected himself, puzzled that he'd been able to say those words without a stab of jealousy.

Claire nodded. "Perhaps I should consider offering you the position, if you wed Tessa. Somehow I don't believe you'd be content as a figurehead."

They both laughed over that, then stopped abruptly when a young steward bustled into the dining room. "Begging your pardon, Miss Talbot. But Monsieur Anton asked me to inquire if you and the gentleman wish to have dinner served, or if you plan to take tea all evening?"

"It can't be!" Ewan consulted his pocket watch. "Where did the time go?"

He could not recall when he'd last lost track of so many hours.

"Give Monsieur Anton our apologies," Claire instructed the steward. "Tell him we will take a late supper, just something light. If that is all right with you, Ewan?"

"Aye, it suits me fine." He patted his stomach. "I hadn't noticed how many tea cakes I was eating. If I keep on like this, I'll *have* to wear a kilt when we reach Strathandrew, for none of my trousers will fit!"

"We cannot let that happen, can we?" Claire rose from her seat, a trifle stiffly. "Though I agree with Tessa, you used to cut quite a dashing figure in your kilt and gillie vest, heading off to fish or shoot."

"Oh, get away with ye!" Ewan winced as he heaved himself to his feet.

"What do you say we take a stroll around the deck?" asked Claire. "A bit of fresh air and exercise might do us both good."

"Aye." Ewan held out his arm to her. More than the sea air or the chance to stretch his limbs, he was convinced any time spent in the company of this remarkable woman would do him good.

If she had guessed how much she could enjoy Ewan Geddes's company once she abandoned her foolish romantic fancy for him, she would have done it years ago. Claire told herself so repeatedly as she wandered the deck on his arm in the gathering twilight.

She could not remember when she'd laughed so hard or so often. The wit they had once used as ammunition for their verbal skirmishes they now turned upon more deserving targets for each other's amusement.

Ewan nodded toward a crewman, swabbing the deck in glum silence. "I reckon somebody lost in the pool."

"Pool?"

"Aye, the cheeky devils were placing wagers on which of the boats would reach me first, or whether I'd drown!"

Claire laughed until she feared her corset would burst.

Ewan lost his battle to maintain an indignant scowl. "I reckon Jockie McMurdo owes us both a pint at the Claymore, once we reach Strathandrew."

By and by their conversation turned to more serious subjects, and Ewan listened to her with an unspoken sympathy that invited her to confide in him. When he talked, she sensed he was giving her a closer glimpse of his true thoughts than he allowed most people.

"This is such a novelty." She stared toward the western horizon, which the setting sun had kindled in all the bright, warm hues of a driftwood bonfire. "Talking to a man about business and having him take me seriously...or at least pretend to."

Ewan ran his hand over the deck railing. "It's not often I get the chance to talk business with a lady and have her even pretend to be interested."

"Did you talk to many ladies about business, back in America?" Claire did not know what prompted her to ask, or why his answer was so important to her.

"A few."

She knew it was too early in their renewed acquaintance to pry, but the brevity of his answer whetted her curiosity.

"Was there ever anyone...special for you in

America, or did you always plan on coming back for Tessa?"

Ewan produced a derisive sound from deep in his throat, something between a chuckle and a growl. "I never dreamed I'd get the chance to court yer sister. I'd reckoned she must have married years ago."

He explained how he had chanced upon the announcement of Tessa's engagement in the *Times.* Claire was forced to agree that Fate had smiled upon the match. She should have known better than to fight a higher power.

Accept what you cannot change. Make the best of what you can get. Claire wished she had mastered those hard but vital lessons long ago. What a lot of unhappiness and fruitless struggle they would have saved her.

It had taken many frustrating years for her to accept that she could never win her father's love. She had finally resigned herself to it, though, and learned to be content with his respect. Now she must accept that Ewan Geddes would marry Tessa, and learn to be content with his friendship. If their recent camaraderie was anything to judge by, perhaps that would not be such a bad bargain, after all.

Ewan stared out at the western horizon, too, with a far-off gaze, as if he could see all the way to America and ten years into the past.

"For quite a while at first, I never had the

time or the money for courting." He shook his head with a rueful half smile. "I might have been a wee bit gun-shy, too, after the trouble it had landed me in."

"T-trouble?"

The sea was surprisingly calm as they rounded the tip of Cornwall, but Claire felt as if a huge wave had lifted the *Marlet,* then sent it plunging down into a deep trough.

"Oh, aye." Ewan turned away from the deck railing and began to walk again.

He did not offer Claire his arm, and she did not reach for it. Instead, she followed close behind him, wishing she had not strayed from the safe subject of business.

"Did ye never wonder why I left Strathandrew so sudden?" he asked. "Or were ye so glad to see the last of me that ye didn't care?"

"I wondered." Claire could coax nothing more from her suddenly constricted throat.

She had wondered, and hoped the timing of his going had been a coincidence. Now she feared she was about to find out otherwise.

"It was bloody daft of me," Ewan muttered. "She was so young and it would have ruined her reputation if anybody else had caught us."

Claire remembered every stinging word of the lecture she'd received from her father on the subject. Ewan must have got one, too. Her only regret, at the time, had been that someone other than her father had *not* discovered them, forcing Ewan to marry her.

Later, she'd been grateful her rebellious wish had not been granted. He would have hated her for what she'd done, and they would have been miserable together.

Ewan turned to her with a shamefaced grin. "I was young, too—that's my only excuse. Lads that age, they don't always think with their heads, if ye know what I mean."

Bobbing a hasty nod, Claire lowered her gaze to avoid his. She hoped he would attribute it to excessive modesty.

"Ye probably wonder what I'm talking about." He lowered his voice. "The night before ye were to sail back home, Tessa sent me a note, asking me to meet her down by the loch after dark. Yer father caught me kissing her and he sacked me."

"I had no idea!" Claire gasped. "When we came back the next summer and found you gone, I assumed you'd grown tired of service and decided for yourself to go to America."

Ewan's large, deft hands clenched into fists and his voice rasped with long-nursed bitterness. "I reckon that's what I hated most about the whole thing."

"My father?"

"No. Well, besides him. I hated that none of it was my decision. I had no choice but to go."

"Were you lonely…at first?"

"Oh, aye." His voice ached with raw longing. "Back home, I was part of something. Part of Strathandrew. Part of a clan. Fishing the same beat and hunting the same hills as my father and his father and on back for who knows how long. Across the water, I felt like I had no place."

How bleak it sounded! Claire's throat tightened and her eyes stung.

"I swore I'd make him pay," said Ewan in a savage whisper. "That no matter how hard it was or how long it took, I'd get a bit of my own back."

His words sent a chill through Claire.

"I'm sorry." She turned and stumbled toward the galley way.

"Claire?" he called after her. "What about supper?"

"Still full from tea," she managed to choke out as she fled below deck.

She did not stop until she was in her cabin, with the door closed and her back pressed against it. Then her trembling knees gave way and she sank to the floor.

She had been wrong in supposing Ewan Geddes a common fortune hunter. Now she wondered if he might have even darker motives for wanting to infiltrate the Talbot family.

He had admitted wanting revenge against her late father. How would he react if he found out that she was to blame for his bleak years of exile?

Chapter Ten

To think, all these years, that he had suspected Claire of tattling to her father about his tryst with Tessa!

Ewan scowled at himself in the shaving mirror after another restless night. He had heard the sincere note of distress in her voice when she'd declared she knew nothing about it. He'd seen her features twist in genuine anguish when she'd expressed her regret over what had happened to him. When she'd fled to her cabin without supper, he'd felt a perfect lout for the second time that day.

Perhaps he should have gone after her last evening, hammered on her cabin door until she came out, then told her the things that had repeated over and over in his dreams the previous night. But it had been the end of a long, exhausting day, and he'd been in the grip of his old grievance. Fearful that he would say the wrong thing and destroy the tenuous bond they'd begun to forge, he had decided to sleep on it instead, hoping he'd be more calm and philosophical in the morning.

If only he could have *slept* on it, instead of tossing and turning all night! Now, surveying the dark circles under his eyes, his ham-fisted butchery of a shave and the hair that went every way except how it should, he worried he might scare the poor lass to death.

When Jockie entered the cabin a few minutes later, he winced at the sight of his old mate. "Call that a shave? Ye look like ye tried to do away with yerself, but made a poor job of it!"

"Get away with ye! It's not that bad." Ewan wetted a corner of the towel and wiped away a few drops of blood, then scooped up a palmful of water from the basin to slick his hair down. "Is Claire…I mean, Miss Talbot, up and about yet?"

"Aye," said Jock. "If ye're quick, ye might catch her at breakfast."

"Thanks." Ewan let Jock help him tie his neck linen. The way he was going this morning, he feared he might strangle himself with it.

Jamming his arms into his coat sleeves, he hurried off and almost collided with Claire at the entrance to the dining room. He spied a few crumbs on the bodice of her dress, which made him wonder if she'd tried to eat quickly and get away before he came.

"Good morning, Ewan." Her tone sounded cordial enough, in a brittle sort of way, and she avoided his gaze as she tried to slip past him. "Enjoy your breakfast."

"Claire." He reached out and caught her lightly by the wrist. "Will ye wait a minute? There's something I'd like to say to ye…about last night."

"Must you?" Her gaze flitted to his face, eyes wide and wary. "Can we not just forget about it? The less said about some things, the better."

He did not loosen his firm but gentle grip on her wrist. "With all due respect, I don't agree. It's like dirt ye sweep under a rug. Nobody can see it anymore, but with no light or air, that bit of dirt can draw bugs or start to stink. Even rot the rug."

She did not like what he was saying. Ewan could see it in her eyes. But she knew he was right and she knew it would be useless to argue with him.

"Very well, then." She turned back toward the dining room, reluctant but resigned. "Though I cannot see what good it will do to stir up more painful memories. The past is best left behind."

"Aye, perhaps. If we could." He let go of her wrist, wishing he didn't have to. "But the past makes us what we are. So, in a way, it's always with us."

Claire pulled a face, as if she were a child and some overzealous nursemaid had just administered a spoonful of foul-tasting but necessary medicine. "I cannot say I care for that notion." She returned to the table and sat back down before the scarcely touched remnants of her breakfast.

Then she drew a deep breath, as if to brace herself for what he would say.

Ewan hauled out one of the other chairs and drew it close to hers. "Listen, I didn't mean to upset ye yesterday evening. Something about going home again made it all feel so close."

He raked his fingers through his hair. "What I'm trying to say is, *my* past made me what I am today. I'm proud of that, even if I'm not proud of all the things I've done to get here." Perhaps all those sleepless hours had not been wasted if they'd made him understand that. "If I'd stayed back at Strathandrew, where and what would I be today?"

He didn't wait for Claire to reply, but answered his own question. "I might have worked my way up to head gamekeeper by now. Married one of the housemaids and struggled to bring up a gang of wee ones on a gamekeeper's pay. Never set foot more than twenty miles from home in my life. And nights when I had a pint too many down at the Claymore, I'd wonder if I could have made something of myself if only I'd dared go across the water when I was young."

"But that would have been different," cried Claire. "As you said last evening, it *wasn't* your choice to go!"

"Not my choice to go, maybe." Ewan shrugged. "But it was my choice what to do once I got there. I could have done what a lot of my workmates did—spent all my wages at the nearest tavern, trying to fill the hole that homesickness chewed in my heart."

"You were too clever for that." Claire's eyes glowed with such admiration it made him almost giddy.

"Not clever." He couldn't lie to her. "Just proud and bloody-minded. I knew yer father reckoned I'd end up in the gutter...probably wanted me to after I laid hands on his precious daughter. I wouldn't let him have that, even if he never knew."

"So you're saying my father ended up doing you a good turn by sacking you and shipping you off to America?"

"I reckon so." Ewan reached out to pat the back of her hand as a gesture of reassurance. "And I don't want ye to feel bad about something that was long ago and none of yer doing, because it all turned out for the best."

When he tried to retract his hand, it insisted upon lingering.

"I wish my father were alive now, to see what you've made of yourself," said Claire. "It would serve him right."

"Miss Talbot!" Ewan feigned outrage. "Are ye saying ye'd want to see yer own father squirm?"

Her eyes narrowed and her lips drew tight, lifting a trifle at the corners to produce a cold smile. "Like a worm on a hook."

Watching her and hearing the chill in her voice, Ewan wondered if his resentment toward the late Lord Lydiard was a pale ghost compared to the fierce bitterness of his lordship's daughter.

She should be relieved that Ewan Geddes was no longer obsessed with revenge...or so he claimed. As another day flew by in congenial companionship, Claire chided herself for having any doubts in the matter. Why must she always be so suspicious?

Ewan was likely right about the past shaping people's present character and situation. That was all well and good if a person was pleased with those. And Claire had been.

Perhaps not pleased, she admitted to herself, but at least content. Ewan's return into her life had forced her to look a little more closely. She didn't much like what she found.

"So, have ye done anything *besides* work for

the past ten years?" Ewan asked as they watched the distant coast of northern Wales drift by. "Was there anyone special in yer life?"

No one whose company she'd enjoyed half as much as his, these past two days. Was it her fancy, or did Ewan sound more interested in the answer to his question than he should be?

"What makes you ask?"

He shrugged. "Ye asked me. I reckon turn-about's fair play."

Though she told herself it was wishful folly, Claire could not help thinking he sounded as if he were trying hard to appear no more than casually interested.

"Very well," she said. "But I thought I told you all there was to tell the night of the Fortescues' ball. I have not been without suitors. In fact, I was plagued with them when I first came out. One or two caught my fancy for a time, but it never took long to discover that the brilliant gleam in their eyes was not love, but greed."

"Are ye sure ye weren't being too hard on some of them?" Ewan's wide, dark brows drew together in an anxious frown.

It should not have looked attractive, but it did. Far too attractive. Claire found herself wanting to kiss away that brooding pucker of flesh above the bridge of his nose. As if she had the ability!

"I mean," he continued, "maybe a fellow started off wanting to court ye for yer fortune.

Like it or not, folks need money for all kinds of reasons, and marrying can be a pleasant enough way to get it."

Claire gave a bitter chuckle. "Pleasant for whom?"

"Both, I hope." Ewan laughed, too. "If the man does his best to give his bride good value for her money."

"Spoken like a true Scot!"

"Never!" Ewan's outrage did not look altogether feigned. "We're a wild, romantic race, don't ye know? Especially the Highlanders and the Islanders."

Dropping to one knee, he grasped the tips of her fingers and began to recite with passionate expression and theatrical gestures, "'My love is like a red, red rose, that's newly sprung in June. My love is like a melody—'"

She could not bear to hear him speak to her that way, even in fun. He could too easily stir up feelings she was struggling to subdue.

So she interrupted him in midquote. "Oh, get away with you!"

A glimmer of wicked glee twinkled in Ewan's gray eyes, making Claire wonder if she should have left well enough alone.

"How about this then? 'So sweet a kiss yester e'en from thee I reft, in bowing down thy body on the bed, that even my life within thy lips I left!'"

A furious blush scorched Claire's cheeks. It would have been better if he'd stayed with the Burns verse, which had been more sentimental than sensual.

"Do get up before any more of the crew see you!" she pleaded. "I will admit that Highlanders are vastly romantic."

She had always thought so, but she was not prepared to admit *that*.

Ewan scrambled up from the deck, still clinging to her hand. "Enough joking, now. I wouldn't be surprised if some of those suitors of yers started out interested in yer fortune. But if they were lucky enough to spend some time with ye, like I have the past two days, they'd soon be glad to have ye for a wife, supposing ye didn't have two pennies to rub together."

Claire tried to compose her features into the superficial smile of someone who had received a flattering but meaningless compliment. Inside, though, her heart felt as if it were being stretched in too many directions at once, while her stomach seemed to have contracted into a hard little knot.

When she mastered her voice sufficiently, she asked, "Are you telling me I might have let a good catch get away?"

Ewan seemed not to notice the quaver in her voice, for he was too busy chuckling. "That's the kind of advice a gillie would give in matters of the heart, isn't it? And who knows, but it might be true. Didn't ye tell me there was a man who once gave ye a run for yer money? What became of him?"

How she wished she could go back to the night of the ball and unsay those words. She was surprised Ewan remembered. He hadn't seemed to be able to keep his mind on anything but Tessa that evening.

"The poor fellow had no idea I cared twopence for him." It relieved the pressure building inside of her to tell Ewan the truth, even if he would never guess she was talking about him. "Not that it would have mattered, of course, because he was in love with someone else."

Ewan winced. "I'm sorry. I should have had better manners than to ask."

"No harm," said Claire, trying to make herself believe it. "It's water under the bridge now, and all for the best, perhaps. It might have turned out we weren't the least bit suited for one another."

For years, that thought had brought her comfort. Now, the better she got to know Ewan Geddes, the more convinced she became that they *were* suited for one another.

Ewan seemed to waver between discretion and candor. Candor won. "Don't ye ever wish ye'd had the chance to find out for certain?"

"I have quite enough regrets in my life without that one." Gently, Claire detached his hand from hers, wondering if he'd realized he was still holding it.

Late that night, Ewan made his way up to the deck of the *Marlet,* clad only in his nightshirt with a cloak thrown over his shoulders. Unlike the previous two nights, he'd slept well, at first. Later he had woken in the darkness as if stirred by some powerful, silent call.

All was quiet on deck apart from the usual soothing sounds of the waves lapping against the hull, the soft creak of timbers and the flutter of canvas. The pale, mournful face of an almost full moon cast its ghostly light on the Irish Sea, glinting off the foam on the waves and imparting a soft glow to the billowing sails.

The first mate had the wheel and he gave a start when Ewan approached him. "Not a time of the night I'd be out, sir, if I had any choice about it. Is there aught I can do for ye?"

"We'll be off the coast of Scotland soon, I reckon," said Ewan.

"Just coming into the North Channel, sir. If ye look off to the east, ye should see the light of Galloway Head before long."

"That sounds like a fine idea." Ewan strode toward the port railing.

Now he knew what had called him. Home.

The wind ruffled his hair, as it had the day before. Tonight it felt different, somehow. Like the hand of the father he barely remembered, pulling off his cap when he came home at suppertime. Overhead, a lone gull screeched. The haunting sound rang in his ears like a cry of welcome.

He gave a start when he heard Claire's voice behind him.

"Is everything all right, Ewan?" She sounded anxious for him. What a change three days had wrought between them!

"Nothing wrong." He turned toward her. "What are ye doing up this time of night?"

The moonlight shone on her hair, pulled back in a loose braid. She wore a dressing gown over her nightgown.

"I couldn't sleep, so I went down to the dining room to fetch myself a *wee dram*." She lifted a glass, as if to prove her story. "On the way back to my cabin, I caught a glimpse of you heading up on deck. Were you having trouble sleeping, too?"

"Aye, a bit." That was as good an explanation as any.

Claire took a sip from her glass, then held it out to him. "There's plenty here for both of us, if you'd care to share."

"I would, thank ye." He savored the mellow fire of the whiskey on his tongue.

It was just what the moment needed. So was her company.

"I envy you this homecoming." Her hoarse murmur was all but lost beneath the muted chorus of the waves and the wind. "I know you've been gone a long while and you've missed it terribly, but at least you had it to come back to."

Ewan didn't understand. "You've got yer own place in London, don't ye?"

"I have a *place* in London. That isn't the same as having a home. If my house in Mayfair burned down tomorrow, I'd grumble about the inconvenience, but then I would buy another and never shed a tear."

He pressed the glass back into her hand. "What about Strathandrew? Would ye shed a tear if it burned down?"

Claire seemed to mull over the notion as she took another sip. "I would. In that way, I suppose Strathandrew is the closest thing to a true home I have. But I've never fooled myself into believing I belong there, the way you do. How did you put it? Fishing the same beat and walking the same hills as your father and his father."

She shivered. "The sea wind gets cool at night. Now that I've had my dram, I should get back to bed."

Was it the night air that chilled her? Ewan wondered. Or loneliness?

"Can ye not stay awhile longer?" He spread his cape. "It's good and warm under here. And there's plenty of room for ye."

She hesitated for a moment. "You're sure?"

"Oh, aye." He moved behind her, wrapping the cloak around them both. "Ye know, I reckon as long as ye love a place, then ye belong there."

"Perhaps you're right." Claire did not sound convinced. "It would be pleasant to think so."

With a sigh, she leaned back against him, her slender curves liberated from their whalebone cage.

Ewan discovered just how warm it could get inside his cloak.

He tried to distract Claire from her melancholy thoughts, and himself from his improper ones. "Say, do ye remember the time ye talked me into taking ye to see the stone circle up the glen?"

The distraction seemed to work on Claire. She chuckled. "I still say I saw a ghost...or something."

"It's a wonder yer father didn't ship me off to America over that."

On they talked for a while, sharing stories from the old days.

"I suppose," said Claire at last, "by morning we should be coming in sight of—"

Before she could finish, Ewan spotted a flicker of light in the distance, as though one of the stars had fallen to earth.

"There!" He raised his arm and pointed, his throat too tight to say more for a moment.

"I see," said Claire. "What is it?"

"The light on Galloway Head," replied Ewan when he recovered his voice. "My first sight of Scotland in ten years."

"Ah!" Claire pressed the glass back into his hand. "That calls for a toast, I think, and there should be just enough whiskey left for one."

Ewan lifted his glass in the direction of the Rhyns, that wee finger of land Scotland thrust down into the Irish Sea.

Claire gave a wide yawn. "Welcome home, Ewan Geddes."

It all overwhelmed him suddenly—the sight of home and her nearness. Before he knew what was what, he had spun Claire around, into his arms. He kissed her the way he had not kissed a lass in many a year. Not since the long-ago night that had cost him so dearly.

He wasn't sure if his veins were full of whiskey or moonlight, or a sweet, tipsy mixture of both. Her lips felt so soft and responsive to the most subtle movement of his. As if she were bidding him welcome.

He was delighted to accept her hospitality.

With a slow, hot swipe of his tongue, he coaxed her lips apart and made a tender but thorough acquaintance of her sweet mouth. One hand played through her hair, while the other... dropped the empty glass.

It shattered on the deck, shattering their moment along with it.

What had he done?

"Mind yer feet!" He lifted Claire clear of the deck and pivoted around to set her down away from the broken glass.

"Everything all right, sir?" called the first mate.

"Just broke some glass here and can't see to clean it up."

"Never mind about that, sir. I'll get one of the crew to give it a swab as soon as they're stirring."

The practical consequences dealt with, Ewan turned to the more important ones.

"I'm sorry, Claire." He let go of her, wishing he didn't have to. "I don't know what got into me just now!"

"Whiskey and moonlight, perhaps." She made it sound so careless. "And feelings running high, looking for an outlet."

"I reckon ye're right."

What she said made sense and he wanted to believe it. Somehow, though, he feared there might be more to it than that.

Chapter Eleven

Ewan was sorry for kissing her.

Claire felt as if her heart were made of glass, and he had dropped it on the deck.

Perhaps that did not matter, though, so long as neither of them cut their feet on the jagged shards, and the whole mess got cleaned up before morning.

Thank heaven for the darkness, she told herself as she stole back down to her cabin. This was not the first time it had been a friend to her—hiding her face from Ewan Geddes after he'd kissed her. At least this time he'd known who she was, even if his reasons had been less than flattering.

In any case, she was the one who ought to be sorry.

She had been able to justify her attempts to

lure Ewan Geddes away from her sister when she'd believed him to be an unscrupulous fortune hunter. Now that she was convinced otherwise, there could be no excuse for her conduct toward the man. She was heartily ashamed of it.

What had possessed her to slip under that cloak with him when the two of them were wearing only their nightclothes? Even Tessa might blanch at that kind of impropriety.

Come to that, what had made him invite her to share his cloak? Had it been nothing more than a rash impulse fueled by drink and the dubious intimacy of darkness? Or could there be more to it? And what might have happened if that cursed glass had not slipped out of his hand?

Claire removed her dressing gown and crawled into bed. Sleep proved more elusive than ever, as the memory of Ewan's kiss and the warmth of his body pressed against hers taunted her. What might he do if she dared to steal into his cabin now? She imagined how he might hold her, kiss her, touch her—until her whole body ached and burned with longing for him.

She rose the next morning dreading the necessity of facing Ewan at the breakfast table. It must be done, though. To avoid him would only arouse suspicion that their aborted kiss had meant more to her than she'd let on. More than she ever wanted him to guess.

To her surprise, the meal proved less awkward

than she'd expected, for both of them took great pains to behave as if nothing had happened. Clearly there were some embarrassments he did not scruple to sweep under the rug.

"So," she asked as Ewan attacked his oatmeal with an appetite, "did the drink and the sea air help you sleep better?"

"Oh, aye." He gave a vigorous nod, but his drawn features told a different story. Was it possible their close contact and kiss had plagued his dreams as they had hers? It would salve her pride a little to think so. "And ye?"

"The perfect tonic." Claire countered his lie with one she hoped was more convincing, then moved on to a less awkward subject. "With fair winds, we should reach Strathandrew by tonight."

Her distraction appeared to work. The tightness around Ewan's eyes relaxed and his smile came readily. "It'll be good to see the old place again. I wonder if it's changed much?"

Claire shook her head. "Time seems to stand still up there. Tessa and I have certainly made no changes since we inherited the place."

Nor had she wanted any. Mr. Catchpole occasionally hinted that a Highland sporting estate was a financial liability. Though she'd had several offers for Strathandrew, Claire had refused to sell. But neither had she made frequent use of it. Her few visits had stirred up too many memories, leaving her restless and melancholy.

"This has always been my favorite part of the voyage," she told Ewan, and reminded herself. "Sailing past all the islands and mouths of the sea lochs."

And looking forward to seeing him again. Noting how much taller he'd grown over the winter, how much broader his shoulders and muscular his forearms. Finding him still so much more alluring than the well-bred young bores whose company she was forced to suffer during the rest of the year.

Every summer she had hoped this would be the one he would notice her. But he never had, no matter how much she'd badgered him. In moments of adolescent despair, she'd often wondered if he recollected her name from one summer to the next.

"Claire?" Her name on his lips, ten years too late, shook her from her bittersweet memories.

"I beg your pardon?" The lapse flustered her. Had the echo of her old longing for him shown on her face?

If it had, Ewan failed to recognize it. "I was asking if ye'd care to join me on deck to point out the sights."

Could she? Return to the very spot where he'd kissed her, and stand near him as if nothing had happened?

"Why, of course." To decline would be an admission that last night had meant more to her than she pretended.

Besides, she craved his company. It was like the bewitched food in a story her nursery maid had once told her, food that made a person hungrier the more they consumed.

If she wasn't careful, she might gorge herself and starve to death.

Ewan was hungry for every glimpse of his homeland.

Fishing villages of whitewashed cottages huddled against the Atlantic winds. Colonies of fat dappled seals lazing on broad, deserted beaches. Humpbacked hills with summits swathed in cloud. Tall, gaunt stacks of rock thrusting from the sea, like accusing fingers pointed at heaven. Dark, towering cliffs seething with seabirds. The ruins of an ancient fortress standing ghostly guardian over the headland it had once protected.

He consumed it all, like a starving man at a banquet table. And Claire Talbot's company added relish to every bite.

"Isn't it strange how low those two bigger islands lie, while the little one rises so high?" She pointed toward them, raising her voice almost to a shout to be heard above the roar of the surf.

"I wonder how that came about?" Ewan observed the cluster of islands for a while, before he found his gaze drawn sidelong to study her, instead.

She had secured her hat in place with a wide scarf, but still had to anchor it against sudden gusts with her hand. That same wind had teased her cheeks to the color of thrift, a tiny pink flower that carpeted the Argyll countryside in spring. As she called his attention to each fresh wonder, her eyes reflected the restless energy of the churning sea.

The *Marlet* raced northward, sails bulging from the wind, its hull rising as it crested each high wave, then plunging into each trough with a belly-wrenching drop. It would have left most folks hanging over the deck rail, retching their guts out. But Claire looked positively exhilarated. Her mood proved contagious.

"If I wasn't so anxious to get home," said Ewan, "it might be a lark to stop 'round and visit some of the islands for a better look."

Claire nodded. "I've often thought that, too. Iona in particular. Perhaps you and Tessa can make a honeymoon tour of the isles."

"Oh, aye." Ewan tried to sound as enthusiastic as he ought to feel. Why did the prospect of touring the isles with Tessa not appeal to him more?

He clutched the railing as another thought struck him. He was not as eager as he should be to see Tessa again, once they reached Strathandrew. For years, she had been the focus of his dreams and plans. Now that they were so close to fruition, those dreams pinched and bound him like an outgrown suit of clothes.

In the past few days, Claire had come to claim more and more of his attention. He could not shake the memory of their brief kiss, nor the conviction that she had responded to his unexpected ardor. Yet today she acted as if nothing had happened. Even last night she'd been cool about it, blaming their indiscretion on whiskey and moonlight.

Perhaps that was what had prompted *her*. Ewan wanted to lay the blame for his own conduct there, as well. But he feared it might not be quite so simple. If moonlight and whiskey had made him sweep Claire into his arms, why did he want to do it again, cold sober and in broad daylight?

He still had not answered that question to his satisfaction hours later, when the *Marlet* glided up the narrow firth toward Strathandrew. Nor had he managed to subdue the urge.

How strange it felt to be standing aboard the Talbots' yacht, watching the staff assemble near the wharf to greet them. Part of him felt he should be down there among them, scrambling for his place, minding Rosie McMurdo's motherly advice to tuck in his shirt and pull up his stockings.

Where was Rosie? There, he spotted her!

Small and stout, standing next to the wraith-like figure of Mrs. Arbuthnot, the housekeeper he'd never much cared for. Alongside Rosie stood Fack Gowrie, the head gardener, and beside him his brother Fergus, the head gamekeeper. An irreverent young minister at the local kirk had once compared the Gowrie brothers to Cain and Abel, for which the elders had promptly raked him over the coals.

Ewan did not recognize any of the junior staff, among whom there had always been a more frequent turnover. Parlor maids left to get married after they'd saved a little nest egg, while footmen and gardeners went to Glasgow or England or America in hopes of bettering themselves.

"This should be a fine surprise for everyone," said Claire as they prepared to disembark. "I wired Mrs. Arbuthnot to expect us, and that we would be bringing a guest, but I didn't mention whom."

Ewan could not resist the urge to adjust his neck linen and brush an invisible fleck of dirt from his lapel. A passing qualm of uncertainty rippled through him as he followed Claire down the gangway. What kind of reception would he get from the folks who'd once been like a family to him?

"Mrs. Arbuthnot, you're looking well." Claire delivered the polite falsehood in a crisp tone as the housekeeper dropped a stiff-backed curtsy.

"I hope it did not put you out too much to make Strathandrew ready for our coming at such short notice."

"Not at all, miss." Mrs. Arbuthnot kept glancing toward the yacht. "We make the house ready for yer coming every summer."

Ewan caught one of the parlor maids rolling her eyes. He could imagine the staff's annoyance at having to go to all that extra work for nothing.

As Claire moved on to greet the cook, Mrs. Arbuthnot cleared her throat to draw her mistress's attention. "Did Lady Lydiard and Miss Tessa not accompany you, after all, Miss Talbot? I thought your wire said all three of you would be coming, as well as your guest."

"I expect my sister and stepmother will be arriving within the next day or two by train," said Claire. "Shortly before we sailed, I received word that Tessa was indisposed and that they would follow as soon as they could.

"I beg your pardon." Claire turned toward Ewan. "I must introduce an honored visitor to Strathandrew, though he is hardly a stranger…"

Catching Rosie McMurdo's eye, Ewan flashed her a wide smile.

"Ewan Geddes!" cried Rosie. She squeezed between Claire and the dumbfounded Mrs. Arbuthnot to throw her arms around him. "Ye look such a fine gentleman, I almost didn't recognize ye, laddie!"

"Cook!" the housekeeper gasped. "Mr. Geddes is Miss Talbot's guest."

"Oh dear!" Rosie pulled back, all red and flustered. "I was so surprised to see the dear lad, I clean forgot."

Ewan grabbed her plump hands before she could get away, and pulled her toward him again. "Thank ye for the warm welcome, Rosie!"

He stooped to plant a hearty kiss on her cheek, savoring Mrs. Arbuthnot's disapproving look. "I was afraid there might be nobody at Strathandrew who remembered me."

"Not remember ye?" Rosie dismissed such a daft suggestion. "After the letters ye sent and all the—"

"I hope ye'll remember some of my favorite dishes and cook them while I'm here." Ewan interrupted her before she could mention the money he'd sent. "I haven't yet met a cook in America who can make *partan bree* or a proper Dundee cake."

The mention of victuals proved a perfect distraction for Rosie. "*Partan bree?* Bless me, lad, yes! I'll have to get ye fattened up while ye're here. Aught ye have a hankering for, just let me know and I'll make it."

The housekeeper cleared her throat again. "I believe we have already discussed the menus, Cook."

An angry retort rose to Ewan's lips, but before

he could spit it out, Claire spoke up. "Surely the preferences of our guests should always dictate our bill of fare, Mrs. Arbuthnot. Why come to Scotland to dine as if we were still in London?"

"As ye wish, miss." The housekeeper's lips pinched together.

Ewan struggled to keep a cocky grin off his face. "Good to see ye again, Mrs. Arbuthnot. Ye haven't changed a bit."

In her case, that wasn't a compliment.

She replied with a wordless curtsy so stiff it looked as though her joints might be in danger of snapping.

The Gowrie brothers looked little changed by the passing years, either, though Fack might have been a tad more stooped and Fergus a touch more grizzled. The gardener appeared almost as glad to see Ewan as Rosie had, while the gamekeeper gave him a welcome barely a degree warmer than the housekeeper's.

As Claire greeted and introduced the junior staff, Ewan basked in their looks of wonderment. He could imagine how he would have felt at their age, seeing a former servant like himself risen to the dizzying social height of honored guest of the Talbots.

Introduced to the round-eyed young gillie, he gave the lad a warm handshake. "Would ye let me borrow yer fly-tying gear for a bit, to see if I can remember how it's done?"

"Aye, sir! Will ye be doing some fishing while ye're here? The trout are big this year. A lot of fight in 'em, too!"

"I'm looking forward to getting a rod in my hands again." The prospect brought a smile to Ewan's lips. "Clears the mind, fly-fishing does. Nothing better."

Claire moved on down the line to a bonny young lass with rich auburn hair pinned up under her cap and a peculiar little smirk on her face, as if she knew an amusing secret.

"This is our newest parlor maid," said Claire. "Rosie's daughter, Glenna."

"Not wee Glenna!" In spite of his denial, he scooped her off her feet and twirled her around. "Why, ye've changed enough to make up for all the rest, lass. Ye make me feel old just to look at ye."

"Welcome home, Ewan." Glenna stepped back in line, her pretty face flushed a bright red. "Don't let Ma torment ye about being too thin. Ye look just fine. Like a proper laird."

Her compliment stirred a strange brew of contrary feelings in Ewan. For years he'd dreamed of this day—returning in a triumph of wealth and success to the estate from which he'd been banished in disgrace. Now, as he glanced from Glenna McMurdo to Claire Talbot, he felt as if he had lost his old place and no longer fit in anywhere.

* * *

Watching Ewan swing the young parlor maid around in his arms, Claire tried to ignore a ridiculous stab of jealousy. She had no claim on the man, after all. And it was obvious the only feelings he entertained toward Glenna McMurdo were a kind of brotherly fondness. Besides, if Claire were foolish enough to envy his attentions to another woman, that woman should be her sister.

For as long as she could recall, Claire had fought against feelings of jealousy toward Tessa. And she had always managed to conquer them. She was not about to poison the one truly loving relationship she'd ever known by giving in to them now.

Once Ewan set Glenna McMurdo back on her feet, Claire turned to introduce him to the rest of the staff, but Mrs. Arbuthnot suddenly appeared at her elbow.

"Begging your pardon, miss, but you might wish to postpone further introductions." She pointed toward the thick, black-bottomed clouds the wind had blown in from the Atlantic.

"Indeed." Claire recalled the capricious Highland weather. "Mr. Geddes is hardly a stranger to Strathandrew. Let us all get indoors before the skies open on us."

The staff needed no further orders to turn and flee up the winding path to the house, the young footmen and gardeners dashing off in the lead, trailed closely by the maids, who hiked their skirts up to make better haste. The cook and the housekeeper followed, Mrs. McMurdo puffing along, while Mrs. Arbuthnot glided beside her. The Gowrie brothers brought up the rear, seeming in no hurry, perhaps because they were accustomed to being outdoors in all weather.

Ewan had not appeared anxious to be on his way, either. But once all the servants had gone, he offered Claire his arm. "That rain's going to take a while to fall yet, I reckon. And we can change clothes at our leisure if we have to. May I escort ye up to the house, Miss Talbot?"

Claire told herself she was quite capable of walking without his assistance. And she should not indulge in any unnecessary contact with him.

In spite of that, she heard herself reply, "You certainly may. Thank you."

She tucked her hand into the crook of his arm. For a moment she allowed her good intentions to slip. She savored his nearness and the sweet illusion that he belonged to her.

"Was I right?" she asked. "Has the place changed much from the way you remember it?"

To her, it felt as if time had slipped backward and she was living out an old dream—walking up from the wharf with Ewan Geddes, arm in arm. Not that her father ever would have permitted it. Nor would the handsome young gillie have offered. He'd have been too busy making sheep's eyes at Tessa, who barely noticed him.

"Changed?" Ewan shook his head and chuckled. "Not any amount. It might look a bit smaller than I recollect. That's about all.

"Now, then…" He reached over with his free hand to pat hers. "How do ye propose we entertain ourselves until the rest of our party arrives?"

Her stomach roiled with shame at his reminder that Tessa and Lady Lydiard would soon be joining them. She had no business indulging in a ten-year-old fancy for the man her sister intended to marry. During their youth, Claire had allowed herself to yearn for Ewan Geddes—only because Tessa had not returned his feelings.

Now that she did, and now that it was clear he had no designs on Tessa's fortune, Claire must lock away those old feelings and never let them back out on any account.

It would not be easy, though.

The jumble of conflicting feelings within her made her answer more sharply than she intended. "You're no longer a servant here, Ewan. You are not obliged to keep me amused. I expect we are both well used to entertaining ourselves, and there will be plenty for you to do at Strathandrew."

Even through the fabric of his coat, she could feel the flesh of his arm grow tense. When she risked a fleeting glance at his face, his dark brows signaled stormy emotions as surely as the sky's dark clouds forecast rain.

"Do ye need to remind *me* that I'm a guest, not a servant?" he growled. "Or yerself, Claire?"

The man was clearly infuriated. Though why, she could not work out.

He shook off her hand and spun about to confront her. "Were ye only willing to suffer my company on the *Marlet* to keep me from jumping ship again? Now that we're at yer fine estate, ye're warning me to keep my distance?"

Claire barely stifled a shriek. The man was as exasperating as he was…compelling!

"How did you ever come to such a ridiculous conclusion?" She stood far too close to him, trading glare for glare. "I was trying to spare you the burden of having to dance attendance on me. Only you could find an insult in that!"

"I've never *danced attendance* on anyone," he informed her in a tone of scorn. "And I'm not about to start. Besides, keeping ye company isn't the same as dancing attendance. Only *ye* would reckon that a burden on a man. I'm here to tell ye it's not, when ye make an effort to be sociable."

It was not much of a compliment, compared to the lavish flattery she'd received over the years. Why, then, did it make her breath catch high in the back of her throat and her knees feel suddenly weak?

Claire knew the answer, but she could not bring herself to accept it, as a gust of rain-laden wind sent them scurrying for the shelter of the house.

Chapter Twelve

By the time Ewan and Claire stumbled into the entry hall of Strathandrew, gasping for breath, they were almost as wet as when they'd been hauled back aboard the *Marlet* from the lifeboat. It seemed nature was prepared to throw cold water on the pair of them whenever they fell to bickering.

The formal elegance of the entry hall and the critical stare of the housekeeper discouraged Ewan from shaking himself like a wet hound.

"Ye'll want to change into dry clothes before dinner." Mrs. Arbuthnot's hushed murmur somehow carried the weight of an order. Her frigid gaze fixed on him, as if accusing him of getting soaked on purpose.

She beckoned a young footman forward. "Alec, show the gentlem— Show Miss Talbot's guest to his room."

As Ewan followed the young fellow up the broad staircase, he glanced back at Claire, who was removing her bedraggled hat. "I'll see ye at dinner, then? Unless ye'd rather I make myself scarce?"

"Don't be ridiculous!" she snapped. "You're a guest at Strathandrew. Of course I shall see you at dinner."

"Just making sure." He took the stairs two at a time to catch up with the footman.

The beautiful, bewigged lady whose portrait graced the first landing seemed to cast him a reproachful look. More fancy folk in silks, satins and lace looked down on him from the walls of the broad upstairs gallery. Ewan wondered if they might be generations of noble Talbot ancestors, contemplating with horror the trespass of a former servant within their domain.

"Been in service here long?" he asked the young footman. His voice erupted with ill-bred loudness in the refined hush of the gallery.

"Two years, sir." The lad barely raised his voice above a whisper, as if he were in kirk.

"How are ye liking it?"

After a pause in which he seemed to weigh the wisdom of answering truthfully, the lad shrugged. "It was this or one of the Highland Regiments, sir. Here I can get home to see my folks now and then. The food's first-rate and the work's not that hard."

Stopping before a fine mahogany door with gleaming brass knob and hinges, he opened it, then stood back to let Ewan enter.

On his way into the room, Ewan flashed the lad a jaunty wink. "And nobody's shooting at ye."

Young Alec grinned. "That's in its favor, too, sir."

"I used to think Mrs. A could hold her own with any bully of a sergeant in the Black Watch," quipped Ewan.

The lad cast a nervous glance over his shoulder before he gave a muted chuckle.

Ewan's own mirth caught in his throat. It wasn't right that smart lads like Alec had so few opportunities in life beyond civilian or military servitude.

Having never known any different, the young footman didn't seem to feel sorry for himself. "If ye want to get out of those wet clothes, sir, I'll go fetch yer trunk."

"A fine idea." Ewan looked around for the dressing screen, but saw none in the richly appointed room.

It lacked nothing else for his comfort, from the dark green hangings on the massive four-poster bed, to the fireplace where a small blaze crackled in a cheery welcome. Still, something about the place made Ewan uneasy. All the more so because he could not put his finger on it.

The footman seemed to interpret his puzzled glance about. "The dressing room is right through there, Mr. Geddes, sir." He pointed to the right-hand wall, where a door stood slightly ajar.

"Aye, of course," said Ewan. "I should have noticed."

"Glad to help, sir." The lad turned to leave.

"Alec?"

"Aye, sir?"

"Ye can leave off with that 'sir' and 'Mr. Geddes' business. It makes me feel like a stranger. This is home to me. Here I'm plain Ewan."

The lad's ruddy face grew even redder. "No disrespect to yer wishes, sir. But if Mrs. A caught me talking that familiar with a guest, I'd never hear the end of it."

"I reckon ye wouldn't." Ewan's shoulders sagged a bit as he headed for the dressing room.

A while later, he emerged in dry clothes, all washed, brushed and eager for a little company. He wanted to find out what had happened around Strathandrew since he'd left. Claire might think time stood still in these parts, but she saw it only for a few weeks every year or so. Mrs. Arbuthnot was such a stickler for "maintaining standards," Ewan doubted anything had changed in the household routine during her tenure.

But even the Talbot's grim housekeeper could not hold back time. Bairns sprouted up into lads and lasses, took a fancy to one another, wed in the village kirk and had families of their own. Meanwhile, their folks grew older and their grandfolks died. There were good harvests and bad, special celebrations, local jokes and minor scandals—all the events that made up the life of a community.

Ewan was anxious to catch up on all of it.

He ducked out of his room, easing the door closed behind him with furtive quietness. Out in the hushed gallery, delicious smells of Rosie's cooking wafted through the breathless air. Ewan followed them to the back stairs. He tread softly, almost on tiptoe, and kept glancing behind him, as if he expected to be caught intruding, and ordered away.

Once he reached the back stairs, principally used by the servants for their discreet comings and goings, he began to relax and feel more at home.

On his way down, he met one of the upstairs maids with a pile of linen in her arms. When she saw him, she gave a strangled squeak of fright and fumbled her load. Ewan swooped to catch the pristine sheets and towels before they tumbled all over the stairs.

"Thank ye, sir." In the faint light from the landing window, the lass's face looked as bleached as the linens. "Is there anything ye're wanting, sir? Ye only have to ring and somebody will come straightaway."

It wasn't possible to summon or demand what he was looking for. "I have everything I need, thank ye, lass. I just wanted to poke my nose below stairs for a wee visit."

She looked at him as if he were clean daft, but all she said was, "As ye like, sir."

Then she bobbed a quick curtsy and headed up the stairs as Ewan continued down.

At the bottom of the steps, he pushed open the swinging door that led to the servants' hall. The long table at one end of the big room was laid for supper, but there was no sign of anyone sitting in the assortment of armchairs and rockers clustered around the hearth at the near end.

Beyond the servants' hall, Ewan could see folks scurrying about in the kitchen, and heard the clatter of pots and pans. The succulent aromas of onions and beef and the mellow fragrance of toasted oats made his mouth water.

He headed toward a side table where Rosie McMurdo was beating some pale yellow froth in a bowl with vigorous strokes. She was concentrating so hard on her task that she didn't even notice him swoop in to plant a quick peck on her plump cheek.

"What's for dinner, Rosie? It smells like heaven!"

Rosie shrieked and her spoon flew up, splashing tiny gobbets of batter all over Ewan's coat, face and hair.

"What are ye trying to do, ye young rogue?" she cried, her fists planted on her ample hips. "Scare a body to death?"

"Sorry, Rosie!" He scraped a bit of batter off his chin, then licked it off his finger. "Mmm! I've waited ten years to taste yer cooking again. I've never had better, in all the time I've been gone."

The cook's vexed look softened. "Oh, get away with ye! I reckon ye've had fine meals in those fancy eating places in America."

"Aye, a few." And at the estates of some of his business associates. He'd never developed a taste for rich fare, however. "It all lacked something in the flavor, though."

Just then, Ewan realized how quiet the kitchen had fallen. He glanced around to find several of the junior servants frozen in place at their tasks, as if they were playing some sort of parlor game. He followed their stares back to the kitchen door, where Mrs. Arbuthnot stood.

"Back to work, all of ye," she snapped. "We have a meal to prepare, or have ye forgotten?"

Her gaze, as cold as a loch in February, turned upon Ewan. "Is there something ye require, sir? There is a bell in yer room, or did Alec forget to inform ye?"

"He told me." Ewan wondered how he could

still feel cowed by a woman he could buy and sell a thousand times over. "And I remember how the bells work. I just thought I'd pop down for a bit of company."

"Ye look as if ye could use another change of clothes before dinner." Mrs. Arbuthnot couldn't have appeared more disgusted if he'd been covered head to toe in fish guts or sheep muck.

"That's my fault," said Rosie. She pulled a handkerchief from her apron pocket, then reached up to wipe Ewan's cheek. "It was kind of ye to drop in for a visit, lad. Another time, maybe, when it's not so busy down here?"

"Aye, Rosie. Sorry to get in yer way."

As he strode back out past the housekeeper, Ewan heard the sounds of the kitchen pick up where they'd left off. He spotted one of the Gowrie brothers sitting near the hearth with a Bible open on his knees. Ewan considered sitting down for a chat with him, just to vex Mrs. Arbuthnot. Then Fergus, the gamekeeper, glanced up with a scowl that informed Ewan his company was not wanted.

He wondered why. Mrs. Arbuthnot had never much cared for him when he'd been a servant here, so her cold welcome came as no surprise. He'd expected better from Fergus, the man who had taught him to shoot and fish.

Pushing open the back stairs door and returning to his room, Ewan knew for certain he had lost his old place at Strathandrew. If he was to have any company at all until Tessa arrived, it would have to be her sister's.

"Oh my." Claire set down her fork after a course of braised beef only to have the dish replaced by one bearing tender white scallops in cream sauce. "Mrs. McMurdo has outdone herself in your honor, Ewan. I hope you're enjoying it as much as you anticipated."

"Oh, aye." He glanced up at her from across the table and smiled. But his voice sounded less enthusiastic than she'd expected. "I never could find a cook in America who knew how to make *partan bree.*"

"The crab soup? Yes, it was marvelous."

"I reckon no one could have made it quite like Rosie, anyway." Ewan lifted a plump scallop on his fork, then closed his eyes, the better to relish its subtle flavor. "Nor queenies so tender."

He sounded appreciative, yet subdued, somehow.

Could it be on account of their earlier quarrel? Could he truly believe she didn't *want* his company? If only he knew how she craved it!

The rain pattered against the large windows that afforded a breathtaking view of the loch in better weather. A small but warm fire crackled in the hearth, making the large formal dining room feel almost cosy. Their seating arrangement contributed to the intimacy of the meal. Until her sister and stepmother arrived, Claire had ordered places to be set for her and Ewan across from one another in the middle of the long table.

"I hope you found the accommodations to your liking?" She worried that her question might sound too stilted or insincere. It was one of those things a hostess was obliged to ask her guests. "I believe Mrs. Arbuthnot put you in Father's old room."

Ewan laughed, and a spark of impudent charm flared in his eyes. "I wondered why such a comfortable room made my hackles rise. Yer father's likely spinning in his grave at the notion of me sleeping in his bed."

A most disrespectful thought popped into Claire's head. "His ghost may be speeding north as we speak to haunt you tonight!"

A tightness within her eased as they laughed together over that absurd notion. A tightness so old and deeply ingrained, she had come to take it for granted as part of her nature. It frightened her a little to begin to let go of it.

"What do ye say?" Ewan's mischievous grin dared her. "Will ye come for a walk with me tomorrow, if the weather's fine? Torment that old ghost a bit by keeping company with a humble gillie boy? Please, as a favor to me?"

Where was the harm in it? Claire asked herself as she tried not to lose herself in his beseeching gaze. Ewan truly seemed to want her company.

Why not indulge in a few of her old dreams? Pretend he had come to Strathandrew as her beau, instead of Tessa's? Despite that meaningless kiss on the deck of the *Marlet,* there was no way she could hope to lure Ewan away from her sister. Nor did she want to, if Tessa truly cared for him. Indulging in a day or two of make-believe would take nothing away from Tessa, therefore it could not be disloyal.

"I suppose you know how difficult you are to refuse when you use that look on a woman?"

Ewan replied with a grin that was equally difficult to resist. "I practice it in the mirror every morning while I shave."

"Indeed?" Something strange and intoxicating bubbled inside Claire. For the first time in her life, she was flirting with a man…and enjoying it. "How very diligent of you."

"So it is." He was flirting back—the rogue! No doubt because he knew neither of them meant to take it seriously. "Surely a captain of industry like yerself will want to reward diligence?"

"And enterprise." Claire postponed her inevitable answer by popping another plump queenie into her mouth. "Very well, then. If the weather is fine, I'll come. Even your considerable arts of persuasion could not induce me to roam about Highland hills in the rain."

"It's a bargain, then!" He looked so vastly pleased, Claire could not help feeling flattered. "I'll ask Rosie to pack us up a lunch, and tell Fergus we'd like a pony to carry it," he added.

"Dear me! How enormous a lunch are you planning to take, that we'll need a pony to haul it?"

"Tramping the hills is hungry work." Ewan finished off the last of his scallops and washed them down with a drink of wine. "We'll want a rug to sit on while we eat. And in case ye get tired, ye can always ride on the way back."

"What makes you so certain I'll get tired?" It was the sort of question to which she would have demanded an answer in their youth. Now Claire asked out of amusement rather than indignation. "Have you done much tramping the hills in America these past ten years? Why, I may need to hoist you over the pony's back to fetch you home tomorrow."

"So ye might, lass." Ewan raised his glass to her, then drained it.

"Whereabouts are you planning to take me?" she asked, as the maid replaced her empty plate with a delectable looking confection of whipped cream, raspberries and toasted oats.

"Someplace special," was all Ewan would tell her before he fell upon his saucer of trifle and devoured every last morsel.

He did not add any blatant flattery about a

special place for special company, but she sensed he meant it. Hard as she tried, she could not help feeling flattered.

Until the moment Claire had asked him where he meant to take her, he'd had a different destination in mind. He'd meant to delay a visit to Linn Riada until Tessa could accompany him. Just then, Ewan knew he could not wait another day. Nor could he escape the conviction that Claire would appreciate the place more than her sister.

Ewan set down his pudding spoon with a sigh of keen anticipation richly rewarded. Only the thought of how Mrs. Arbuthnot might gloat over such crude manners kept him from licking his saucer clean of his favorite *cranachan* pudding.

"A splendid meal!" Claire touched her lips with her napkin, then set it beside her own well-scraped saucer. She turned to the serving maid. "Do convey our compliments to Mrs. Mc-Murdo."

The lass gave a silent, smiling nod as she collected the dishes.

"Having plates come back to the scullery empty is the best compliment ye can give Rosie," said Ewan.

How well he remembered the cook anxiously watching dishes return below stairs—exulting over the empty ones and taking barely touched plates as a grievous insult to her skill and effort.

Sometimes he had waylaid serving staff on the back stairs and gobbled up the leftover food on several plates just to spare Rosie's feelings.

Claire rose from her seat. "I'll retire so you can enjoy your brandy. Feel free to make use of the billiard room."

She motioned to a set of elaborately carved double doors behind him. "It's just through there."

Ewan got to his feet. "I know where it is."

"You do?"

"Aye. In the old days, I used to catch the odd glimpse through the windows of his lairdship and guests playing."

Since he could fish and shoot better than any of the gentleman, billiards had represented a skill that set them apart from him. Once he'd begun to make his fortune, he had set to work mastering it.

"I beg your pardon." Claire winced. "I should have asked if you play."

Perhaps. But he liked that she'd assumed he could. "Oh, aye. I'm good, too."

Claire's chagrin evaporated in a gust of laughter, as if she understood what that signified, and sympathized. "A pity my father isn't here so you could challenge him to a game."

She did understand.

"Why don't ye take his place, then?"

"Me? You must be joking!"

"Why not? I can't very well play without an opponent."

That made her stop and think. "I suppose not, but I'd be no good to you. I haven't the least notion how to play."

"I could teach ye." He used the tone and look that had persuaded her to come walking with him.

For a moment she seemed almost ready to agree. Then she drew back, shaking her head. "Billiards is a man's game."

"Aye. So's running one of the biggest shipbuilding firms in the country. Ye mastered that quick enough, and I'll bet ye didn't have as good a teacher as me."

Claire's perpetually guarded look relaxed and her fine, clear eyes sparkled. "Your modesty is touching!"

How beautiful she looked! And how much he wanted to make her laugh again. "Modesty's an overrated virtue."

As she chuckled at his quip, Ewan knew how Rosie McMurdo must feel when a whole tray of plates arrived back in the scullery, picked clean.

"Come on, now." He pressed his advantage. "It's not like tossing the caber. There's nothing about billiards that should give a man an advantage over a woman. It's all in the precision of yer shots and yer strategy."

Claire crossed her arms and looked at him with narrowed eyes.

For a moment Ewan feared she might guess… guess what?

"Are you doing this just to shock poor Mrs. Arbuthnot?" she asked.

"Of course not. That would just be a lucky by-blow."

"Very well, then." Claire circled the table to join him. "But you'll find no honor in besting a poor novice."

He opened one of the billiard room doors and held it for her to enter. "I don't reckon ye're going to stay a novice very long."

"I don't intend to." She gave a defiant little toss of her head and Ewan found his fingers itching to nestle in the fine, silken strands of her hair.

For days, he'd been plagued by these feelings for her, as intense as they were baffling. First he had tried to dismiss them. Then he had tried to explain them. Both to no avail.

Now Ewan wondered if he ought to explore them to find out how deep they ran.

Before Tessa arrived.

Chapter Thirteen

"That's one of the things I love about the Highlands," said Ewan the next morning, as he and Claire led a well-laden pony up into the hills. "If ye don't like the weather, ye haven't got to wait long for it to change!"

"It works in reverse, too." Claire cast a dubious glance at the serene blue sky. "Do you suppose the fine weather will last until we get back?"

"I reckon it might." Ewan sucked in a deep breath of fresh Argyll air. "There's not much of a wind to blow clouds our way. Like my old Gran Cameron used to say, God rest her soul, 'we might as well enjoy the sunshine, for we won't keep the rain away by fretting about it.'"

"A wise woman, your grandmother." Claire resolved to take her advice...though not about the weather. She must soak up the sparkling warmth of her stolen time with Ewan and not spoil it by fretting about the future. "She used to keep house at Strathandrew, didn't she?"

Ewan nodded. "That was how I got into service here."

"I don't remember her all that well." Claire vaguely recalled a pair of wide-set gray eyes, much like Ewan's. "Just being very sorry when I heard she'd passed away and that we would be getting a new housekeeper."

"I remember Gran telling me yer ma hired her and Rosie." Ewan patted the pony's neck.

Perhaps that was why old Mrs. Cameron had paid special attention to her when all the other servants made such a fuss over Tessa.

Ewan caught her gaze with his. "So what did ye think of our billiards game last night? It's not that hard once ye catch on, is it?"

"Most diverting," said Claire. "With enough practice, I might give you some real competition one of these days."

What she had enjoyed, more than the game itself, was the instruction she'd received from Ewan. When he'd wrapped his arms around her to demonstrate the proper way to hold a cue, she had savored his touch to the very marrow of her bones. Only by biting on her lip had she been able to stifle a sigh of delight.

Now she glanced away, so he would not see that delight reflected in her present gaze.

He must not have noticed, for he sounded casually cheerful when he asked, "Does that mean ye'll play me again tonight?"

"Why not?" Claire strove to sound equally casual. "With only the two of us here, it doesn't make much sense to part company after dinner."

How much longer would the two of them remain alone? Claire pushed that foreboding thought to the back of her mind and locked it in a dark cupboard, along with her fear of the heartache she would suffer once Tessa reclaimed her beau.

"I have a piece of advice," said Ewan, "that should help yer game."

Something in his tone warned Claire it was likely to be an impudent suggestion.

"Indeed?" She rallied, welcoming the distraction from her locked-up worries. "And what might that be?"

"Don't wear a corset." Suppressed laughter bubbled beneath his audacious suggestion. "It makes it too hard for ye to bend over the table to make yer shot."

Perhaps thinking she was too shocked to reply, he rattled on. "It's only me to see ye, anyway, and I think ye've got a fine figure without squeezing it all out of shape. Ye're not wearing a corset now, are ye?"

"Ewan!" A furious blush tingled in Claire's cheeks. "That is *not* a proper question for a gentleman to ask a lady!"

"Aye, well, I'm no gentleman, am I? So confess, lass. Yer secret's safe with me."

"As it happens, I am quite unencumbered at the moment." It was hard enough to catch her breath while tramping through the hills without being stifled by a corset!

"There, ye see?" Ewan looked her over with obvious admiration. "No corset and ye look as bonny as I've ever seen ye."

"In this?" Claire glanced down at her sturdy tweed skirt and waistcoat and the billowing sleeves of her old-fashioned blouse. "You must be daft!"

"I am not! Now I'll admit I'm no authority on ladies' fashion. I only know what I like. Tweed suits ye better than all that fussy silk and lace some lasses get themselves up in."

Claire wasn't certain that reflected well on her femininity, but she had to admit she enjoyed the ease of movement this outfit afforded her. "Very well, then. I promise to dispense with my corsets...*if* you will wear your kilt to dinner."

He looked vastly attractive in the one he was wearing now, with the black leather gillie vest over a loose shirt. The sight of him, as much as the steep slope they were climbing, made Claire gasp for breath.

Ewan laughed. "Ye've got yerself a bargain."

For a while they saved their breath for walking, until they were out of sight of the house and high on a ridge with a magnificent view of the loch.

"Let's rest here awhile." Ewan lifted a brown jug from the pony's pack. He pulled out the wooden stopper and passed the jug to Claire.

She gave it a suspicious sniff. "Whiskey?"

That was the last thing she needed.

Ewan shook his head. "Cider. Some of Rosie's best."

He spread their picnic rug upon the heath. When Claire had settled herself on it, he sat down beside her.

She took a deep drink from the cider jug, then handed it back to him. "This place *is* beautiful. No wonder you've longed for it."

A familiar but intriguing sight caught her eye. She pointed toward the ruin of an ancient castle on a small island at the far end of the lake. "Do you know anything about that place? Father always forbade Tessa and I to go near it when we went rowing in the loch."

"Eilean Tioran? Aye." Ewan set the cider jug down after he'd had a drink. "They say it was the stronghold of a branch of the Cameron clan. No enemy ever successfully attacked the castle by water. According to one old song, a sea serpent kept guard out in the loch, smashing the boats of any foe who tried to sail against the Camerons."

The earnest tone in which he recounted this preposterous tale warned Claire not to laugh.

"Red Kenneth Cameron fought at Stirling Bridge and again under Robert the Bruce at Bannockburn." Ewan gazed toward the island castle, his eyes shining with pride. "Murdo Cameron fell at Flodden Field, and Alec the Martyr was executed after Kilcrankie. They were bold warriors."

And he, the descendent of bold warriors, lairds of a serpent-guarded castle, had been reduced to a servant of foreign masters on the land they'd once ruled. Little wonder he'd had a chip on his shoulder.

"What became of the Camerons and their castle?" she whispered.

"Treachery." Ewan's hand balled into a fist and his chiseled jaw tensed. "We were betrayed by the McCrimons. The daughter of their chief was betrothed to Angus the Fair. All her family came to the wedding feast at Eilean Tioran, and while they were making merry, one of the McCrimons threw open the sea gate and let in English soldiers."

"You must hate the English."

"When I was a lad, I wanted an easy target to pin all my troubles on. But once I got to America, I started reading some history whenever I had a spare minute. I found out it wasn't as cut-

and-dried as all that. There were plenty of times through the centuries when we Scots were worse enemies to ourselves than anyone else could have been."

Could that be said of her, too? Claire wondered, as she gazed out at the ancient Cameron stronghold, rising from the mist.

"Highlander against Lowlander," Ewan mused, shaking his head. "Clan against clan. The kirk all splintered into groups killing each other in the name of God. The few times we've truly come together as a nation, no one could stand against us."

"Is Eilean Tioran what you brought me to see?" Claire asked.

"Eh?" Ewan started, as if he had temporarily forgotten her. "The castle? No. It was you who pointed that out. The place I'm taking ye is still a ways ahead. I reckon we'd better be off if we're going to get there and back before dinnertime."

He got to his feet, then held out his hand to hoist her up. The strength and warmth of his grip sent a bittersweet rush of longing through her—for more intimate touches from him. How she wished she could go back to that night on the deck of the *Marlet* and fold herself into his embrace once more.

"Are ye all right, Claire?" His voice held a tender note of concern. "Ye look sort of dreamy-eyed."

"I was just thinking about that romantic old castle and all the history it's seen."

Her excuse was true in part. Mixed up with all her thoughts about Ewan had been one about the abandoned castle. Like this stolen time with him, Eilean Tioran was a romantic dream from the past that could never be anything but a fantasy.

"Are ye sure that's all?" Ewan did not sound convinced.

"Of course." Claire strove to look and sound like the "sensible sort of person" her stepmother had commended her for being. "What else could it be?"

She hoped he would never guess.

What else *could* have made Claire Talbot look like that?

For one delirious moment, Ewan had thought she'd fixed him with the soft, brooding gaze a woman reserved for her *muirneach*...her beloved. And in that instant, a strange thing had happened to his own vision.

Sometimes, if a stag was shot away up in the hills, it would be flung across the pony's back to be brought home. Then it was the gillie's job to throw his coat over the pony's head, to keep it from taking a fright. Now, Ewan thought he knew how a pony must feel when that blinding coat fell away at last, and he could see again.

What he saw, after being blind to it for too

long, was that he had begun to fall in love with his old adversary.

How could it be, though? What kind of fickle creature was he, to transfer the allegiance of his heart in a matter of days from the one who had held it for over a dozen years? And how could he be so daft as to vest his love in the one woman who could never return it?

Claire's voice, breathless and a trifle sharp, penetrated his bemusement. "I hope whatever you have to show me will be worth the exertion."

He glanced over to see her clinging to one of the straps that secured the pony's pack. Her face was flushed and shiny, and several strands of her hair had fallen loose around her face. She looked almost as if she had been caught in the prelude of lovemaking.

Images of the two of them enjoying a lusty tumble in the heather sent a rush of heat through his loins and stirred the pleats of his kilt.

It took all his will to keep his voice from breaking when he answered her. "It will be, I promise ye. And all the better for the challenge of getting to it. I reckon I don't have to tell you that nothing worthwhile ever came easy."

His words seemed to stir something in her, for her blue-gray eyes flashed with determination that Ewan found altogether provocative. "You're right, of course. Striving makes the eventual reward all the sweeter."

"Aye." She understood, in a way he'd never expected a woman to do. "Venison always tastes best after a long stalk over rugged country. The most delicious salmon is the one that puts up the toughest fight."

From beyond the next rise, he caught the wild, nimble music of hill water. "It's only a wee bit farther now."

"Good!" Claire pushed a fallen wisp of hair off her brow. "I have had all the pleasure of a challenge I can stand for one day."

As he shared a winded chuckle with her, Ewan circled around behind the plodding pony until they were both on the same side of the beast. He wanted to be close to Claire, with an unobstructed view of her face when she first glimpsed Linn Riada.

He hoped it would not be like Strathandrew, diminished from the glory of his cherished memories.

"Oh, Ewan!" She groped for his hand, squeezing it with such force he almost cried out.

The glow of wonder in her eyes assured him it was as spectacular as it had ever been. He turned his gaze upon the ribbon of water, plunging and tumbling over the high rocks into a wee hidden glen. The sight squeezed his heart and made him catch his breath.

The angle of the sun's bright rays hit the fine mist thrown up by water glancing off the rocks.

The golden light splintered into dozens of tiny rainbows.

Ewan had been here many times and long thought it the rarest place in the world. But he had never seen it like this. The shimmering colors accounted for only part of the magic. The rest he found in the misty glow of Claire's eyes and the rapt tremble of her lower lip.

Might it have made a difference if he'd brought her here a dozen years ago? Before all her interest and energy had been committed to the family empire? Before her dauntless heart had been poisoned by a succession of men too selfish and stupid to realize she was worth more than any amount of gold?

It might. But what of it? If *might have been* and *if only* were rocks, his countrymen could build a cairn as high as heaven to lament their broken dreams and lost opportunities. Why should he be any different?

"So," he asked once he'd mastered his voice, "was it worth the climb?"

She turned toward him, her eyes still shining with wonder. "If you don't know the answer to that question, Ewan Geddes, you aren't nearly as clever as I thought you were. It would have made a climb halfway to the moon worthwhile. I cannot believe I have been coming to this part of the world for so many years, without ever guessing a place of such beauty was nearby."

Ewan drank in the sight of her, as she gazed in awe at the waterfall. "Sometimes the beauty that's near at hand is the hardest to see."

Would she understand what he meant? Was he being too blatant? Too subtle? All his life Ewan had been confident of his own charm, when he chose to exercise it. Suddenly, he cared too much to be sure of himself.

The pony shook its mane and whinnied, bringing Ewan back to earth. "I reckon somebody's trying to remind us he toted a lunch all the way up here, so we'd better get busy and eat it."

"Somehow, it doesn't seem quite right to eat an ordinary lunch in such a magnificent setting." Claire lifted the rug off the pony's back and spread it on the ground. "We ought to be dining on manna from heaven, or golden apples from Olympus. Quaffing the Fairy King's enchanted mead."

Ewan chuckled as he unstrapped the picnic hamper and let the pony loose to graze. "I never took ye for a fanciful lass. What's all this whimsy ye're spouting?"

"I've never been in such a fanciful place." Claire stooped and broke off a spray of heather, then drank in its subtle, fresh perfume. "I feel like I've strayed into the world of fairy stories, and the wee folk might pop out at any moment and grant me three wishes."

Lifting her face to the sun, she began to spin 'round and 'round.

"That's the heights making ye light-headed." Ewan caught her in a dizzy wobble and lowered her to the picnic rug. "Have another drink of cider and try one of Rosie's *bridies*. I reckon they've got more flavor than that manna stuff."

He slipped the cider jug into one of her hands and a wee golden-brown pie full of meat and taties and onions into the other. "There's oat cakes, too, and a bit of smoked salmon. And there's cheese and Dundee cake. Nothing too fine or fancy, just good Highland fare."

Claire washed down a big bite of *bridie* with a long swig from the cider jug. "Mmm! I was wrong. This is the perfect food to eat here—a banquet fit for a Highland chieftain!"

"I'll tell Rosie ye said that. She'll be tickled."

They enjoyed the rest of their picnic in the relaxed silence of good comrades, serenaded by the lilting music of the hill water. Every time he glanced at Claire, Ewan felt as if his heart was plunging over Linn Riada with all its beauty... and peril.

"I reckon we'd better head back." Ewan began to pack the remnants of their lunch into the basket. "Mrs. A will blame me if we're late for dinner."

"She's quite a gargoyle, isn't she?" Claire was

not disposed to think well of anyone responsible for making them leave this enchanting place. "I probably should dismiss her, but she does keep a tight rein on the place while we're in London."

"It's not just her." Ewan didn't sound anxious to leave, either. "With guests to feed, Rosie will be cooking her heart out. I've seen what it's like in the kitchen when a meal gets held up. It's a lot of bother for the staff."

"I suppose it must be." With a faint sigh of regret, Claire rose and folded up the picnic rug.

A qualm of guilt seized her when she recalled the number of times dinner had been delayed at Strathandrew without anyone in her family sparing a thought for the turmoil it might cause below stairs. "You must admit, this isn't an easy place to leave."

Her insides twisted tighter when she remembered that she had been the cause of his long exile from Linn Riada and all the other places he loved so well. Could whatever prosperity he'd found in America compensate him for their loss?

"I won't gainsay ye." Ewan stood for another long moment staring at the waterfall, as if eager to etch it in his memory.

The angle of the sun had altered, so the spray no longer spawned the dozens of miniature rainbows that had caught Claire's breath with their uncanny beauty. But it was still an enchanting sight.

Something moved her to approach and stand beside Ewan, her arm pressed lightly against his—sharing one *last* look, as he had shared the first with her. "Thank you for bringing me here. I'm honored."

Was it her oversensitive imagination, or did he edge away from her when he replied, "Ye make it sound as if it's something that's mine to give. Linn Riada is on Talbot land. It's always belonged to ye."

"What's the good of owning something if you don't know it?" For years her heart had been his, and lately he had reclaimed it, without ever knowing about either.

They reloaded the pony in thoughtful silence, then set off.

"Are we not going back the same way we came?" asked Claire. Her legs and backside felt stiff and a little sore after their steep walk, followed by a long sit on the rocky heath.

"We can, if ye like," said Ewan. "But I've already seen what I wanted to see over there. The way we're headed, ye can sometimes catch sight of the stags all gathered. Have ye ever seen that?"

Claire shook her head. "Father didn't approve of girls coming anywhere near a hunt."

"It's quite a sight."

Though not one they were destined to see that afternoon, as it happened.

They had been walking for some time in a westerly direction over gradually declining slopes when Claire shaded her eyes against the setting sun and asked, "What's over there? Another ruined castle?"

Glancing in the direction she'd pointed, Ewan shook his head.

"A stone circle?" If so, she would make certain they gave it a wide berth.

Everyone else had thought it a fine joke, but she *had* seen a fierce blue-painted face staring out at her from behind one of those eerie ancient stones. A dozen years later, the vivid memory still gave her chills.

"It's nothing worth seeing," Ewan insisted in a gruff tone that only piqued her interest.

"Are you sure it's not a castle?" She peered toward the regular piles of stone. "From this distance, it looks very like that Eilean Tioran place."

"It's *not* a castle!"

"What is it, then?"

"It's a village." Ewan heaved a bitter sigh. "Or what was left of one after folks were evicted so the laird could sell this land to yer family. He'd already moved his clansmen off the hills to pasture sheep. When that wasn't profitable enough…"

His voice died away for a moment, then he found it again. "Gran told me how the laird's factors set fire to the thatched roofs with old and sick folk still inside the cottages."

The wind rustled a forlorn sigh through the barren branches of a twisted tree. Claire fancied it bore an acrid whiff of smoke from long ago. "That's terrible! What became of those people— the ones who weren't killed outright?"

Ewan's gaze swept over the forsaken piles of stone. "Some found passage to America. Others went to Glasgow to find work. Young men enlisted in the Highland Regiments. Lassies went into service on estates like Strathandrew. A few fools tried to farm a bit of land farther up the coast that was no good for hunting."

"Your family?" Claire almost couldn't bear to ask. But neither could she bear not knowing.

Ewan tugged on the pony's lead to make it walk faster. "Pa never did fall to stealing sheep, that I know of. We might have been better off if he had."

Claire cringed to recall the heartless quip about sheep-thieving she'd flung at Ewan the night of the Fortescues' ball. "Can you ever forgive me for being so unfeeling? I swear, I never would have said such a thing if I'd known about...all this."

"I know." The temperate tone of his voice held a pardon. "It's not like I've never had reason to regret things I've said in anger."

His response emboldened her to ask, "What *did* your father do?"

"Worked himself to death, and my ma along with him, on a piece of rock that wasn't fit to farm. They were so worn down when the bad harvests of the forties came, they sickened with diphtheria. Afterward, I went to live with Gran at Strathandrew."

Claire wanted to tell him how sorry she was. But all the conventional words seemed inadequate. Besides, Ewan hadn't finished talking. Perhaps the best thing she could do for him was not to speak, but to listen with a compassionate heart.

"Gran had tried to talk Pa into taking a job as a stalker at Strathandrew, but he was too proud. I remember him quoting Burns, though I didn't know what it meant back then. 'The English steel we could disdain, secure in valor's station; But English gold has been our bane—Such a parcel of rogues in a nation!'"

Claire reached for his hand. "I shouldn't have asked. You wanted a nice visit home to see all your old haunts. Now I've stirred up these dreadful memories, instead. I *am* sorry."

She was sorry on her own account, too. For spoiling a day that had promised to be idyllic—one she could have looked back on with delight for years to come.

No matter what happened.

Chapter Fourteen

Well, a fine cock-up he'd made of that!

Ewan glowered at himself in the shaving mirror as he dragged a comb through his hair in a halfhearted effort to make himself presentable for dinner. Not that it mattered.

If Claire Talbot had been disposed to look on him with anything more than polite sufferance, his self-pitying blather about the Clearances would soon put a stop to it.

"What possessed ye to go that way in the first place, ye daft fool?" he growled at his scowling reflection.

He'd known the old crofts lay in that direction. He could just as easily have brought Claire home by another route. Then, when she'd seen them and asked, couldn't he have made light of it, instead of making the whole thing sound so…tragic?

He had wanted to show her the waterfall—to share one of his treasures with her. Perhaps as a way of letting her see there were riches a person couldn't earn...or inherit. They belonged to anyone with the spirit to go looking for them, regardless of rank or worldly wealth.

The waters of Linn Riada gave rainbows, music and magic to laird and gillie alike. In some mysterious fashion, sharing all that with Claire had put them both on the same footing. It might even have given him a slight advantage, for he'd been the benefactor and she the recipient of his gift. The crofter village had reversed all that, making her feel sorry for him.

Shooting one final grimace at his reflection, Ewan headed for the dining room, bracing himself for a damn awkward evening. In spite of that, he still found his stride quickening as he descended the grand staircase. He'd been apart from Claire for less than an hour, yet he could hardly wait to see her again.

As he entered the dining room, Ewan checked his headlong rush.

Lost in thought, Claire stood before the huge windows that provided a fine view of the loch. Each pane of glass in the vast array had been scoured to a transparent sparkle. She wore a gown the color of bluebells that carpeted the Argyll woodland in spring. The style was simple, yet becoming to her willowy figure. Ewan could tell that, true to her word, she'd forgone the unnatural constriction of a corset.

For a few sweet moments that passed all too quickly, he drank in the sight of her, as refreshing as cold, tart cider after a long day's stalk in the hills.

Then, with the mysterious intuition of a wild hind in his sights, she sensed his presence and turned toward him. "Ewan, I'm sorry. I was just enjoying the view."

The sincere warmth in her tone and gaze thawed any awkwardness on his part.

He grinned. "That's all right. So was I."

Perhaps she did not understand his impudent bit of flattery. Or perhaps she preferred not to acknowledge it, for any one of a dozen reasons.

Her smile of welcome changed to a look of sweet earnest as she skirted the long dining table to approach him. "Would you like a sherry before dinner? I think Mrs. McMurdo would prefer us to get started soon."

Ewan strode forward, meeting Claire in the middle of the room. "I don't need a drink to rouse my appetite." He pulled out her chair and held it for her. "Our walk took care of that."

Glenna McMurdo peeped into the dining room just then. When Claire responded to her questioning look with a nod, she hurried away again.

"About our walk," said Claire, once Ewan had

taken his seat opposite her. "It got me thinking, and I have an idea I'd like to discuss with you."

"With me?" He could not imagine what.

She nodded. "I cannot think of a better person to consult."

Her confidence warmed him. "If it's an opinion ye want, I'll do my best to offer a sensible one. What's this idea of yers?"

Glenna returned with a tureen of her mother's cock-a-leekie soup, the hearty aroma of which set Ewan's mouth watering. Claire waited until the girl had ladeled generous helpings into their bowls, then returned to the kitchen.

"Seeing that village and all the empty countryside made me wonder if Mr. Catchpole isn't right about Strathandrew, after all. It does seem a waste to keep so much land for the use of a single family—particularly now that Father is no longer around to host his shooting parties."

"Are ye thinking of selling the place?" The notion took away his appetite, even for Rosie's fine cooking.

"Not selling," Claire assured him. "At least not all of it. I couldn't part with this house. It's as much a home to me as anywhere. But I wonder if there isn't some way to make the estate more productive and of benefit to the local people?"

"What are ye proposing, lass?"

"I'm not certain. But surely between the two of us, we can come up with a few ideas."

She looked so eager, Ewan could not keep a tiny flicker of enthusiasm from stirring inside him.

Lifting his spoon to his lips, he savored a mouthful of Rosie's nourishing, flavorful soup. "I reckon we can, if we put our heads together."

Claire looked at him as if he'd just given her an expensive gift. For the rest of the meal, they tossed ideas back and forth about farming and fishing, kelp harvesting and whiskey distilling. Even some far-fetched ones like building a hotel and using the *Marlet* to fetch folks from Glasgow on holiday excursions.

"I have one more favor to ask you," said Claire as she set aside her spoon after a helping of rich Clootie dumpling.

"Name it."

"Whatever enterprise we decide upon, I shall be much too occupied with Brancasters to oversee it myself."

"Aye?" Did she want his help to hire someone?

"I was hoping...you might consider...managing it for me."

"Me?"

"Who better? You're obviously a smart, forward-thinking businessman. I'll pay you twice whatever your American employer does, and you'll be able to live here in the Highlands. See here—what are you laughing about? I'm quite sincere in my offer."

"I know ye are, lass." Ewan struggled to rein in his runaway mirth. He was touched by her faith in him and excited about her plans for Strathandrew. But if Claire only knew how much her generous offer would cost her if he accepted it! "It's not that."

"What, then?" She sounded impatient with his unexplained frivolity. "Can't you see what a perfect arrangement this could be for all of us? You and Tessa wouldn't have to go away to America. She could come and visit in London whenever she liked."

Tessa? Her sister's name on Claire's lips stifled any laughter that remained in Ewan. How could he have forgotten so quickly the lass who had held his heart for over ten years?

She would be here soon. What would he do then? Cast aside the love he'd finally won, for another he had no chance of winning?

What had come over Ewan? Had she offended him with her offer of a job?

When she asked him, during their billiards match, he was quick to protest. "Offended? No, Claire. Honestly, I'm flattered that ye'd be willing to give me that kind of responsibility and pay me such a handsome salary."

Curious? He hadn't sounded flattered when she'd first raised the idea. He'd sounded surprised, then amused by the notion. Then, suddenly, he'd gotten very quiet and thoughtful. Unlike last night, he seemed to be going out of his way to keep his distance from her.

"You'll do it, then?"

He was bending over the billiard table to make a shot when she asked. His cue struck the ball with far too much force—even a beginner like her could tell. It slammed into her ball so hard that both nearly flew off the table. Ewan grumbled something under his breath that sounded like a curse.

"Let's not get ahead of ourselves, all right?" He straightened up, holding his cue so tightly that his knuckles whitened. "Ye've got Tessa and me all married off and living in Argyll and making arrangements for visits. In case ye've forgotten, the lass is still engaged to another man!"

"Yes, but..."

"Ye said yerself she's changeable in her favors. What if yer sister gets here and announces she's come to her senses? That she'd just as soon stick with that Stanton chap, after all?"

Could even Tessa be that foolishly fickle?

"Is *that* what you're worried about?" Relieved to discover she hadn't damaged the fragile bond of respect and affection growing between them, Claire could speak of his eventual marriage to her sister without flinching. "You think I'll jinx your romance with Tessa by talking as if it's all settled?"

"Aye." Ewan relaxed his death grip on the billiard cue. "Something like that."

But there *was* more to it. Claire sensed a change between them that his explanation could not account for. And it was not a change for the better.

The memory of those tumbled piles of rock that had once been homes haunted her. As did Ewan's infamous account of how the Highlanders had been dispossessed. She'd been selfish and wasteful to hold on to Strathandrew as a way of clinging to the past and her memories of Ewan.

"What do you say to this, then?" She forced herself to meet his shadowed gaze. "No matter what happens between you and Tessa, my offer will stand."

Ewan's bold brows knit together. "It will?"

Was this only another way of trying to hold on to him? Claire asked herself. "If it's something you would like to do, I cannot think of a better man for the job."

"That is a handsome offer." Ewan leaned against the billiard table. "Do ye need an answer from me right away?"

Claire shook her head. "Take all the time you need."

"I promise ye I'll give it serious thought." A deep yawn followed his words. "For now, though, I'm ready to call it a night, if ye don't mind. I'm not used to tramping the hills in the fresh air like I once did."

Stifling a pang of disappointment, Claire feigned a little yawn of her own. "Nor am I. A good night's sleep sounds like a fine idea."

If only she could be certain of getting one.

Ewan replaced his cue on the rack. "I thought I'd do a little fishing tomorrow. Would ye care to join me?"

"Do you really want me to?" Would it be possible to recapture the easy camaraderie they'd shared earlier today?

For a moment, he hesitated. But when he answered, Claire could not doubt the ring of sincerity in his voice. "Aye, I do. I wouldn't have enjoyed myself half so well today if ye hadn't come."

"Thank you, again, for inviting me." Claire moved toward the rack and replaced her billiard cue. Her path took her within a hairbreadth of Ewan. "I can't remember when I've enjoyed myself so much."

She had never been an impulsive person. After rescuing Tessa from several scrapes into which impulsiveness had landed *her,* Claire was more than ever inclined to weigh her decisions and act upon them in a restrained, prudent manner. But as she brushed past Ewan, determined to leave the room first rather than be deserted by him, a compelling impulse seized her.

One she was powerless to resist.

Leaning toward him as she passed, she surged up on her tiptoes and grazed his cheek with her lips. "Good night, Ewan."

Before his subtle scent intoxicated her into doing something even more reckless, she fled the room and did not look back.

"What was that all about?" Ewan murmured to himself. Pressing his hand to his cheek where Claire had kissed him, he listened to her footsteps retreating up the staircase.

Glenna McMurdo peeped around the door frame. "What was all *what* about?"

"None of yer business, missy!" With a guilty start, Ewan snatched his hand away from his face. But where Claire's lips had brushed, his cheek stung like fury. "What are ye doing, sneaking around, anyway?"

"Sneaking, indeed?" Glenna crossed her eyes and stuck her tongue out at him, the way she'd often done as a child when he'd teased her. "I'll have ye know I'm busy cleaning up after yer fine dinner!"

The seething stew of contrary feelings inside him vented in a burst of laughter. It was good to know at least one person at Strathandrew was not awed or resentful of his new status as a guest of the family.

"A fine dinner it was, lass. Tell yer ma I said so. Well served, too."

Glenna cocked her head in the direction of the kitchen. "Why don't ye come down and tell her yerself? She felt that bad about shooing ye out when she was fixing dinner last night. It's just that she was so nervous with Monsieur Anton hanging about."

Ewan shook his head. "I should have known better than to get in the way at a busy time like that."

"It's not busy now," said Glenna. "Just me and Maizie in the scullery doing dishes. Ma'd love a wee visit with ye."

"What about Mrs. A?" He didn't fancy another run-in with the housekeeper.

"Gone to bed early with a headache," said Glenna. "Not much wonder she's got one, clenching her teeth the way she has since ye got here."

"Fack and Fergus?" He didn't want to go where he wasn't wanted.

"Taking advantage of Mrs. A's indisposition to pop into the village for a pint with the crew from the *Marlet*." Glenna planted her hands on her hips the way Ewan had often seen her mother do. "Now, are ye going to come and have a cup of tea with Ma, or is Fergus right and ye've gotten too grand for us?"

"He says that?"

Glenna shrugged as she headed back into the

dining room. "Mutters it under his breath, but nobody pays him any mind. Ma says he took it hard when ye left."

Ewan followed her. "All the more reason he should welcome me back."

"Ye can't always tell how folks feel by the way they act." Glenna piled the last few pieces of china and cutlery onto a tray. "Like Miss Talbot."

"What's Claire...I mean, *Miss Talbot,* got to do with this?" Ewan demanded.

Glenna rolled her eyes. "Do ye not recollect how she used to fuss at ye all the time?"

"Aye." He tried to help Glenna clear the table, but she waved him away. "The two of us were like oil and water back then. We've both done a bit of growing up in the meantime."

If only he'd realized that before he'd set about pursuing his boyhood dream of winning her sister.

"It's more than a *bit of growing up.*" Glenna hoisted her tray and headed for the kitchen. "Make yerself useful by catching doors for me, will ye?"

Ewan hurried to keep ahead of her as she strode toward the back stairs. "I don't know what ye're talking about, lass. Are ye sure *ye* do?"

"Aye. I knew what was what when I was eight years old, watching the pair of ye. Claire Talbot fancied ye, but ye wouldn't look at her twice unless she insulted ye to get yer attention."

"Ye're daft!" Ewan staggered on the stairs and barely escaped rolling all the way to the bottom.

"I'm not the one falling down stairs, am I?"

"That had nothing to—"

Glenna acted as if she didn't hear his protest. "Lads do it all the time—pulling yer braids, threatening to put bugs on ye, acting the fool—anything to get ye to pay them some mind."

Her words struck Ewan dumb, for he recalled doing some of those things to make Tessa notice him.

"Most lasses are clever enough to know what it means." Glenna breezed into the servants' hall, heading for the scullery. "When the shoe's on the other foot, and one of them is trying to make a lad take notice, it's hopeless."

Claire? Sweet on him? Ewan could not have been more disoriented if he *had* fallen down the back stairs and landed on his head. Part of him continued to insist that Glenna was talking nonsense. Another part was not so sure.

"Mam," Glenna called out, "I've fetched ye some company!"

"Company?" Rosie emerged from the scullery, drying her hands on her apron.

When she spied Ewan, she held her arms open to him. "Come sit by the fire and have a cup of tea with me, lad, and let me look ye over proper. Did ye have a good dinner?"

"Topping, Rosie." He stumbled into her embrace, then let her lead him into the servants' hall. "You'll have seen for yerself, we all but licked the plates clean."

"Aye, it's good to see ye have an appetite."

"The lunch ye packed for us was fine, too. If I'm not careful, they're going to have to widen the doors to let me out when it comes time to leave."

Rosie gave him a gentle cuff on the arm, then dropped into her rocking chair by the hearth. "Get away with ye. I'd be well enough pleased if ye put on a pound or two. Now sit yerself down and tell me what ye've been doing in America to make all that money. It's legal, I hope."

"Aye, Rosie, all legal." Ewan laughed as he settled himself into the armchair beside her. He knew a few captains of industry who could not make that claim. "Just a lot of hard work and a wee bit of luck."

"I hope ye could spare what ye sent us, lad."

"Oh aye," Ewan assured her, though without quite as clear a conscience as he'd avowed his honesty.

The little bit he'd sent in those early years had sometimes been a sacrifice. But he'd been glad to do it just the same, to put Rosie's mind at ease about him, and to feel a connection to home. He hadn't missed much larger sums he'd sent in recent years.

As Rosie had bidden him, he told her about

America, minimizing his early hardships and homesickness. She told him about all the doings on the estate and in the village. Except for everyone growing older, little appeared to have changed in the ten years he'd been gone.

While part of his attention was fixed on their conversation, another part of his mind pondered Glenna's preposterous claim that Claire Talbot had once fancied him.

"What about ye, lad?" asked Rosie when she'd finished reciting a list of couples who'd gotten married in the past ten years. "Have ye got a sweetheart back in America?"

"N-no." The question caught him off guard. "Been too busy to do much courting." His conscience prodded him to mention Tessa, but he could not get the words out.

"So *that's* why ye came home!" Rosie beamed. "Ye've got yerself all set up and now ye want to find a wife."

Before he could do more than open and close his mouth like a freshly netted loch trout, Glenna appeared from the kitchen bearing a tray of tea and oat cakes. "If Ewan's going to find himself a wife, he'll need to get better at recognizing when a lass has a fancy for him."

Giving an exasperated shake of her head, she set the tea tray down on a small table beside her mother's chair. "When I told him Miss Talbot used to be all calf-eyed for him, he wouldn't believe me."

"Tell yer daughter she's daft, Rosie." Now that he'd begun to mull over the notion, Ewan could not summon quite the same degree of certainty.

"Do ye mean ye never knew?" Rosie poured his tea, then added a wee dollop of cream and a single small lump of sugar, just the way he liked it.

When she saw from his face that he was in earnest, she treated him to a look that mingled amusement and pity. "The poor lass took it so hard when ye went away. I don't think she ever knew it was her father's doing."

Ewan took a sip of the hot strong tea. It felt as though his world had shifted, changing the land-scape in ways he could not recognize.

"Speaking of weddings…" Glenna passed the plate of oat cakes to Ewan. "Geordie Cameron and Winnie MacLeod are getting married to-morrow. That's why the men all went down to the village for a pint, to help Geordie celebrate."

"I'm glad to hear they're getting along better than they used to at school." Ewan chuckled. "I remember the time Geordie dipped the end of one of her braids in the master's inkwell. Win-nie gave him a black eye for his pains."

His own words fairly clouted him in the stom-ach.

"Oh aye." Glenna's pretty mouth stretched

into a wide grin. "That's the way of it sometimes. The MacLeods are having a ceilidh tomorrow night to celebrate the wedding, and a
bunch of us from Strathandrew are going. Why
don't ye come along? I'm sure Geordie and Winnie would be glad to see ye."

"Aye," Ewan nodded, taking another long sip
of his tea. "I just might."

If he could convince Claire to come as his
guest.

Chapter Fifteen

"You want me to go *where*?"

Claire's cast went awry, sending her line flailing in Ewan's direction. The hook snagged his cloth cap and jerked it off his head into the river.

He let out a whoop of surprise followed by great rolling gusts of laughter that threatened to knock him off his feet.

"If ye'd rather not come to the ceilidh with me, just say so, lass!" he gasped between heaves of laughter. "Ye don't have to try and drown me!"

Suddenly the mild morning air felt icy cold against her blazing cheeks. A dozen years seemed to have melted away, and she was sixteen again. Only this time the handsome young gillie was paying attention to her.

Reeling her line back toward shore, she

masked her flustered feelings with a tart answer. "You don't look in much danger of drowning to me. And if you had taken a tumble into the water, it would have served you right for ruining my cast by popping a question out of the blue like that!"

"Popping the question?" Ewan chuckled as he waded into the shallows to retrieve his cap. "I could understand *that* throwing yer cast off, or making you want to drown me for my presumption. But I was only inviting ye to a party in the village."

He disengaged her hook from the sturdy tweed, then shook the cap off and put it back on his head. "It's to celebrate the wedding of a couple of my old schoolmates. Geordie and Winnie used to fight like cats and dogs when they were younger. Almost as bad as ye and me at that age."

His words made Claire fumble her fly rod. Did the man realize what he'd said?

He was certainly in a chipper mood this morning. A good night's sleep seemed to have banished the strange awkwardness that had possessed him so suddenly last night. Or perhaps it was being back on the river with a rod in his hand. The friendly gurgle of the water seemed to invite a person to cast her worries off and let the current float them away.

Spellbound, Claire watched the lithe grace of

his line whisking out and back over the water, tempting the hungry fish to snap at his lure. Was he casting bait for her, too, with this tempting invitation and his provocative remarks? And if so...what was he fishing *for?*

The past several days had been the happiest of her life. Even the knowledge that it could end at any moment did not spoil her enjoyment of their time together, but added a sweet poignancy that made her savor it all the more.

But beneath the surface of her happiness, a treacherous current of yearning tugged at her. The yearning for something more than a few days of make-believe. With his charm, Ewan made her want it. With his kindness, he made her believe she might deserve it.

"Do wish your friends every happiness for me," she said when she had finally mastered her voice. "But please don't feel obliged to cart me along. You're here as my guest, not as a hired companion."

Ewan turned his head to answer, but at that moment a fish decided it liked the looks of his dry fly, and latched on. Claire set aside her own rod to fetch the net. Then she perched herself on a large rock to watch the fight.

A strenuous battle it was, too, on both sides. More than once Claire thought the fish must have got away, only to see the line stretch taut again. More than once she lunged forward with the net, only to watch a silvery form slither out of the shallows to fight on.

By the time he landed the creature, all twenty squirming pounds of it, Ewan's face was flushed and his forehead beaded with sweat. He subsided onto the rock where Claire had been sitting to watch him.

"Let's get one thing straight, shall we?" He pulled off his cap and dragged his forearm across his brow. "This shouldn't be an obligation...for either of us. I've enjoyed yer company the past few days. Am I fooling myself to believe ye enjoyed mine?"

Claire kept her eyes fixed on the river, not daring to meet his discerning gaze in case hers should betray her. But she could not bring herself to tell him any less than the truth. "You aren't fooling yourself, Ewan. I've had a perfectly marvelous time with you."

She congratulated herself on keeping her voice steady.

"Well, that's fine, then." He lunged sideways, catching her hand in his. "We'll have some more marvelous time tonight. Have ye ever been to a Highland ceilidh?"

There was something different about the way he held her hand. Or was she only fooling herself? Either way, she could not shake off his touch.

"It's a party, isn't it? Like the gillies' ball Father used to give at the end of the hunting season?"

"Aye, something like that." Ewan chuckled. "But louder and faster, with more to drink."

"Will there be dancing?" From her fifteenth summer until the year he'd gone away, she had hoped with all her heart that Ewan Geddes would ask her for a dance at the gillies' ball.

"Eightsome reels until yer feet ache." He spoke in a coaxing tone that Claire would have found difficult to resist…if she'd wanted to. "Singing and stories and toasts. Piping and fiddling. Cakes and ale and maybe something stronger."

This might well be their last evening together. Part of her wanted to spend it alone with him. Perhaps that was not the best course, though. With a crowd of other people around, she might not be so tempted to say or do something to betray her feelings for him.

"What do ye say, then?" Ewan winked and gave her hand a squeeze.

"You're certain it won't make your friends uncomfortable to have me there—the Lady of Strathandrew?"

This time she watched his face carefully, to make certain he was telling the truth. She'd cheerfully let him go without her rather than spoil the wedding celebration. Well, perhaps not *cheerfully*...

He mulled over her question, and she could tell what his answer would be. She steeled herself to insist he go without her.

"It might be a wee bit awkward at first," he admitted. "I hadn't given it much thought."

Claire stifled a sigh. At least he hadn't lied to her. She sensed he never would.

"But," he added, "that's apt to be as much on my account as yers. After ten years over in America, I'm a bit of a stranger in these parts, myself."

"So you want me for company in case nobody else will dance with you?" She couldn't resist teasing him.

"It's not like that. Anybody who comes in goodwill is welcome at a ceilidh. After a few dances and a pint or two, everybody's yer friend, anyway."

That had a vastly appealing sound.

"In that case, Mr. Geddes—" Claire rose from their rock perch to bob a little curtsy "—I'd be honored to go with you."

Ewan shifted his grip on her hand and brought the backs of her fingers to his lips. "The honor... and the pleasure...will be all mine, lass."

"It doesn't look like we've anything to worry about." Ewan leaned over on the driver's bench of the small pony cart to whisper in Claire's ear. "The ceilidh's already started. I doubt anybody will even notice we're here."

A spate of rain in the afternoon had given way to a fine, warm evening, so the festivities were being held out-of-doors. Lanterns hung from tree branches and perched on improvised tables, though it was not yet dark enough to need them. The hearty smells of fish, meat and bread wafted on the evening air along with the rollicking music of several fiddles, some tin whistles and a hand drum.

Since the bride's father was the local brewer and tavern keeper, ale flowed freely, while two sets of dancers whirled through an eightsome reel. Ewan knew the men would pass around whiskey flasks to supplement the refreshments later on.

Most of the Strathandrew staff had already arrived and were taking an eager part in the festivities. Claire's little Welsh maid was dancing with Jockie McMurdo, while Glenna spun around on the arm of Alec, the footman. When she caught sight of Ewan and Claire together, she shot him a knowing grin.

Clutching Claire's hand, Ewan threaded his way through the crowd in search of the bride and groom.

"Ewan Geddes, we heard you were home from America!" Winnie pulled him down for a kiss on the cheek. "Is this just a visit, or are ye planning to stay?"

"I meant it just to be a visit, but now that I'm back...I don't know."

"Geordie, love!" Winnie reached over and tugged on the coat sleeve of her bridegroom. "Look, it's Ewan, come all the way from America! Isn't it good to see him again?"

"That it is, lass." Geordie wrapped one arm around his bride's hips, while extending his free hand toward Ewan. "We're glad to have ye here to celebrate with us, Ewan."

"I hope ye don't mind. I brought a friend, Claire Talbot. I'm staying at Strathandrew as her guest."

The newlyweds gave Claire a warm welcome, inviting her to have something to eat or join in the dancing.

"Aye." Ewan almost had to shout to make himself heard above the fiddle music and the general hubbub. "Dancing sounds like a fine idea. We'll work up an appetite for that good food. Geordie, ye're a luckier man than ye deserve after the way ye tormented this poor lass while we were at school."

He slipped a handkerchief out of his coat pocket, knotted to hold several gold coins. He wished he could give them more, but knew this would be all they would take without embarrassment.

"A wee something for a wedding present, Winnie." He dropped the little bundle into her hand. "Don't let this rascal put upon ye, now."

The music came to an end on a long drawn out chord, after which the dancers applauded, then dispersed, flocking to the refreshment tables. The musicians each took a quick drink, then raised their instruments again.

Ewan nodded toward the broad, flat bit of ground where fresh eightsomes were marshaling. "Dance, Claire?"

"I should like that very much." In the soft light of the setting sun, her smile took on a special glow. Did this dance mean something more to her than he knew?

He had no time to ask, for they were soon swept up in the spirited music and movement of one reel, then another. Every time his hand came in contact with hers, it felt different than the other lasses'. The skin of his palm tingled, as if warmed suddenly after coming in from the cold. When the steps of the dance separated them, his gaze followed her with jealous intensity. He begrudged every moment it took for Claire to find her way back into his arms.

When Captain MacLeod, the bride's uncle, made bold to claim a dance with Claire, Ewan surrendered her hand reluctantly. Someone pressed a mug of cold ale into his hand, after which he retreated to watch from a distance.

"Ye look like ye're having a good time." Glenna suddenly appeared at his side, her voice barely audible above the music.

"Oh, aye." Ewan tipped up his mug for another drink, not taking his eyes off Claire.

"I've never seen Miss Talbot so lively." Something in Glenna's tone warned Ewan she was making more than a casual observation. "She's aye bonny when she smiles and her eyes get that sparkle."

He nodded.

"I always liked her," said Glenna, "for all she's quieter than her sister. The way she speaks to the servants, ye get the feeling she respects what ye do, without making a big fuss."

"And?" If the lass had something to say, Ewan wished she'd spit it out. This reel was almost over, and he wanted to be well placed to claim Claire again in case one of the other lads took a notion to dance with her.

"I'm thinking I should have kept my mouth shut about her being sweet on ye. I wouldn't have said anything, but I thought ye must have known."

"What's that got to do with anything?" Ewan drained his ale, then handed the empty mug to Glenna.

She grabbed him by the shirtsleeve before he could get away. "Be kind to her, Ewan, ye hear me? Don't go amusing yerself with the lady."

Colm MacLeod's ale was good and strong, and Ewan had downed his pint fast. His head and his heart felt full to the brim with froth.

"I promise, lass." He wrapped his arm around her shoulders and gave a hearty squeeze. "I hope ye have no objections if I let her amuse herself with me."

He didn't stay to find out, for the reel was winding down to its final bars.

The captain bowed to Claire as the music ended. "Would ye care for another round, Miss Talbot? Ye step as light as thistledown!"

"Why, thank you, Captain." Claire fanned her flushed face with her hand and answered in a breathless voice. "But I believe I must rest and have a drink before I do any more dancing."

Ewan seized his cue to cut in. "Can I get ye a mug of ale, lass? Or cider, maybe?"

She turned toward the sound of his voice with a smile and a look that set him dizzy. "Cider please, if it wouldn't be too much bother."

"No bother at all." He drew her away from the dancing toward the table where drinks were being dispensed.

Claire subsided against him. Ewan could feel her heart pounding, and it made his pound faster. "I haven't danced like that in years. I'm so glad we came."

"I'm glad *ye* came." He had almost enough ale in him to ask the question that had been burning in his mind since last night. When Glenna had made him see his past...and perhaps his future, in a whole new light.

They finished their drinks in time to join the next reel. After another vigorous spell of dancing, they refreshed themselves with both food and drink. Then they danced some more.

"Ye're just in time," said Winnie's sister awhile later, when she passed Ewan yet another pint for himself and a mug of cider for Claire. "After this next reel, they're going to have the toasts, so save a bit of yer drink."

Ewan promised they would. Then he found them an empty bench, under the broad boughs of an old oak tree, where they could rest their feet while they watched the festivities. Claire tossed back her cider so fast he was obliged to fetch her another for the toasts.

"Go a little easier on this one, lass," he warned when he placed the refilled mug in her waiting hands.

"I'll try." She took a sip that lengthened into a substantial drink. "But I'm thirsty, and this is so refreshing!"

He could not gainsay her. The MacLeods had a well-deserved reputation as good brewers, and Ewan suspected they had put by a few kegs of their best ale and cider to celebrate their youngest daughter's wedding.

"This isn't like the mild stuff Rosie makes."

He tried again, for he feared one of them might need to keep their wits later, and it wasn't going to be him. "It's *hard* cider."

Claire nodded and clinked her mug against his. "It's *fine* hard cider. Remind me to buy a few kegs of it to take back to London." A wee bubble of laughter burst out of her. "Perhaps *this* could be part of our business enterprise for Strathandrew!"

"Perhaps it could, lass." Though at the moment, business was the very last thing on his mind.

Yes, indeed! This was fine cider and a fine night for a fine party. Unlike the social functions she'd been obliged to attend in London, Claire didn't much care if she ever went home.

Another reel broke up. This time the fiddlers set aside their instruments to take up brimming ale and cider mugs instead. The groom got everyone's attention long enough to propose a toast to his new in-laws for the grand ceilidh they'd hosted.

Claire was more than eager to drink to that.

Other toasts followed, some in English and a few in Gaelic that Ewan translated for her. It was a haunting, musical language, she decided, far more outlandish-sounding than French or German or any of the other foreign tongues of which she could understand at least a few words. A language for extravagant, poetic endearments, capable of seducing a woman without half trying.

"This is the last one," said Ewan as Captain MacLeod rose and lifted his mug. "A toast to the bride and groom for their life together."

The captain spoke a phrase of rolling, lilting words that everyone else present seemed to understand.

"May you hereafter be blessed," Ewan whispered, "with plenty of fish in your net. Plenty of oats in your kettle. Plenty of peat on your hearth. Plenty of bairns in your cradle."

The last bit sent a ripple of laughter through the crowd.

"And plenty of love in your hearts," Ewan concluded.

Claire drank the toast with the rest, despite some reservations. Not that she begrudged the newlyweds any of those things. "Rather modest hopes for your friends, don't you think?"

"Do ye reckon?" Ewan glanced down at her. "I'd say that old wedding toast covers the most important things in life. Enough to eat and keep warm."

He lifted his hand to cup her cheek. "A family to love."

Those impossibly sweet words sounded almost like an offer. Especially when accompanied by his chaste but intimate touch.

"Claire, I've got something to ask ye." The

intensity of his gaze excited and dismayed her in equal measure.

She wanted to brace herself for his question with one last drink, but she had emptied her mug after the last toast. "What do you want to know?"

He opened his mouth to ask, then hesitated and looked around. "This may not be the best place to talk about it. Do ye mind if I fetch ye home?"

And bring this night to an end one moment before she must?

"Couldn't we stay for one more dance? It looks as though they're getting ready to start again."

One of the musicians had picked up his fiddle and was sliding his bow in a tentative caress over the strings.

"There'll be some singing now." Ewan glanced up into the darkened sky. "Besides, the wind's changed. Clouds starting to blow up."

Perhaps it would be best to start for Strathandrew. All that cider was going to her head. If she had any more, she was liable to say or do something to embarrass herself and tarnish the memory of her time with Ewan. Besides, she was curious to find out what he would ask.

"Very well, then. Home it is." As she surged up from the bench, her head began to spin. She might have fallen if Ewan had not risen and slid his arm under hers to keep her upright.

"None too soon for ye, I'd say." He chuckled as he steered her toward the spot where he'd left the pony cart.

"I can walk perfectly well, Ewan Geddes," Claire insisted, though she made no effort to pull herself out of his arms. "I got up a little too quickly, that's all."

"Aye, and put down a load of hard cider too quickly."

As they made their way toward the pony cart, Claire's maid came running over to them. "Are you going home now, miss? Shall I come along to get you ready for bed?"

The little Welsh girl sounded willing, though perhaps not eager to leave. No more eager than Claire was to have any company but Ewan's on the ride back to Strathandrew.

"I can manage on my own for tonight, thank you, Williams." She waved the girl away. "You stay with the others and enjoy yourself."

"Thank you, miss. If you're sure?"

"I am quite resolved."

Jockie McMurdo drew Miss Williams back to the party.

"Don't worry about getting up too early tomorrow," Claire called after them. "I'm certain I shall be sleeping in."

"Come along, then." Ewan tugged her toward the cart. "Before we both end up sleeping along the side of the road somewhere."

Sleeping by the side of the road on a warm summer night didn't sound like such a hardship, if it meant lying in his arms. Claire barely resisted the urge to tell him so. Perhaps it was that lovely cider at work. The reasons for keeping all kinds of secrets no longer seemed as compelling as they once had.

As she and Ewan drove away from the ceilidh, a Gaelic song wafted on the night air. Though Claire could not understand a single word, it was impossible to mistake the poignant edge of longing, for it struck an answering chord within her.

"So," she said after they had driven a little way in silence, "are you going to ask me that important question? Or was it just a ruse to get me away from the ceilidh before I drank any more cider and made a fool of myself?"

Ewan shook his head. "It wasn't a trick. I'm just wondering if it's such a good idea to ask, after all."

"You make it sound ominous." Claire listed sideways until her head rested against his arm. She wasn't sleepy…exactly. Just very, *very* relaxed. "I think you might as well, though. Otherwise, you'll never know. Then you'll always wonder about it and wish you'd asked when you had the chance."

"I reckon yer right, lass." He gave a soft chuckle. "Ye talk surprising good sense for having so much of Colm MacLeod's hard cider in ye."

A giggle gushed out of Claire. The kind that would have set her teeth on edge if she'd been sober. "Sensible—that's me. Even my stepmother says so. Sensible and unemotional. Almost as good as talking to a man."

Her brainless giggle turned into a pathetic little hiccup of a sob. "Do you think I'm as good as talking to a man, Ewan? Is that why you've liked keeping company with me this week?"

"No, lass, no!" He pulled the pony to a stop, then twisted about to wrap his arms around her.

Oh, it felt lovely! The clouds had pretty much covered what was left of the moon. Still, Claire wondered if there was enough of its light to mix with MacLeod's ale and make Ewan kiss her. Without any stupid glass to break this time, and bring him to his senses.

She felt his lips against her hair—a good start. She lifted her face.

Ewan didn't kiss her, but he did press his brow to hers. "Much as it pains me to agree with Lady Lydiard, ye are a sensible person, Claire. I have enjoyed yer company and getting to know ye. But *not* because ye're anything like a man!"

That was some comfort at least.

"Now," he murmured. "About that question of mine..."

To hell with his question! How could she give an answer that made any sense with his lips so maddeningly close to hers?

"This business with Geordie and Winnie got me to thinking. When *we* were young and foolish, and tormenting the life out of each other, I don't suppose ye ever…had a bit of a fancy for me?"

He sounded as though he found the notion preposterous. If she denied it, he might believe her, even as she clung to him.

"Congratulations, Ewan Geddes. You've finally figured it all out…ten years too late."

"Ah, lassie." He ran his hand over her hair until he cupped the back of her head, tilting her face a fraction of an inch higher. "Are ye certain it *is* too late?"

She parted her lips to answer. But before she could get the words out, Ewan kissed her, searing every sensible thought from her mind with the delicious heat of his mouth.

This was an altogether different kiss than the one that had taken them both by surprise on the deck of the *Marlet*. This time Ewan knew what he was doing and had every intention of continuing to do it, even if whiskey glasses began to fall around them like raindrops!

Chapter Sixteen

Ewan had fallen so deep into their kiss, he didn't even notice the first raindrops falling upon them. If MacLeod's cider tasted half as good from a jug as it did on Claire's lips, they would make a fortune selling it!

Even more delicious and intoxicating was the certain knowledge that she had once cared for him. If she had back then, when he'd been a young fool, blind to her wit and beauty, surely he could make her care again. The challenge of winning her, and the forthright eagerness of her response to his kiss, fired his blood.

But the changeable Highland skies seemed bent on putting out any kind of fire. Drop after drop of rain kept falling, until he could no longer ignore them.

"I have to get ye home, lass." It would be a

wonder if she understood a word, for he could not bring himself to lose contact with her lips as he spoke. "Before we both get soaked to the skin."

"Why?" asked Claire in a lazy, dreamy tone that sounded anything but sensible. "Is it raining?"

"Aye, ye daft lass. Pouring!"

It seemed the pony had more sense than either of them, for it started moving forward without any signal from Ewan. The closer it got to a warm, dry stable, the quicker it trotted. Ewan had no choice but to take the reins and exert some control over the beast so the cart did not end up overturned in the ditch. When it hit a bump in the road, jolting them, Claire squealed and threw her arms around his waist.

The rain had slackened a good deal by the time they reached Strathandrew.

"Come on, Claire, we're home now." He tried to dislodge her arms from their grip around his waist.

She murmured something incoherent, then laughed to herself, but clung to him tighter than ever.

Ewan shook his head. "I thought cold water was supposed to sober folks up. Be a good lass, now, and let go, so I can get ye into the house."

With difficulty, he managed to pry himself loose and scramble down. Then he hoisted Claire over his shoulder and staggered toward the side door.

Luckily, it was not locked.

Once inside, he climbed the back stairs as quietly as he could manage with an unconscious woman slung over his shoulder and his balance none too steady. He expected Mrs. Arbuthnot to appear at any moment and give him a blistering dose of her righteous wrath.

When he finally reached the top of the stairs and gazed down the wide second-floor gallery, Ewan let out a groan.

"Claire!" He lowered her from his shoulder and gave her a gentle shake. "Which one of these rooms is yers, lass?"

Her head hung limp, but she managed to bear a little of her own weight. At first Ewan thought she could not hear him, but then she laughed. "I don' care. Put me in any one you like. Put me in *yours!*"

She laughed even louder, and when he tried to hush her, she hurled her arms around his neck. Off in the distance, Ewan thought he heard footsteps. Part of him wondered why he should care if the housekeeper caught them together. But a greater part still felt like an intruder—in the house under false pretenses and needing to mind his behavior so he didn't get turfed out.

The footsteps sounded as if they were getting closer, and his room was the nearest one.

Before he had time to think better of the idea, Ewan lurched toward his door, leaning Claire against it while he turned the knob. It slid open faster than he'd expected, sending the two of them sprawling onto the floor.

He had just enough presence of mind to kick the door shut before the whole room began to spin. By the time that subsided and he could see straight again, he was shivering from the chill of his wet clothes.

Claire lay still beside him, but her face had a pale, waxy look he didn't like. He pulled her closer to the hearth, glad for once that Mrs. Arbuthnot insisted on fires being laid in the guests' rooms no matter what the season. Fetching the extra blanket from the foot of his bed, he tucked it around Claire.

"This isn't the most comfortable spot to sleep off too much cider, lass." He trailed the back of his fingers down her cheek. "We'll do better for ye soon, though. I promise."

He ducked into the dressing room, where he fumbled out of his wet clothes and into a dry nightshirt. Then he grabbed his dressing gown with the intention of wrapping Claire in it.

She didn't appear to have stirred a muscle while he'd been gone. The warmth of the fire had brought some color back to her face, though. A look of peaceful contentment softened her spare, delicate features. The rain had teased stray tendrils of her hair into a winsome halo of tiny curls that no amount of primping could duplicate. Ewan found himself drawn to her more intensely than ever...if that were possible.

Hovering over her, he pressed a kiss to her cheek, then pulled back the blanket and tilted her onto her side. Next he began to wrestle with the long row of tiny buttons down the back of her gown.

"Here I thought tying dry flies took deft fingers!" he muttered as he fumbled with the stubborn wee things.

When Claire stirred and let out a tipsy chuckle, he protested, "I'm doing my best, but I never claimed I had much practice at helping ladies out of their clothes."

Like plenty of other challenges he'd undertaken in his life, he just kept at it until his persistence yielded results.

"There!" he said when the last button finally came undone. "No wonder ye need a lady's maid, lass. What were ye thinking, telling yers to stay at the ceilidh as late as she pleased?"

Letting Claire roll onto her back again, he tugged the sleeves from her arms and eased her out of the wet gown. Thinking himself almost finished, he was amazed to discover the quantity of petticoats and other undergarments he still had to tackle. One by one, he shifted her out of them, then removed her slippers.

As he rolled the silk stockings down over her slender calves, Claire smiled and purred in her sleep, giving a provocative little twitch of her hips. The sight roused Ewan, searing away any chill that might have lingered in his flesh.

Could he find the restraint to *behave* like a gentleman...even though he wasn't one?

Now, for instance. The few underclothes Claire still had on weren't even damp. But that did not stop him from having a go at the row of hooks down the front of her corset. He told himself he was doing it so she could sleep more comfortably. But he didn't altogether believe his own excuse.

Why did women bind themselves up in such miserable contraptions? he wondered as he struggled with one uncooperative hook. He didn't admire the exaggerated figures corsets forced their bodies into, and he detested the hard stiffness, just where they should be soft and yielding.

In fact, he had never found a single thing to like about them...until this moment. Now, he had to admit there was something mighty appealing about the way a woman's flesh burst out of one when it came off!

Claire gave a sigh of pleasure when hers finally fell open—the kind of sound Ewan might have hoped to coax from her if they'd been lovers. How he wished they *were* lovers—hoped they could be. That and so much more. If only she were wrong, and he was not ten years too late!

He sat for a moment, watching the soft flicker of firelight play over her bare arms and shoulders. Beneath the sheer confection of fine linen, lace and ribbon that covered her upper body, her small, perfect breasts fairly pleaded for the attention of his hands and lips.

Or was that his own desire doing the pleading?

Either way, he found himself reaching for her, just as her eyes drifted open. He froze, wondering if she was sober enough to realize what had happened and make a fuss.

"Ewan?" She didn't look frightened or angry. "Where am I?"

He pulled his hand back from where it hovered over her breast, aching to touch. "Ye're in... my room, lass. Ye see, it started to rain on the way home from the ceilidh and ye...nodded off, so I had to carry ye into the house. Then I didn't know which room was yers and..."

"I remember." She gave a slow nod. "I told you to bring me here."

"Aye, so ye did."

With languid grace she raised one bare arm and stared at it, as if it she had never seen it before. "You took off my clothes."

It was not an accusation, just a statement of fact that appeared to surprise her somewhat.

"Aye, I did. They were wet, and I was worried ye'd catch cold in them, so I…" He picked up the dressing gown to explain how he'd intended to put it on her.

She didn't give him the chance.

Her lips curved in a befuddled grin. "Are you going to ravish me?"

"No!" he insisted with as much sincerity as he could muster when his body throbbed with desire for her. "It's like I told ye…the rain and…I couldn't find yer bedroom…and yer clothes all wet…"

"No?" Claire's grin puckered into a pout. "Well, I wish you would!"

Her hand slithered toward him like a fair, tempting serpent, coming to rest on his leg. "Is there any way I can persuade you to change your mind?"

Persuade him? Was the lass daft? It was taking every crumb of willpower he had to stop himself!

"Now, Claire, ye don't mean that." He tried to move out of the range of her touch, but his body refused to cooperate. "It's all that cider in ye. Too much of it can make folks a wee bit…randy."

"Randy?" She giggled. "Is that what you call it?"

She began to caress his thigh through his thick cotton nightshirt in a way that roused him unbearably. "*You* made me randy ten years ago, and you still do."

That was not the kind of thing he needed to hear, just now.

"I'm flattered…I reckon. But this isn't the right time or place." His body protested that for what she—and he—wanted, there could be no *wrong* time or place.

"Have you not had enough ale to be randy for me?" She removed her hand from his leg and struggled to sit up. "I could fetch you some more."

"Ye're in no shape to fetch anything," he told her as she sank back onto the carpet. "And I swear, it isn't that ye don't make me rand—I mean, that I don't find ye attractive."

He thought of mentioning Tessa, but discarded the idea. He felt guilty enough about the sudden transfer of his affections from one Talbot sister to the other.

"This was yer father's room," he reminded her, hearing the desperation in his own voice. "What do ye reckon he'd say if he could see us now?"

"I know exactly what he'd say." Claire fixed him with a haughty glare uncannily reminiscent of her late father. "He'd say, 'My dear, you are too wealthy, too clever and too plain for a man ever to want you *except* for your fortune.'"

For a moment, outrage burned in Ewan even

hotter than desire. "He said *that?* To his own daughter?"

He wished Lord Lydiard's ghost had haunted the place, so he could give the arrogant nobleman a piece of his mind. "The miserable, bloody bast—"

"That's it!" Claire interrupted his indignant curse.

"Eh?"

"I can *pay* you!" She raised herself on her elbows. Her blue-gray eyes glittered with the silver of newly minted shillings. "Name your price for one night. I'm sure you'll be worth every penny!"

Though she fixed him with an adoring smile, and the flimsy fabric of her undergarment pulled even tighter over her inviting bosom, Ewan felt as if the ale in his belly had suddenly gone sour. His throat tightened and it was all he could do to keep from spewing his guts out.

He'd fooled himself into believing Claire must have the same kind of feelings for him that he'd come to have for her. He'd hoped they could be a man and a woman in love, as equal partners. But that wasn't the kind of feeling she had for him at all, nor had she ever.

She was only randy for him, and proposing to pay for his services. A fortune for a single night, but that did not make any difference. If he accepted her proposition, there would be no equality. He would be her servant, required to know his place and not expect anything from her beyond his wages.

"Well, Ewan, what do you say? I promise I'll be totally discreet. No one need ever know about our little...tryst."

What did he say? Couldn't she tell he was too shocked and disgusted to speak? Or did she assume he'd be willing to do anything for the right price?

He hadn't mastered his outraged pride enough to speak, but he could still move—to put as much distance as possible between the two of them. Because, in spite of everything, he still wanted her with a fierce lust that might master him if he let it. Lurching to his feet, he staggered a step backward, toward the dressing room door.

But he was not quick enough for Claire, who thrust out her foot to rub against his bare leg. "If you're shy about using my father's bed, we can always go to my room, instead. I'll tell you which one it is this time."

How part of him wanted to oblige her!

"Stay here if ye like." He stalked toward the dressing room. "Or go back to yer own bed. Either way, you'll go alone, for I won't spend another night under this roof!"

"But Ewan!" she wailed. "What's the matter? Have I said something wrong? After the kiss you gave me on the way home, I thought you mightn't mind making love to me."

He didn't dare turn around or his resolve might crumble. And his pride along with it. "I'd tell ye what's the matter, Claire, but ye're too drunk to understand. Come to think of it, I'm not sure ye would, even if ye were sober."

Slamming the dressing room door shut behind him, he pulled on whatever clothes came to hand—anything to keep him from going in his nightshirt to the railway station, where he would catch the next train south. He'd send for his trunk later.

Coming to Strathandrew had been a mistake. Returning to Britain had been a mistake. He'd tried to rewrite the past, only to find it was etched in stone as hard as the Grampian Hills. Whatever he might have made of himself in America, to people like Claire Talbot he would always be a servant.

Claire flinched when Ewan slammed the door behind him. She was sober enough to recognize the anger in his voice, but not sober enough to work out what it meant. Apart from the obvious, that she would not be spending the night in his bed, or he in hers.

When she'd opened her eyes to find him bending over her, removing her clothes, she'd assumed she must be dreaming. All her suppressed desire for him had fused with Mr. Mac-Leod's potent cider to make her blurt out that scandalous proposition. She knew there were many reasons why it was wrong, but at the moment, they'd all eluded her.

Were any of them truly as compelling as her desperate need for him? Recalling the look of disgust on his face and the way he had recoiled from her touch, she knew there was no hope of that need ever being satisfied.

She had believed that once before, when he'd disappeared off to America, leaving her with nothing but the memory of a single stolen kiss. Over the years she had come to accept her chaste lot in life. Then Ewan Geddes had returned, a man grown. He had gone out of his way to revive all those old feelings and make her achingly aware of everything she'd been missing.

Feeling a strange sensation on her face, she dashed her hand across her cheek. It came away wet.

Claire hated to cry. It never solved anything. Quite the contrary. It squandered time and energy that might be put to more profitable use, and it exposed a person's vulnerability.

At the moment, she had no choice in the matter. That deceptively sweet cider had demolished the iron-clad self-control she'd spent a lifetime forging. Tears coursed down her cheeks in spite of her. Soon sobs retched up from the depths of her heart. Yet, in some bewildering fashion, this passionate release of her emotions felt vital and satisfying.

She didn't want Ewan to see her this way, though. She tried to crawl away and hide somewhere, but she was too weak and dizzy to do more than sit up with her knees bent in front of her, and bury her face in her arms.

Her tears had almost spent themselves when she heard the dressing room door open. She tried to stifle her sobs, but they were like wild things on a rampage after having been caged for too long.

"Aw, what are ye taking on like that for?" Ewan's voice held a mixture of pity and disdain that ignited a spark of anger in Claire, too fierce for her tears to quench.

Though she shrank from exposing the ravages of her weeping, she raised her head to glare at him. "Why did you make me confess my old feelings for you, Ewan? Why did you flirt with me at the party and kiss me on the way home? Just so you could make a fool of me?"

Her questions made him flinch even as he protested, "I never heard anything so daft!"

She'd been daft, all right—daft to trust him! "It's the kind of cruel trick I'd have expected from you, once. I thought you'd changed."

The scoundrel did not even have the decency to look properly ashamed of himself. "But I haven't changed, have I? At least not as far as ye're concerned. I'm still nothing to ye but a hireling to do yer bidding."

Now who was daft? She'd never thought of him that way, even when he'd been in service to her family. And certainly not now.

A fresh wave of misery broke over her. She knew it was the drink making all her feelings so raw. Tomorrow she might repent everything she said and did tonight. But she could not keep her emotions bottled up inside her a moment longer.

"You made me feel beautiful for the first time in my life," she cried, "but it was all a lie! You really find me too repulsive to touch…even for money!"

With that, she hid her face in her arms again, wishing he would go and let her lament in peace. Her accusation hung in the brittle silence until she began to wonder if he'd slipped away without her hearing.

"Get one thing through yer fuddled head, Claire Talbot." Ewan hurled his answer at her as he swept out the door. "It's not *ye* I find repulsive. It's yer damn money!"

The rain had eased to a fitful spatter by the time Ewan strode back out the side door and headed for the village on foot. He could have taken the pony cart or saddled up one of the horses from Strathandrew's stable, but the explosive mixture of feelings inside him demanded some physical outlet. Walking was the safest one he could think of.

Besides, he didn't want to be beholden to the Talbots for any more favors. He'd had about as much of their *hospitality* as he could stomach.

The whole humiliating confrontation with Claire ran through his mind again and again. To think she'd had the gall to be angry with him! Accusing him of leading her on, the way some women in America had enticed him, trying to get their greedy hands on his money.

Just thinking about it made him feel dirty.

He was far from proud of his conduct in the past week, to begin with. He had left Tessa with an unspoken understanding that he would propose to her as soon as she broke her engagement. Even if his feelings had changed, which he now questioned, he shouldn't have kissed another woman—especially not her sister!

A noise on the road ahead shook Ewan out of his guilty reflections. A small procession of bobbing lights moved toward him, accompanied by the sounds of people laughing and talking in louder than usual tones. Damn! It must be the rest of the Strathandrew folks returning from the ceilidh.

Ewan froze in his tracks for a moment, then jumped the ditch and scrambled up a bit of a hill to find cover behind some bushes. He felt like a rank coward, sneaking off without a word to any of them, but he couldn't abide the prospect of having to dodge their questions about where he was bound at this hour of the night, and why.

With a pang of regret, he listened as they passed by, picking out Rosie's voice, Glenna's and Jock's. What sort of gossip would there be among them when he was discovered missing? How would Claire explain his abrupt departure?

Once the sound of their passing faded in the distance, he got back on the road again and continued toward the village. With no sounds but the wind in the leaves, and little to see but shadows and stars, there was nothing to distract him from the tribunal of his conscience.

What in blazes had made him imagine himself in love with Claire Talbot, of all people? Could it be the time they'd spent together? Or perhaps some perverse reaction to their old friction? Or could it be that she represented the kind of challenge he'd never been able to resist?

Whatever it was, he'd made a fine fool of himself over the whole business. Now, for the second time in ten years, he was leaving Strathandrew in disgrace. The power and fortune he'd accumulated in the meantime did not ease the heartache of his going one bit.

Few hours in Ewan's life had ever passed so slowly as the long, dark ones while he waited for the train station to open. When the stationmaster finally appeared, he was running late, perhaps having overslept after the ceilidh.

"When's the next train south?" asked Ewan, unfolding banknotes from his wallet.

He hoped it would not be long. He wanted to be well away from here before his doubts and regrets about last night overwhelmed him.

"There's only the one a day," said the stationmaster, "for this is almost the end of the line. "The northbound train should be coming through anytime now. It'll go on to Mallaig, then turn and come back this way, heading for Fort William. That's when ye'll get on—around three this afternoon."

Three!

"Can I just get on when it comes through the first time?"

The stationmaster looked at him as if he'd sprouted green hair. "And go all the way to Mallaig and back for nothing? Why on earth would ye want to do that?"

"Maybe I'd just like to see the country up that way, all right?"

The stationmaster's brow furrowed. "I don't know. It's not included in the fare, and if all the carriages were full…"

"Have ye ever seen the train full on the way to Mallaig or back?"

"Well, no…but—"

Ewan unfolded another banknote. "Then give me a return ticket to Mallaig."

"Ye mean, besides yer single to Glasgow?"

"That's right." Ewan shoved the notes under the wicket.

The stationmaster shook his head. "It's yer money, I reckon."

"Aye, it is."

Off in the distance, a whistle blew.

"Early," grumbled the stationmaster. "Wouldn't ye know it."

"Can ye just hurry with those tickets?" Ewan glanced out the station window at the approaching locomotive. "I don't want to miss that train."

After a few anxious minutes, he found himself on the platform, ticket in hand, ready to put plenty of distance between him and Claire. When the door of one of the carriages opened, Ewan hurried to climb aboard.

Just as Tessa Talbot disembarked and threw herself into his arms. "Ewan! How did you know I'd be on this train? Have you been coming here every morning to meet it? You dear, dear man!"

"I...well...that is..." He was too tired and too stunned by her sudden appearance to know what to say.

Luckily, she didn't appear to require an answer. "What an adventure I've had getting here!"

Ewan recovered his voice at last. "Are ye feeling better? Where's yer ma?"

"Hot on my heels, I should imagine." Tessa latched on to his hand and towed him away from the train. "I was dreadfully worried she'd catch up with me in Glasgow."

At his puzzled look she replied, "I never was ill, you know. Mama detained me, then sent that note to the *Marlet* telling you to sail without me. I must say, I was rather hurt that you and Claire didn't wait."

"I'm…sorry about that. It was all so sudden and I thought ye might—"

"Oh, that's all right." Tessa pressed herself against him, but the only burning desire he felt was to get on the train. "I should have known Mama would try some trick like this to keep us apart. I'm certain she thought I just needed a few days away from you to come to my senses."

If only she had.

Tessa shook her head, a willful glint in her eyes. "She only succeeded in making me more determined than ever to marry you."

"Marry me? But I haven't—"

A shudder went through the train, then its wheels began to turn. Ewan was tempted to break away from Tessa and jump on it, but he feared she'd only follow him. Besides, he'd barged into the poor lass's life from out of nowhere, made her fall in love with him, only to fall *out* of love with her. He owed her every courtesy.

"We'll show my mother and everyone else!" For such a delicate creature, Tessa had a grip like a blacksmith. "If I want to marry a gillie, or a butcher, or a…dustman, they can't stop me!"

Was that all he was to her—a gesture of rebellion?

Not that he had any right to sit in judgment, he supposed, after the way he'd behaved of late. Besides, he was beginning to wonder about the motives behind his feelings for her.

"We have to do it *now,*" Tessa muttered to herself in vehement tones. "Before she gets here and tries to interfere. I'll show her I'm not some vapid little debutante she can wed off to some chinless baro—"

"Hold on a minute, lass." Ewan dug in his heels and swung Tessa around to face him. "Do *what* before *who* gets here? Where are we going?"

He hoped he'd jumped to the wrong conclusion.

Tessa laughed and threw her arms around his neck. "This is Scotland, remember? Land of elopements. I want to go get married—*now!*"

Chapter Seventeen

For one blissful instant, when she woke in Ewan's bed, Claire could not remember anything that had happened after they'd left the ceilidh. Ignoring the queasy sensation in her stomach and the tight ache in her head, she gave a slow, sensual stretch, accompanied by a throaty little chuckle.

Oh dear, what had she done?

Then her tardy good sense woke up. Oh dear, what *had* she done?

Ewan was not in bed with her. Was that a good sign or bad?

A pile of her clothes lay on the floor beside his dressing gown, but she was still wearing her chemise and pantalettes. That definitely counted as good.

Claire plundered her memory, though she

feared what the search might yield. Perhaps if she started with the last thing she *could* recall with any clarity, then worked her way forward, she might get somewhere.

She remembered the ceilidh…the dancing… the toasts…the cider. After that, events began to blur.

Ewan had wanted to ask her a question. Had he asked it? What had it been and how had she answered?

Oh, no! She remembered. Both his question… and her answer. What had possessed her to confess the truth? It had been one thing to enjoy his company for the past few days, to *pretend* there was more between them than there ever had been, or could be.

She had never meant to take it further. Not even if Ewan had shown an interest. Which, of course, he never would.

Would he?

The vivid recollection of a kiss stirred in her sluggish memory. Perhaps she was only confusing last night with that other night on the deck of the *Marlet*.

No. This kiss had been much longer, deeper and more satisfying than the other—much too good to have been a product of her imagination. But if he *had* kissed her, what had it meant, and why had he stopped?

Her memory grew even murkier at that point.

Dredging words and images out of it was like trying to see across the Strand during a winter fog in London. Might it prove as dangerous as trying to cross a busy street in such a fog?

The distant, muted sound of footsteps startled Claire bolt upright, making her head spin and throb at the same time. Whatever had happened between her and Ewan last night, she did not want any of the servants finding her barely clothed in his bed.

Crawling out from under the covers, she struggled into her gown, though it was hopelessly crumpled and still damp. She could not begin to fasten all those fiddly buttons down the back. How had she *unbuttoned* them, last night? The harder she tried to remember, the worse her head spun, but it was no use.

Had Ewan undressed her? It seemed the most likely explanation. Given the circumstances, it could not have been a very romantic or sensuous undertaking, yet how Claire wished she could recall it!

Once she'd managed to get herself a little more modestly dressed, she gathered up her other garments and peeped into Ewan's dressing room. Perhaps, after putting her to bed, he'd gone to sleep in there.

A glance into the little room yielded no sign of him, though the floor was littered with discarded clothes, including his nightshirt. The sight of it made Claire even more uneasy.

Struggling to remember if she knew where Ewan had gone, she crept to the door of his bedchamber. There, she listened for sounds of movement out in the gallery, but heard nothing. With any luck, the servants might be late getting to their morning chores after last night's festivities.

Claire eased the door ajar and peeped outside. Finding the gallery deserted, she fled to her own room as quickly as her spinning, throbbing head would let her.

Her memory chose a most inopportune moment to return.

Some subtle combination of sound and scent in the gallery must have triggered it. Sensations overwhelmed her, as fresh and vivid as when she had first experienced them, last night. She recalled being bounced about as Ewan carried her up the back stairs. It had been everything she could do to keep from retching all over the carpet.

She'd quickly recovered when he set her on her feet, though. Ah, the warm tickle of his breath in her ear when he'd asked which room was hers!

A mortified whimper left her lips when she recalled her reply. *I don' care. Put me wherever you like. Put me in your room.* Evidently he'd taken her at her word.

Claire roused suddenly from her memories to find herself standing in the middle of the gallery, the back of her gown gaping open and most of her underclothes in her arms.

Before she blundered into one of the servants, or they into her, she ducked into her bedchamber. Tossing her clothes into the dressing room, she donned her nightgown and crawled into her own bed. Perhaps if she slept for a while, she could begin this day all over again.

But sleep eluded her. The memory that had come back to her out in the gallery must have been acting like a stopper wedged tight in the mouth of a jug. Once it popped free, the rest gushed forth with bewildering speed and intensity. If only she could forget them again!

As she recalled waking to find Ewan undressing her, a delicious tingling heat swept through her body. A clammy, bilious chill followed hard upon it when she remembered inviting him to ravish her. Then, when he'd been gentleman enough to resist her invitation…she'd offered him money for his *services?*

Rolling onto her stomach, Claire buried her face in her pillows to muffle a wail of anguish.

The locomotive gave a long, plaintive whistle as it pulled out of the station on its way to Mallaig. Ewan felt like throwing back his head and letting out an answering wail.

"Hold on a minute, Tessa." He dug in his heels before she hauled him all the way to the kirk. "We can't just go get married without a by yer leave to anybody."

"Of course we can, darling." Tessa laughed, but she did not loosen her grip on his arm. "It's called eloping. Couples with beastly families do it all the time."

But how many lived to regret it?

"Ye're still engaged to the Stanton chap. Or did ye speak to him before ye left London?"

What would he do if she had broken her engagement at his urging? Marriage would be the only honorable course. Though people like Lady Lydiard might believe otherwise, honor was as important to Ewan as to any nobleman.

"No, I didn't speak to Spencer." At least Tessa had the grace to look properly ashamed of her admission. "I caught Mama sending him a message to come at once. Not that it would have made a particle of difference in my feelings. That's when I decided to take matters into my own hands and run away to you."

"So ye traveled all the way here by yerself?" The realization hit him like a blow. "From London?"

He shuddered to think of her changing trains in a rough town like Glasgow. If anything had happened to her, he'd never have forgiven himself. "Yer ma must be worried sick!"

He'd never thought the day would come when he'd feel sympathy for Lady Lydiard.

"Why are you fretting about my mother?" cried Tessa. "Did you not hear what she tried to do to us?"

"Don't be too hard on her." It astonished Ewan to hear himself speaking those words. "She was only trying to do what she thought was best for ye."

After the previous night's festivities, there weren't many people out and about in the village that morning. All the same, Ewan and Tessa were beginning to attract attention from the few children and old folks going about their business.

"Speaking of yer ma," said Ewan. "There's only the one train a day from Glasgow. She can't possibly get here before tomorrow morning, can she?"

"I suppose not." Tessa cast him a wary look, as if to say she couldn't fully trust any man who would take her mother's part. "What has that got to do with anything?"

"It means there's no tearing hurry to get to the kirk," said Ewan. "After the trip ye've had, ye must be tired? Hungry?"

Tessa started to shake her head when a wide yawn overtook her, and her stomach rumbled. "Perhaps a little. I didn't notice it while I was traveling—it was all such a terrific adventure. But now that I'm here…"

"Can ye walk as far as Strathandrew?" Ewan cringed at the thought of seeing Claire again, but he owed it to Tessa to look after her now.

She yawned again. "I think so." Plastering herself against him, she rubbed her cheek against the sleeve of his coat. "I can do *anything* as long as I have you with me."

He had to admire the lass for her spirit, even if he didn't approve of her dangerous impulsiveness. "It sounds like ye managed pretty well on yer own, coming all the way up here. Just a wee bit farther, then ye can rest and fill yer belly with some of Rosie's good cooking."

"Oh yes!" Tessa listed against him as they walked. "I'm so longing to see Rosie and all the others." She chuckled like a mischievous child contemplating a most amusing prank. "What did they say when you told them you and I will be getting married?"

What had come over him? Ewan wondered. There'd been a time he'd gladly have walked across hot coals for the chance to have Tessa Talbot linger this close to him. Now all he wanted to do was put a bit of distance between them before he suffocated!

"I haven't told them. I didn't think it was my place to say anything just yet."

"Not your place?" She gave his arm a token swat. "Why, you're talking like a servant. If you're the man I'm going to marry, then of course it's your place to tell whomever you like."

"I didn't mean *that* kind of place." Though he told himself she deserved his forbearance, Ewan could not soften the sharp edge of his voice. "It wasn't my place to speak because nothing was settled when we parted in London, and ye were still engaged to another man."

"Gracious! What's made you so testy, darling?"

Before he could invent a halfway plausible excuse for snapping at her, Tessa worked out one of her own. "It's having to spend all that time with no company but Claire's, isn't it?"

In a way, perhaps—but not the way Tessa assumed.

"I know you two have never got on, and she can seem rather stiff and cool...."

Remembering Claire Talbot sprawled on the floor of his bedchamber like a large, wanton rag doll, casually inviting him to have his way with her, almost made Ewan burst out laughing. Her proposition still outraged him, but now that a little time had passed, parts of what had happened struck him as funny.

Or maybe he was only giddy from lack of sleep.

"It's just her way, poor thing," said Tessa. "She does work terribly hard, you know, to make a success of Brancasters. And she's so clever about business. It's not her fault she doesn't know how to get on with men. She's had so many of them court her just to get their hands on her fortune. That must make it very hard to trust people, don't you think?"

Ewan made some vague noise of agreement.

He knew. Better than Tessa would ever guess.

Once her memory of the night's events returned, there could be no question of Claire going back to sleep.

As she sipped a cup of strong coffee in the breakfast room, she wondered if she would ever enjoy a tranquil night's sleep again, after what she had done to her sister.

She'd driven Ewan Geddes away. Not in the manner she had originally planned, but he was gone just the same. And Tessa's chance for happiness might well be gone with him.

He was a good man who had loved Tessa devotedly for a long time. And he was no fortune hunter. Quite the opposite, in fact—a little too proud and independent. Now that she understood why, Claire could not blame him for either trait.

Ewan Geddes was also a strong man, which Tessa needed. He would not put up with any nonsense, even if it meant jumping into the ocean rather than being held on a ship against his will. Even if it meant quitting Strathandrew in the middle of the night, rather than suffering the unwanted demands of his hostess.

Claire rested her aching brow against her hand and slowly shook her head over her disgraceful behavior. Would she *ever* scrape together the tattered shreds of her self-respect? For her sake, perhaps it was better if she had driven Ewan out of their lives. How could she ever look him in the face again, after what she'd done?

The sound of approaching footsteps and voices forced Claire to rally her shattered composure. Life must go on and, as ever, she must find a way to accept what had happened and make the best of it.

Then the breakfast room door burst open and Tessa dashed in, towing Ewan behind her. Claire wished the floor would cave in and swallow her up, or the ceiling would collapse on top of her— anything to keep her from having to face him again, so soon.

She rose from her chair and opened her arms to her sister. "Dearest, I'm so glad you've arrived at last!"

Shame and regret over her recent actions made her more demonstrative than usual. She clutched Tessa in a warm, tight embrace of unspoken repentance.

"Heavens, Claire!" Tessa kissed her cheek, then drew back, chuckling. "One would think you hadn't seen me in months rather than just a few days. I'll admit, it does seem longer than that. Wait till I tell you all that happened."

She spun about, calling to Glenna McMurdo, who hovered just inside the door. "Could we get something to eat, please? I'm famished and I expect Ewan is, too, after coming into the village so early to meet my train."

"Aye, miss." The maid hurried off.

Tessa reached for Ewan's hand again. "Wasn't that sweet of him to do? Especially since he had no way of knowing for certain I'd be coming today. I thought of sending a wire to let you know I was on my way, but I had only a little bit of money, and I wanted to make sure it would last."

Those words distracted Claire from her desperate effort to avoid Ewan's gaze. "Only a little money? I don't understand, dearest." She glanced past Tessa and Ewan toward the door. "Where is your mother?"

"I don't know," Tessa announced with an air of blithe indifference. She collapsed onto a chair, pulling Ewan down on the one beside her. "And after what she did, I don't much care, either."

Wilting back onto her own chair, Claire listened with growing alarm as Tessa related the story of her mother's attempts to keep her in London. Fortunately, she seemed to have no suspicion that Claire might have been in league with Lady Lydiard, perhaps because the pair had never cooperated in anything before.

"When I heard she'd summoned Spencer, that was the last straw," said Tessa. "I took what pin money I had on hand and slipped out of the house. It was the most marvelous adventure traveling north all by myself.

"I got on the wrong train in Manchester and was so afraid I'd miss my connection to Carlisle. But people were ever so kind. Apart from that boy who tried to steal my reticule…and that sailor who appeared rather the worse for drink."

"Oh, dearest, how awful!" Claire's hand trembled as she lifted her coffee cup to her lips. "Thank heaven you reached here safely!"

To think that while Tessa had been braving such dangers, she had been larking about the Highlands, pretending that her sister's beau belonged to her!

A welcome distraction appeared at that moment in the shape of Glenna McMurdo, bearing a tray well laden with breakfast foods. The savory smells of eggs, fried ham and kippered herring made Claire's gorge rise. Ewan did not appear very hungry, either, taking only a slice of bread and butter while Tessa heaped her plate.

"When I saw dear Ewan waiting for me on the platform," she said between bites, "I knew it had all been worthwhile. I was determined to find a parson and get married at once, before Mama could turn up and start interfering again."

"You're married?" Claire fumbled her cup, splashing lukewarm coffee all down the bust of her morning gown.

She had repented spoiling her sister's chances. If Tessa and Ewan wanted to marry—well, she loved her sister and respected him more than any other man she'd met. She wanted them to be happy together. Yet hearing they were already wed felt like someone was gouging her heart out with a dull knife.

"Not yet." Intent on her breakfast, Tessa didn't seem to have noticed Claire spilling her coffee. "But soon."

From his chair beside Tessa, Ewan might not have glimpsed the incident, either. Claire hoped he hadn't.

"Sensible man that he is," Tessa continued, "Ewan pointed out that Mama cannot arrive any earlier than tomorrow morning. He wanted to make sure I had a chance to eat and rest before the wedding. Isn't he a darling?"

Claire forced the corners of her mouth up. Her sister's innocent question twisted that invisible knife in her chest. Her nerves were so overwrought that when Tessa dropped her cutlery on her plate with a loud clatter, Claire flinched back, gasping.

"I have the most marvelous idea!" Tessa

turned toward Claire and grabbed her hand. "While I have a little nap, could you call on the parson and ask if he'll come here to conduct the ceremony this afternoon? Then we can have a nice fancy tea to celebrate. I'll pop down to the kitchen and ask Rosie to get busy baking a wedding cake."

As Claire struggled to find her voice, Ewan spoke up for the first time since he and Tessa had arrived from the village. "Go have yerself a good lay down. *Then* we can talk about weddings and such."

His tone was neither loud nor sharp, but his words rang with a firm resolve that even Tessa seemed prepared to accept. "Oh, very well. But I don't want to wait too long. Mama will only find some other way of coming between us, if we do."

"If yer ma or anyone else *can* come between us," said Ewan, "then we don't belong together and it's just as well we find out first as last."

Anyone else—those words had an ominous sound. Had they been meant for Tessa? Or as a warning to her sister?

Tessa yawned and rubbed her eyes. "Perhaps you're right. I will not let opposition from my mother or anyone else sway me. In fact, the harder they try, the more determined I become."

Ewan patted the back of her hand. "Ye are a

determined lass. No doubt about that. Now, get yerself off to bed for a few hours before ye fall asleep where ye're sitting."

The practical, solicitous fondness of his words made the back of Claire's throat ache. Not for all the world would she deprive her sister of it. Yet how she longed to have a man like Ewan speak to her that way!

"Gracious!" Tessa rose from her chair and stretched. "I don't know why you insist on postponing the wedding when you're acting like a husband already."

She stooped to press a kiss on his brow. "I hope you don't have any ambition to tyrant over me once we're married. I won't stand for it, you know."

Ewan got to his feet. "That's one thing I *can* promise ye, lass."

He followed Tessa as she departed the breakfast room.

At the last moment he was within earshot, Claire could hold her tongue no longer. "Ewan!"

"Aye?" He paused in the door and turned to glance back at her, his features tensed in a grim, anxious look.

Now that she had his attention, she could not think what to say. This was not the time to talk about what had happened last night, even if he would listen to her.

"Are…are you going to have a sleep, too?" He

looked as if he could use one. Apart from everything else, she was sorry for that.

Ewan pursed his lips and shook his head. "No. I'm going to pack. The train south will be coming back through the village later today and I plan to be on it."

"But…Tessa? The wedding?"

"There's not going to be a wedding, Claire. Not today, for sure. Once yer sister's rested enough to think straight, I'm going to tell her."

Chapter Eighteen

After what had happened last night, Ewan should have savored the look of distress on Claire's face when he told her he'd be leaving, and not likely marrying her sister.

But he couldn't.

If she thought of him as nothing but a servant, she should be glad to see him go and let Tessa wed the "right sort" of fellow. Or maybe he was reading too much into that look, because he didn't want to face the truth.

It might only be a hangover that made Claire appear so miserable. Considering how much cider she'd drunk last night, and how fast she'd put it away, she had good cause to be feeling poorly the morning after. Maybe she was embarrassed about getting tipsy and almost ending up in bed with the man her sister wanted to marry.

Or maybe she was worried he would tell Tessa what had happened.

If Claire could believe him capable of such ungallant conduct…! Ewan's waning anger blazed afresh, but rapidly burned itself out. Considering some of the things he'd said and done this past week, he didn't deserved his own good opinion, let alone hers.

"Are you coming, darling?" Tessa's summons jolted him from the stern verdict of his conscience.

"Aye, lass, I'm right behind ye." He hurried to catch up with her.

Was he being fair to Tessa? he asked himself. Was he right to dismiss her feelings for him as nothing more than a rebellious fancy? Or was he trying to make himself believe it, to soothe his guilty conscience and excuse his behavior with Claire?

There was one way he might find out. And if he was right, it might fix some of the upheaval he'd caused by barging back into her life after all these years.

"Tessa?" Ewan reached for her hand when he caught up with her at the top of the stairs. "There's something I've been wanting to tell ye."

"Can't it wait, darling?" She leaned against him as they walked down the gallery. "I'm ever so sleepy after that lovely breakfast."

She stopped in front of a door that must lead to her bedroom.

"Aye, lass." He needed to take an unsparing look at the motives behind his feelings for her. Or behind the feelings he'd *thought* he had. "I reckon it'll keep till ye're better rested. Have a good sleep."

He turned toward his room, and the packing that awaited him.

"Darling?" Tessa had not released his hand. Now she tugged him back toward her. "Aren't you forgetting something?"

She greeted his bemused look with a chuckle. "—Aren't you going to kiss me? It's quite ridiculous to think of us getting married when we've never even kissed."

"I told ye how I feel about that, Tessa. And we did kiss, remember? It was a long time ago. Maybe ye've forgotten it."

"You can't put me off with that excuse. I'm certain I would remember if you'd kissed me, Ewan Geddes."

He'd flattered himself that she would. But it had been ten years ago. Tessa had probably been kissed by several other men since. He had never forgotten it, though.

"That last summer?" Even as he tried to prompt her memory, the flesh between his shoulders crinkled. "Remember—the night before ye sailed back home? Down by the dock?"

"Are you certain it was me?"

"It was dark…but ye wrote me a…" A note. An unsigned note that he'd assumed must have come from Tessa. How blind could one man be?

"Poor darling." Tessa reached up to stroke his brow. "I didn't pay you much mind back then, did I? I promise to make up for it once we're married."

So Tessa hadn't cared for him, back then. She couldn't have nursed a fallow desire for him all the years they'd been apart—the way he had for her. He would have a lot to think about before he boarded that train for Glasgow later today. He needed some accurate measure of Tessa's present feelings for him, to help sort out the whole bewildering tangle.

"Married…aye. Let me just tell ye quickly what I was going to say about that. Then ye can sleep on it."

"Oh, very well." Tessa leaned back against her door. "Since you're so determined to have it out. What is this important news of yours?"

When he heard the soft tap on his door a while later, Ewan assumed it must be the young footman, Alec, sent to help him pack. It had the deferential sound of a servant's knock. The kind that said, *Pardon me for intruding, but would it be too much trouble if I come in, now, and do my job?*

"Aye, come on in!" he called from the dressing room. "I could use yer help. Did some of my shirts get taken to be laundered? And have ye seen my silver cuff links?"

The footman did not answer. Claire did. "I'll ask Mrs. Arbuthnot about your shirts. I expect the cuff links are somewhere about. When did you last have them on?"

What had brought her here?

Ewan emerged from the dressing room with a waistcoat folded over his arm. "Sorry, I thought ye were somebody else. What can I do for ye?"

It was the question of a servant, born and bred.

"What would I *like* you to do for me?" asked Claire. "Or what are you *able* to do for me?"

He'd intended to talk to her before he left Strathandrew, to make certain everything was out in the open and understood between them. But he wished she hadn't come here. It was too potent a reminder of last night.

"Tell me the first of those," he said, "then I'll tell you the second."

"Very well." She inhaled a deep breath, then forged ahead. "What I want…what I wish, is that you could forget what happened last night and not hold my intolerable behavior against my sister. Drunk or sober, I should never have thrown myself at you that way. I cannot begin to tell you how much I regret the distress I must have caused you."

Ewan could see the distress it caused *her* to speak of it. Her face looked pale and pinched. Her wary gaze flitted around the room, seldom daring to meet his. Her bearing suggested someone braced for a blow. She looked so ill at ease, his heart went out to her in spite of himself.

"I wouldn't say ye *threw* yerself at me." He tried to ease the tension between them with a little teasing. "Ye could hardly sit up."

He immediately regretted his misplaced attempt at humor, for it appeared to fluster Claire even worse. Her lower lip quivered until she caught it between her teeth, and she blinked furiously in an effort to fight back tears. It wasn't any hangover making her look like that. Nor had she mentioned him keeping quiet to Tessa about last night, but seemed to assume that he would behave with honor.

"I will never forgive myself if I have spoiled Tessa's chances with such a fine man." Her voice broke on those last two words, but before Ewan could reply, she rallied.

In spite of her obvious dismay at having to plead with him, she seemed determined to have her say. "I swear, if you marry my sister, I will never do anything to embarrass or insult you again. I won't drink anything stronger than tea in your presence."

If their positions had been reversed, would he have been able to master his pride to plead like this with *her?*

Perhaps she glimpsed a softening of his expression that gave her hope. "Reconsider, Ewan, I beg you. Tessa is a dear girl. You've loved her all these years without any hope. Don't lose her now because of my folly. You can live here at Strathandrew and run the business we talked about. You'll hardly ever have to see your wife's odious relations. Please? For Tessa's sake and for your own?"

When she looked at him like that, he wanted to grant her anything she asked. But for his own sake and for Tessa's, he must not let her persuade him.

He set the waistcoat he'd been holding on the bed. "If it helps, Claire, I don't hold what happened last night against ye. I reckon we all have...needs we keep under control most of the time, like a big dog on a leash. One drink too many is like trying to walk the dog over slippery ground. It's easy for the beast to run away with us."

Claire let out a quivering sigh. "Then you'll stay? If you'd rather wait and have a proper wedding, I promise I'll intervene with Lady Lydiard so she won't give you any trouble over it."

He hated to squash her fragile sense of relief. "Ye don't understand, lass. I haven't changed my mind about marrying Tessa, though that has nothing to do with..."

He'd been going to say it had nothing to do with her or last night, but that wasn't true. "Ye said I've loved Tessa all these years. After giving it some hard thought, I see that's not true. I only wish I'd realized it before I barged back into all yer lives and turned everything upside down. But I'm glad I had the sense to see it before we rushed into something that would have been bad for both of us."

Did he owe Lady Lydiard his thanks for giving him a few days to come to his senses? It galled Ewan to think so.

"You can't mean that!" All Claire's distress seemed to vaporize into passionate anger. Eyes that had once held mournful mist now flashed with silver lightning. "Feelings like those don't flourish for ten years, then disappear in a few days!"

As it had when they were young, her antagonism rubbed against his pride to kindle an answering spark. "Maybe not, if the feelings are true to begin with and if neither of the folks have changed in the meantime."

"Are you saying you didn't love my sister when we were young?" she demanded. "You gave a very fine imitation of it."

"I'm sure I did, for I was convinced that was what I felt." Ewan looked back on his behavior

with hard-won perception. "Mooning about...
watching her from afar...showing off for her...
dreaming of her—that's the way a lad goes on
about any bonny lass. And for me, I reckon it
was all mixed up with wanting something better for myself."

"Are you saying you only cared for my sister
as a—a symbol of your ambition?" Could she
look that indignant on Tessa's behalf, if she had
any true feelings for him?

"Look, I'm not proud of it. No more than ye
are of getting drunk and offering me money to
share yer bed. I was young then. I don't know
if it's the same for lasses, but for lads it's like
three or four years of being drunk on a brew of
all the bloody queer feelings raging inside ye.
Ye make a damn fool of yerself as often as not,
and ye aren't responsible for a lot of the daft
things ye do."

Again Claire caught her lip in her teeth. But
this time, Ewan guessed she might be trying to
curb a wayward grin. "It is no different with
girls."

"Well, there ye go." It did not give him nearly
the satisfaction to score that point off her than it
would have once upon a time.

"Tessa may not realize it yet, but she never
loved me, either. Not the way it should be between a grown man and woman. I'm some kind
of forbidden fruit to her. If I'd never been a ser-

vant, if I was some toplofty blueblood with her ma nagging her to marry me, she'd throw me over as quick as she did that poor Stanton chap. Quicker, maybe."

He thought for a moment. "I reckon she cares more for Stanton than she knows, if she's stayed with him this long in spite of her ma's approval."

Again Claire looked as if she wanted to laugh. Then she grew sober again. "That's a great deal for you to have figured out in such a short time."

Ewan shrugged. "I'm smarter than I look."

"I've never underestimated your brains, Ewan Geddes."

She deserved a less flippant answer. "The truth is, maybe I'm *not* as smart as I look. I've had clues over the years about my own feelings, I just never tallied them all up before and made myself take a good hard look at the sum. It's not easy letting go of something ye've hung on to for a long while."

Was that what she had done? Claire wondered. Clung to her old feelings for Ewan Geddes long after she should have let them go? Had she truly loved him, or had her feelings been tainted by something else—perhaps the need to compete with her beautiful sister for attention and love?

"Must you go right away?" she asked. "Could you not stay a few days and break the news to Tessa more gradually?"

Ewan considered her request, then slowly shook his head. "I reckon a quick break will be kinder in the long run."

Part of her wanted him gone. He posed too grave a threat to her self-control. Another part could not abide the prospect of losing him from her life again.

"If you would like to stay…or go away for a while, then come back later, I meant what I said about you running a business here at Strathandrew. I still believe it's a worthwhile idea and I'm convinced you're the perfect man for the job."

Was this just another way of buying his presence in her life? In part, perhaps, she conceded after a ruthless scrutiny of her motives. But there was more to it. She had promised him the job offer was for business reasons, independent of personal considerations. She owed it to him to keep her word about that.

Ewan considered her offer for a few moments. "Ye don't think the whole thing would be too awkward between ye and me?"

Devilishly so, and more on her part. All the same, if he wanted the job and was willing to take it, she must not let her apprehension stand in his way.

"I expect it *will* be awkward between us for a time. But we aren't sixteen anymore, Ewan. We've both knocked about the world enough to know that everyone makes mistakes now and then. We all do things we wish we could undo."

"Oh, aye." He seemed to sigh the words more than speak them. "I reckon we both made mistakes last night. Ye've had the character to own up to yers and make an apology. Ye put me to shame."

What on earth was he talking about?

Her puzzlement must have shown on her face, for Ewan asked, "Do ye remember what ye said to me last night?"

A blistering blush suffused her face. It surprised Claire to discover she had any embarrassment left after last evening. "I'd prefer it if we could both forget everything I said and did."

"Aye, there's some things I'd like to forget, as well. But there are other parts I want to remember always. Like dancing with ye at the ceilidh, and hearing ye confess ye fancied me once upon a time."

It had been so much more than a fancy, and by no means confined to the past. If she emptied a keg of hard cider, she might find the reckless nerve to tell him so. Or perhaps not. All the cider in the world could not sweeten the bitterness of humiliation she had tasted last night.

Tasted? Nay—drained to its vilest dregs.

"Why didn't ye tell me it was ye I kissed that night by the dock, not Tessa?"

His words staggered Claire. "What? And give

you reason to hate me more than you did already? I'm sorry for what it cost you, Ewan, but I swear I had no idea until you told me a few days ago. And what good would it have done to tell you? The truth wouldn't have changed anything."

"It might have made me realize yer sister didn't care anything for me, back then. It might have helped me not feel so bloody guilty about the fancy I found myself taking to ye."

Ewan took a step toward her. "I should never have kissed ye, Claire. Not last night. Not that night on the *Marlet*. And for sure not that night ten years ago."

He took another step.

Claire pressed herself back against the door, as if his words were weapons and he were threatening her with them. What had possessed her to come here?

"Please…" She fumbled with the doorknob. "…you made your feelings abundantly clear last night. I don't need to hear any more."

Berating herself for being a coward, but unable to dredge up the courage to face him a moment longer, she turned to flee.

But the door would not budge.

She grappled with the knob, twisting and pulling in a frenzy to escape.

"I won't hurt ye, Claire." He stood so close, she could feel the warmth of his breath on her ear. "At least, no more than I have already."

Reluctantly she lifted her gaze to see Ewan's strong brown hand resting high on the door, holding it shut.

"Ye may not want to listen to me, lass, but I reckon ye need to, for ye're not really *hearing* what I'm trying to say."

Perhaps this was what she needed. To purge any foolish wisp of hope from her heart. And to atone for her behavior last night.

"Go ahead and speak your piece, then." It took every scrap of nerve she possessed to turn and face him. "I assure you, I understand better than you think."

One glimpse at his face and she wished she'd had the sense to keep her back to him. He looked tired and troubled. But that only made her yearn for him all the more. Whatever her feelings had once been for him, they had since ripened into love.

"I hope that's not true, Claire, or I'm wasting my breath." He shrugged his broad shoulders and flashed a grin that held more wariness than mirth. "I've got nothing to lose by trying, now... except my pride. And I reckon I'd be better off with less of that."

"Perhaps we both would."

He gave a slow nod. "Ye and me may be more alike than either of us would care to admit. I hope ye'll pay better mind to what I have to say than I pay to myself sometimes."

Thrusting out his lower lip, he blew a puff of breath that stirred the lock of hair hanging over his brow. "I'm sorry I kissed ye because I had no right while I was still claiming to care for yer sister. Last night, ye accused me of leading ye on, but I swear I wasn't trying to do that. I was just so confused by my own feelings."

"You were?"

"Aye. That was one of those clues I should have figured out. A man who's in love doesn't spend all his time thinking about another lass and wanting to kiss her every time he gets half an excuse."

She heard what he was saying. She wanted to understand and believe, but her guarded heart refused to grasp it.

Ewan seemed to sense her doubt. "What I felt for Tessa was the fancy of a lad for a lass, because she was bonny. What I feel for ye is the love of a man for a woman who's bonny...and clever, and passionate and proud."

He removed his hand from the door. "If all ye can ever feel for me is what I used to feel for Tessa, then I guess there's no more to be said and I'd ought to get out of yer lives before I cause any more trouble for all of us."

Had she misunderstood him—hearing what she so desperately wanted to hear? Or if she had heard right, what could have made him say such things? "I told you, I don't want your pity, Ewan, if that's what this is about."

"Ye think I'd tell ye I love ye, because I feel sorry for ye?" He sounded as though he had never heard anything so foolish.

"I don't know. Would you?"

"No!" He slammed his palm against the door. "—Haven't ye listened to anything I've said, lass? I've finally figured out that it's not right to mix love up with other feelings. Not ambition. Not rebellion. And sure as hell not pity!"

Claire drew back at the severity of his outburst. The fierce strength of his declaration felt like a golden hammer pounding against the thick sheet of ice that had long encased her heart. That ice had been her prison, but it had also been her protection. Could she do without it?

Ewan's blast of outrage seemed to dissipate as quickly as it had erupted. With slow, tender restraint, he raised his hand to her cheek. And when he spoke, the gentle sympathy of his tone warmed her. "Look, I know plenty of men have had a hand in convincing ye that ye'll never be loved for who ye are—starting with yer own pa. I hope wherever he is, he's having to answer for that foolishness."

Her father had not been the wisest of men. She had rescued Brancasters from enough of his mismanagement to know it. Yet she had idolized him and craved any love he had left over for her. Could she accept that he'd been wrong about her?

"I'm not asking ye to believe me all at once," murmured Ewan. "I'm only asking ye to pretend for a few minutes that ye believe. Would that be so hard?"

Slowly, Claire shook her head. Had she not done a good job of pretending when they'd first come to Strathandrew? Too good, perhaps. The movement of her cheek against the palm of his hand felt so comforting, she soon found herself nuzzling into his caress.

"Good." The corners of Ewan's wide mouth curled in a slow blossoming smile that melted more of her ice palisade. "Then tell me this—if ye could believe that I loved ye, could ye love me? Not just wanting me to serve ye in bed, but as a partner ye could trust and respect, as well?"

Fear told her that was too dangerous a question to answer truthfully, without the convenient excuse of drunkenness. As Ewan had said, she had nothing to lose except her pride. But pride was important to her. In the past, it had enabled her to carry on when she'd been tempted to surrender to despair.

"I've never felt any other way about you." She struggled to coax her voice above a whisper. "Though I made an awful botch of it last night, trying to tell you so."

As if it possessed a will of its own, her hand

rose to graze his cheek. "I find you a most desirable man, and I would give most anything to… enjoy your company in bed. Never as a servant, though. A master, perhaps. A teacher. But not a servant."

Ewan hoisted his shoulder, to catch her hand between it and his cheek. "In that case, I reckon I could stay at Strathandrew a wee bit longer."

The breath she'd been holding escaped in a soft, hopeful sigh. "You could?"

"Aye. Ye see, I need to mount a campaign to convince ye of how I feel about ye."

With their hands still pressed to each other's cheeks, he lowered his face to hers, angling his lips until they were poised in a perfect position for a kiss. "It's going to take a great many walks in the hills, I reckon. More billiard matches in the evenings. I'll have to brush up on my Burns to recite ye lots of love poems."

Like the enchanted hill water, his gray eyes sparkled with rainbows, tempting her to chase a dream.

"It all sounds too good to be true."

"That'll be part of the challenge. To make ye believe it's good enough to be true. To make ye believe ye deserve it to be true."

He chuckled—a sound as sweet and intoxicating as hard cider. "Lucky for me, I've always enjoyed a challenge."

His lips were so close to hers, she could feel

their movement as he spoke, and the warm whisper of his breath. If he didn't kiss her soon, Claire feared she might swoon or scream or otherwise embarrass herself and spoil the moment. She would not bid him, though, like a mistress bidding a servant. Instead, she waited, trusting that he would satisfy the desire he had kindled.

Ewan did not disappoint her. Nor did he keep her waiting and wanting.

His lips closed over hers, unhurried, but not uncertain. With a deft swipe of his tongue, he beguiled her mouth open, then treated her to a kiss that put Claire in mind of Mrs. McMurdo's cranachan trifle—soft, sweet, rich…and mildly intoxicating.

"I reckon it's only fair to warn ye," Ewan murmured when he had sated her with his kiss. "This sort of thing is going to be a key strategy for convincing ye how I feel. And this…"

The hand that cupped her cheek began a slow, delightful descent, down her neck, toward her bosom, where it came to rest in a tantalizing caress. "It was everything I could do to keep my hands off ye, that first night we played billiards. From now on, unless we have company, I'm not even going to try."

Her mouth went dry and her knees grew weak just contemplating the prospect. They grew weaker still when Ewan's lips followed the trail his hand had blazed down her neck.

"I'll serve ye notice about something else, too." His words became kisses against the sensitive flesh of her neck.

"And what might that be?" Her question emerged in a breathless whisper as she inclined her cheek to nuzzle against his hair.

The hand fondling her bosom made way for his approaching lips by sliding down to her waist.

"If I catch ye wearing a corset again," he threatened in a husky purr, "ye'll leave me no choice but to take off yer clothes and relieve ye of it."

A hot, sweet shiver rippled through her.

"I'm wearing a corset now." She arched against him, painfully self-conscious of such wanton behavior, yet reveling in it at the same time. "It's a very tight one. Laces up the back. Fiendishly difficult to get off. I doubt you could if you tried."

"Do ye, now?" Ewan glanced up at her, the fires of sweet sin blazing in the depths of his eyes. "That sounds like a direct challenge to me. I'm afraid ye leave me no choice but to carry ye over to that bed and prove I'm more than a match for laces and whalebone."

She did not protest as he hoisted her into his arms and strode across the room, flinging her down upon the bed. But after he'd thrown off his coat and begun crawling toward her with lithe, predatory grace, she could not resist a further teasing challenge.

"You aren't still bashful about carrying on like this in my father's bed, I hope?"

"Hang yer father!" Ewan swooped in to kiss her with fierce, wild ardor worthy of some romantic Highland chieftain of old. Claire wondered what sort of challenge might provoke him to make love to her among the ruins of the ancient castle. Perhaps even wearing a kilt?

Chapter Nineteen

⋘∽⋙

Who'd have guessed Claire Talbot had it in her to be such a beguiling little minx? Ewan thanked heaven he'd discovered the truth in time!

He kissed her hungrily as he wrestled with her clothes. "If this damn hook doesn't give way soon, I'm afraid I might tear yer pretty dress."

She grappled for his hand, caught it and raised it to the neck of her gown. "Rip away!" she urged him with a wanton chuckle. "I believe it might prove quite stimulating."

Stimulating—the word all by itself stimulated him. Let alone having Claire whisper it in his ear in that seductive tone while the backs of his fingers pressed against her breasts.

Highland passion waged war on sensible Scottish thrift and trounced it soundly. His fingers tightened over the cloth and twisted. Then he gave a good, hard, sudden yank. The sweet screech of rending cloth almost made him lose control of himself.

"There now!" He pulled the gown off her as he'd done last night. Only this time with a more cooperative partner and far less indecision on his part. "I've only a dozen or so layers left to peel away."

Claire gave a giddy, infectious laugh. "Would you like some help?"

"I told ye…" Ewan kicked off his shoes, then pried off her slippers and tossed them onto the floor. "I like a challenge. Besides, undressing's half the fun. It's near as good as taking the pretty wrapping paper off a present."

Claire's carefree bubble of laughter shattered. "I hope you will not be too disappointed by what you find under all the pretty wrapping."

That would be his greatest challenge, Ewan realized. Not bringing her pleasure in bed, but convincing her she pleased *him*. Persuading her that she deserved all the tenderness he could lavish upon her.

"Oh, *muirneach!*" He gathered her into his arms, glad of a chance to marshal his self-control. "I'll let ye in on a wee secret."

"What secret?" Her tone sounded doubtful, but she nestled into his embrace clad only in her petticoats and other underclothes. "And what does that word mean—*mor-nuck?*"

"It means darling one, or favorite or beloved. Ye can also use it to mean a loving touch." He demonstrated by cupping her breast in his palm. "And this is the secret. When a man loves a woman, however she looks—tall, tiny, slender, stout, dark, fair—*that* becomes the yardstick he measures beauty by from then on."

"I hadn't thought of it that way." Claire searched his gaze, perhaps seeking to weigh the truth of what he'd told her.

Ewan was able to stand her scrutiny with perfect assurance. Where he had once reckoned golden curls the height of perfection, they now seemed a bit too obvious for his taste. The soft, tawny hue of a fawn suited him much better these days.

"Now that you mention it, though—" Claire raised one long, slender forefinger and traced the tip over his full, brooding brows, a feature he'd never been particularly proud of "—I've often thought certain gentlemen of my acquaintance needed a stronger brow to be truly handsome."

"There, ye see?" Ewan caught her finger and lowered it to his lips, planting a kiss upon the tip. "Ye knew that in yer heart, even before I told ye. I promise ye, I *will* like what I find. And I'll leave ye in no doubt of it."

"Now…" In a sudden movement, he sat up and tossed her across his lap, reaching for the laces of her petticoats and corset. "Are ye going to let me finish unwrapping my parcel?"

Perhaps the way he handled her tickled. Or perhaps his reassurance had sunk in, freeing her to become playful again.

She twisted toward him until her hand could reach the buttons of his shirt. "I have some unwrapping of my own I'd like to do, and I'm rather impatient about it."

Ewan laughed as he untied her petticoats and she fumbled with his buttons. A woman like Claire would make every day and every activity a fresh, zesty challenge. He only wished he'd been wise enough to recognize it years ago.

"Hold still now!" he said when he'd shed his shirt and she her petticoats. "I don't need any distractions while I figure out how to unlace this corset of yers."

The sensation of her wriggling over the lap of his trousers was a potent distraction, indeed!

He wrestled for several minutes with the intractable undergarment until the laces gave way at last.

"There!" He pulled it off her, then threw it with some force toward the hearth. "Remind me to light a fire and burn the fool thing, will ye?"

"So you conquered it, after all." Claire threw her arms around his neck and rewarded him with a firm, confident kiss. "Resourcefulness is a fine quality in a lover!"

Ewan savored the intoxicating sensation of her breasts against his bare chest, with only a flimsy barrier of linen and lace covering them. "Aye, and in a husband, too. I warn ye, Claire, I want ye for my wife. But I'm willing to wait until ye're convinced I really do love ye."

The news of his fortune would surely convince her, as it had dissuaded Tessa from her misplaced fancy for him. He didn't want to get into all that now, though. He just wanted to bring Claire the pleasure she'd denied herself for so long. And to satisfy the desire that had been building within him over the past several days.

Before his mention of marriage could alarm her, Ewan sought to divert her by fondling her breast through the fine linen of her undergarment. "What do they call this thing yer wearing?"

Claire did not answer for a moment, her eyes closed, relishing the sensation of his intimate touch. When she finally heeded his words enough to reply, her voice was husky with desire. "A chemise, I think...or a camisole."

"It's very pretty," Ewan murmured. "Almost worth the bother of shifting that miserable corset. It's a shame ye have to cover it up with outer clothes."

A look of disappointment twisted Claire's delicate features when he lowered his hand from her breast. When he slipped his fingers beneath her chemise and began again without even that delicate fabric to muffle his touch, she wriggled and heaved a long, rippling sigh.

"Ye like that, do ye?" As if he needed to ask.

"Mmm." She nodded, and the strong, steadfast blue of her eyes seemed to shimmer with heat.

He dropped a soft kiss on her neck, then nuzzled her ear. "I'll let ye in on another secret."

"I like your secrets," she replied in a breathless whisper. "Tell me."

He nudged the bottom of her chemise up with his wrist, to bare her bosom for the attention of his lips and tongue. "I'm just getting started."

"Oh, my. I don't know how much more of this I can stand."

Ewan lowered his head and swiped his tongue over the firm, roused flesh of her nipple. "I have great faith in yer powers of endurance, *muirneach*."

He only hoped his own endurance could match hers, long enough to bring her the pleasure she deserved.

Ewan loved her and wanted to marry her. Like seeds sown on parched, stony soil, those ideas refused to penetrate and take root, at first. Gradually, however, the warm rain of his kisses and the tender harrow of his touch began to make Claire's doubtful heart more receptive.

Step by sweet, seductive step, he coaxed her to abandon any lingering doubts she might harbor about her appeal as a woman—discarding them like pieces of clothing tossed onto the floor. And for each garment he removed, he gave something else to take its place—special kisses, caresses and whispered endearments, tokens of his desire for her.

How glad she was that he had not made love to her last night, after all, when her senses might have been muddled and her memory clouded by a haze of cider fumes. Now she savored each sensation, feeling beautiful and desirable and cherished for the first time in her life. His *muir-neach*.

She eased her tight control of the yearning that had simmered within her from the moment she'd glimpsed Ewan Geddes again. Kindled by his ardent attentions, that yearning swiftly gathered power and heat, until it consumed her in a brilliant blaze of rapture.

When Ewan hovered over her, she opened herself and welcomed him inside her. She found fresh delight in the swift hiss of his breath and the tightening clench of his muscles with every fevered thrust. Until a great shudder went through him and he quenched his cry of release in a long, deep kiss.

Ewan had not gotten any sleep the previous night, and Claire very little. Now, with desires sated and happiness finally within their grasp, they sank into deep, untroubled slumber.

A frenzied rapping on the door brought them both awake again, disoriented and alarmed by the racket. In the first confusion of waking, Claire groped for the edge of the bedspread, to cover herself. Then she glimpsed Ewan's bare chest and hard, lean thighs in the falling darkness and her flesh tingled with an aftertaste of ecstasy.

"Aye," Ewan called in a hoarse, impatient voice to whoever was on the other side of the door, "what is it?"

"Mr. Geddes," answered the young footman, "sorry to bother ye, sir. Would ye by any chance know where we might find Miss Talbot? Lady Lydiard is anxious to speak to her. We've looked high and low, but we can't find her anywhere."

Ewan rubbed his eyes as his lips stretched into a broad grin. Claire jammed her hand over her mouth to keep from betraying her presence with a burst of giggles.

"I reckon I know where I can find her." Ewan's tone sounded perfectly innocent. "Just give me a few minutes and I'll fetch her for ye."

"Thank ye, sir. I'll tell her ladyship. We were getting worried something might have happened to Miss Talbot."

As the footman's muted footsteps retreated

down the gallery, Ewan turned toward Claire, pressing her down onto the bed again.

"Something *did* happen to Miss Talbot," he whispered, then gave her a deep, luscious kiss that made Claire squirm with eagerness to take him inside her again. "I hope she isn't sorry it happened."

Even in the dim light of evening, she could make out the anxious set of Ewan's bold features. She could not bear to leave him in any doubt.

"Do I look sorry?" She ran one hand through his crisp dark hair, while the other skimmed over the firm, spare flesh of his flank in an admiring caress.

His body roused to her touch at once.

He brought the tip of his nose to rest against hers. "Ye look tempting as sin. But I reckon we'll get no peace until ye go find out what her ladyship wants. I wonder how she got here."

"Rode her broomstick?" suggested Claire, setting her pent-up laughter free.

More laughter sputtered out of Ewan until the bed trembled with their fruitless efforts to contain it.

"Hush, now!" said Ewan with a final chuckle. "Or somebody's going to figure out ye're here. Then ye'd have no choice but to marry me unless ye want yerself and Brancasters caught in a scandal."

He rolled off the bed and began to collect his clothes.

"What makes you think I'd mind having to marry you?" Claire caught her chemise when he tossed it to her, then slipped it on.

Ewan perched on the edge of the bed and began to pull on his own underclothes. "If ye decide to marry me, I want it to be *yer* choice. Not something ye were forced into, by me or anybody else."

To think she'd assumed he must be a fortune hunter! The lump of shame that swelled in Claire's throat almost gagged her. She knelt behind Ewan, wrapped her arms around his chest and lowered her head to rest on his shoulder.

"Thank you," she whispered.

He reached back and ruffled her hair. "I've got a lot to make up, not paying ye any mind when we were young."

Before Claire could reply, he bent forward to scoop her gown off the floor. He examined the tear that ran from the neckline halfway down the bodice. "I owe ye a new dress, too."

"I am at least as much to blame for that as you are." She snatched the gown from him and began to pull it on. "If you can lend me one of your coats to throw around my shoulders, and check the gallery to see if the coast is clear, I might get back to my room and change clothes without anyone being the wiser."

"Let's be quick about it, then." Ewan climbed into his trousers. "Before her ladyship gets tired of waiting and comes looking for you."

Claire shuddered to think of it.

By the time she had put on enough clothes to cover herself decently, Ewan was fully dressed and had a coat all ready to wrap around her.

"I'll go check out the hall." He gave her a last quick kiss, then slipped through the door, which Claire held slightly ajar behind him.

"All clear," he whispered, beckoning to her. "I'll go stand guard at the back stairs until ye get safely to yer room."

Pressing her fingers to her lips to hold in nervous laughter, Claire clutched Ewan's coat around her and bolted for her bedchamber.

Just as she was closing the door behind her, she heard Ewan's voice boom out. "Aye, I found her. She'll be along in a minute or two. How did her ladyship get here, anyway?"

She didn't have time to stand and eavesdrop, Claire reminded herself. Pulling off Ewan's coat, and her torn gown, she bundled them into the deepest corner of her wardrobe. Then she grabbed a shirtwaist she could wear without the aid of a corset, and dressed as quickly as possible.

After pinning her tumbled hair into a proper looking coiffure, she fortified herself with a deep breath and stepped back out into the gallery, where she found Ewan waiting for her. He looked her up and down with a gaze of blatant admiration—the kind that would have kindled only suspicion in her if any other man had stared at her that way.

He offered her his arm. "Ye're looking very well, Miss Talbot. Not a hair out of place. Nobody would suspect what mischief ye've been up to."

No doubt he was right. Anyone looking at her would see no change in sensible, business-like Miss Talbot. Yet she felt like a new person, with a changed attitude toward herself and the whole world.

"I doubt anyone would be surprised to discover *you'd* been up to mischief." A tone of fond flirtation sweetened her old tart banter.

Ewan greeted her words with a hearty laugh and an affectionate squeeze of her arm. "Aye, ye skewered me proper, lass! I should know better than to match wits with ye, but I can't help myself."

She tilted her head to rest against his shoulder. "I hope you'll never try."

A beguiling image rose in her mind of the two of them, years in the future, bantering over the breakfast table while several dark-browed, merry-eyed youngsters laughed at their silly mama and papa.

"Only, please don't make me laugh in front

of my stepmother," she begged him. "Lady Lydiard may think I've gone off my head, and try to have me committed to Bedlam."

Claire made a wry face, though she was not entirely in jest. Her stepmother was liable to take almost as dim a view of Claire's courtship with Ewan Geddes as she had of her own daughter's. She'd been counting on Claire to remain unmarried, eventually passing her vast fortune along to Tessa's children.

Halfway down the front staircase, Claire could hear the sound of voices from the parlor.

"In that case," said Ewan as he tried to disengage his arm, "maybe we ought to—"

"No." She clung to him tighter than ever. "I happen to be in love with you, and I don't care who knows it."

Another reason she was loathe to let him go, Claire could scarcely admit to herself, let alone Ewan. She had wanted him so long and with so little hope, she could scarcely bring herself to trust this sudden taste of happiness.

Would she wake up in her own bed, alone, to find it had all been a dream? Would Ewan come to his senses and realize it was her beautiful, high-spirited sister he truly cared for, after all? The solid substance of his arm provided a source of reassurance she could cling to when those kinds of doubts assailed her.

The low rumble of a man's voice carried from

the sitting room. Claire glanced toward Ewan, her brow raised. "Who could that be?"

"I reckon it's that Stanton chap. Glenna told me he and Lady Lydiard caught the train as far as Lyonsay, across the loch to the west. Then they hired a boat to bring them here. Her ladyship is an aye resourceful woman. I'll give her that."

They hurried toward the sitting room door, then stood for a moment, staring.

Lady Lydiard had, indeed, arrived.

She sat on the sofa, staring toward the big bay window, where Spencer Stanton was laying down the law to Tessa in a firmer tone than Claire had ever heard him use before. Tessa appeared to be taking his lecture with a surprising air of meekness.

"Have you any idea what could have happened to you?" Spencer plowed a hand through his hair. "Or how worried we were for your safety? I was quite frantic and so was your mother. You must promise me you'll *never* do anything like this again."

Tessa opened her mouth to reply, but before she could get the words out, Spencer spotted Claire and Ewan.

"Is this the scoundrel who had the gall to court you behind my back?" he demanded, striding toward them at a pace that alarmed Claire. "The one who sent you flying the length of the country all on your own, into heaven knows what kind of danger?"

Ewan raised his hand and answered in a peaceable tone. "Aye, I'm the scoundrel. But if ye'll just give me a minute to explain…"

Spencer must have decided the time for explanations had long passed. As he charged the length of the room, he'd pulled a glove from his pocket. Now he struck Ewan with it. "I demand satisfaction, sir!"

Ewan flinched from the blow. His hand closed over the glove and he tore it out of Spencer's hand. "Ye arrogant English ass! I'm the one who'll have the satisfaction of trouncing ye!"

"Ewan, no! Spencer, please!"

Claire tried to come between the two men as Tessa exclaimed, "A duel, over me? How romantic!"

A duel? How idiotic! Surely they wouldn't.

"Claire?" Spencer stared at her as if she had gone mad. "Don't tell me this blackguard has got his hooks into you, as well?"

"Watch who ye're calling a blackguard, Sassenach!" Ewan gave Spencer a shove.

"Do you know who this man is?" Spencer asked Claire, his finger pointed at Ewan.

Were people *always* going to harp on the fact that Ewan Geddes had once worked for her family? Claire began to understand her sister's impatience with such prejudices.

"Of course I know," she snapped. "Our acquaintance goes back a great many years."

"Then it doesn't bother you that he owns Liberty Marine Works, one of Brancasters' biggest rivals?"

"I know he works for—"

"Not *works for,* Claire—*owns!* When I returned to London, your Mr. Catchpole brought me a message from that investigator you'd hired. He had managed to delve a little deeper into this fellow's background."

"Ewan?" Claire drooped into a nearby armchair. "Is this true?"

"It is." Tessa piped up. "He told me so before I went to lie down. Not which company, just that he had an enormous fortune. He said he wanted me to come to America with him, because I'd be a perfect hostess and win all the grand society folk over, on account of my being the daughter of a peer."

She sounded altogether disgusted by the prospect.

Suddenly Claire's old doubts and suspicions returned to bedevil her—all the stronger for her fleeting glimpse of love and happiness. Had Ewan wooed her as part of some underhanded business dealing, to revenge himself upon Brancasters for her father's treatment of him? Had he wanted her as an entrée into American society when her sister had proven unwilling? Or was

there some other inscrutable reason, far easier
to believe than the preposterous possibility that
he loved her?

"Claire." Ewan knelt beside her and tried to
take her hand, but she pulled it back. "I'm sorry
ye had to hear like this, *muirneach*. I was going
to tell ye, I swear!"

"Bravo, Claire!" cried Lady Lydiard. "I see
your plan has worked perfectly!"

A bewildered silence greeted her words. One
her ladyship wasted no time filling. "Claire recognized you as a fortune hunter the moment she
laid eyes on you, Mr. Geddes."

Ewan leaped to his feet. "Fortune hunter?
What are ye blathering on about, woman?"

Had Lady Lydiard not heard Spencer's rev-
elation? Claire wondered. Or had she not understood what it meant? Whatever else Ewan
Geddes might want from her, he had no use for
her money.

Clearly her ladyship did not realize that, for
she continued in a tone of contemptuous triumph. "Between us, we contrived that the two
of you should come to Strathandrew by your-
selves. Claire predicted you would pursue her,
instead of Tessa, once you discovered her greater
fortune. Now that my daughter is safely out of
your clutches, Claire no longer needs to pretend
to be taken in by your wiles."

"I don't believe it," Ewan murmured, more

to himself than to anyone else in the room. "I mean I *do* believe it. What I can't believe is that I didn't see it."

He looked dazed, as if someone had clouted him hard on the head with a heavy object. Claire felt as if that had happened to her, too. His gaze fell upon her, a dark mirror that perfectly reflected her own hurt and anger.

Would he believe her if she tried to explain? Or should she salvage her pride by pretending her infatuation with him had all been a ruse?

Chapter Twenty

Claire had thought him a fortune hunter, had she? She'd strung him along to *protect* her sister from him?

As brutal truth battered down a cushioning wall of disbelief around his heart, Ewan felt the pressure of his temper rising, like a boiler with a stuck valve. Any minute it might explode, blowing his relations with the Talbot family to kingdom come.

And not a bad thing, either, if *this* was what they thought of him.

Lady Lydiard gave a haughty little sniff of triumph. "I suggest you pack your bags, Mr. Geddes, and quit this house at once. The sooner you return to America and leave this family in peace, the better it will be for all concerned."

Perhaps it would be, for him. At last he might

be able to put all this nonsense out of his mind and stop pining for things that could never be. He could turn his energy toward making a real life for himself in America, instead of just marking time by accumulating money. Before he left, though, he'd offer jobs to any of the Strathandrew staff who wanted to come and work for him.

Well, maybe not Mrs. A...

His gaze came to rest on Claire's stricken face. Would it be better for her if he went away—the one man who'd been prepared to love her for more than her fortune?

Perhaps she read that question in his eyes, for she mustered her composure and rose to address her stepmother. "May I remind your ladyship that Mr. Geddes is here at *my* invitation. He will continue to be welcome at Strathandrew until I say otherwise."

Was he hearing right? Ewan wondered. He told himself not to make too much of it. Like as not, Claire just wanted to put her toplofty stepmother in her place. Besides, why should he care whether she wanted him to go or to stay?

He'd swallowed his pride once already to confess his true feelings for her. He'd mounted a campaign to win her trust, like a new servant *on approval,* trying to win a permanent place in her affections. He wasn't about to slink off across the ocean before he had a chance to thrash all this out with her. He deserved an apology, or at the very least an explanation.

"Go!" He pointed at Tessa, her mother and her fiancé, then motioned toward the door. "All of ye. Now! This is between Claire and me!"

Spencer Stanton puffed out his chest like a stag challenged by a rival. Unlike wild harts, who tended to mill about meekly while the stags fought, the two women squawked in outrage.

"He's right." Claire herded them toward the door. "Go, now, please!"

"I shall be waiting just outside," Stanton assured Claire as he glared at Ewan. "If you need me, call out."

Ewan glared back. What did the Englishman think he was going to do—sling her over his shoulder and make off with her out the window?

"That won't be necessary," Claire insisted. "I can take care of myself."

For some reason those words stirred Ewan's sympathy against his will.

"Well!" Lady Lydiard pulled a handkerchief from her reticule as she swept from the room. "To think I should live to hear myself spoken to in that tone."

"Oh, Mother!" Tessa sounded thoroughly exasperated. She clutched Stanton's arm as the two of them followed Lady Lydiard.

Claire closed the door behind them all with restrained but resolute force. Then, after a moment during which Ewan sensed her gathering her wits and mettle, she turned to face him.

"You know," she said, "if you had told us all the truth about your fortune from the beginning, it would have saved everyone a great deal of bother."

Ewan braced for battle, ready to give as good as he got. "Would it have made any difference, Claire? Or would ye just have suspected me of something worse?"

Seeing a flicker of doubt cross her face, he knew he had scored his point. Before she could rally, he strode toward her. "Is that all this week meant to you—a great deal of bother?"

When he saw the anguish in her eyes, he felt like the scoundrel and blackguard Stanton had called him.

"This has been the happiest week of my life, damn you!" She flew at him, giving the lapel of his coat a token pounding with her fist. "Don't you dare make fun of it!"

"I'm not making fun, I swear." His arms closed around her and held her against him. "This week has meant more to me than ye'll ever know."

He intended to release her if she tried to pull away. But he could not let her go without one last embrace, however fraught with conflicting feelings.

To his surprise, she made no effort to draw back.

"Be fair." He nudged her chin with the knuckle of his forefinger. "Ye were the one who first said *bother*. What was I to think?"

"I don't know, Ewan." She shook her head. "What are either of us to think about any of this? I cannot blame you if you hate me for what I did…what I tried to do."

Her obvious remorse and her passionate admission that this had been the happiest week of her life went a great way to appease his wounded pride and cool his hasty temper. He tried to imagine himself in her place.

"I don't hate ye, Claire." He pulled her back down to the chair where she'd been sitting, then sank onto the ottoman at her feet. "I know ye were only trying to protect yer sister. If I *had* been after her fortune, it was a good plan."

He smiled, trying to ease the strain between them. But he could not coax an answering one from Claire.

"I know what it's like," he said, "when folks make up to ye just for yer money. That's why I didn't say anything about owning Liberty Marine. It may have been part of why I was so stuck on Tessa all over again—because she seemed to want me in spite of thinking I wasn't well off. It never crossed my mind she might want me *because* she thought I wasn't well off."

He shook his head. "A bonny lass, yer sister, but a strange one."

It wasn't much of a jest, Ewan would have been the first to admit. Still, it troubled him that his words did not bring even a ghost of a smile to Claire's lips. Had what he thought he'd found with her been so fragile that this foolish business was enough to shatter it beyond repair?

Ewan Geddes, pursued by female fortune hunters? Claire could scarcely believe it. Not that it was difficult to imagine women wanting him. But not for his money alone.

"I suppose I can see why you didn't want to let people know the true extent of your wealth."

Being able to understand and excuse his mild deception did not make her feel any better. Neither did the indications that he might be prepared to forgive what she had done. He was giving her credit for far more noble motives than she had truly acted upon. Much as she wished she could accept his pardon and move forward, she cared for Ewan too much to deceive him further.

"If your plan had occurred to me," she admitted, "I might have been tempted to pay a visit to America in hopes of finding a man who could love me for myself alone."

Ewan clasped her hands. He looked relieved, yet still vaguely worried. "I've saved ye all that trouble, haven't I? I've got more money than I know what to do with, so I couldn't possibly be after yer fortune."

"Nor I after yours." That was one thing she could offer him. But would it be enough?

"That's right, eh?" His smile was so infectious, Claire could not help but return it—a wan imitation at least. "And I'm pretty sure ye didn't take up with me just to vex her ladyship and shock all yer friends."

"I don't have many friends," said Claire. Then, in case that should sound too much like pity-mongering, she quipped, "And vexing my stepmother is only a fortunate by-blow."

Ewan laughed, though a shadow still lingered in his eyes. "Is it all settled between us, then, *muirneach?* I know we used to enjoy quarreling with one another when we were young. Now, I reckon we're both wise enough to see there's more fun to be had kissing and making up."

He raised one hand and tapped his finger gently against her lips. "What do ye say?"

"Of course!" The words burst out of her, though not in the cheerful tone they called for. "There's nothing I'd like better!"

"Then why do ye sound as though I've just tortured ye into a confession?"

"Because…" She might as well tell him the truth, before she lost her nerve or her remaining scrap of integrity. "…when I came up with that scheme to trick you into pursuing me instead of Tessa…"

"Aye? No wonder ye were so amazed when I jumped off the *Marlet*."

"Yes...well, I see now that my plan was nothing but...an excuse to get you for myself." She looked away, unable to face him.

"I reckon yer plan worked, didn't it." Ewan sounded more amused than anything. "Though not for quite the reasons ye intended."

"Ewan, didn't you hear me? I schemed to steal you away from my own sister, the way I stole that kiss you meant for her ten years ago!"

"So ye did. And I kissed ye—twice more—when I was supposed to be looking to marry yer sister. It seems to me we've both done wrong by poor Tessa, though I'm finding it hard to feel sorry for her. In the end, I think ye did her and me a favor by giving us some time to come to our senses."

"You don't think I'm quite despicable?"

"Oh, aye. Now and then. That business of flaunting yer jewelry." Ewan clucked his tongue. "And suspecting me of being a fortune hunter in the first place—that was low."

His teasing tone tempted Claire to smile, and to hope, in spite of herself. He angled himself around on the ottoman until she had no choice but to look him in the eye.

"Does it change how I feel about ye, though?" He pretended to weigh the matter, then flashed a roguish grin as he shook his head. "I've done my share of things I'm not proud of. I've misjudged folks. I've acted selfishly. I hope I've improved some with age, but I can't swear to it."

Ewan's common sense words touched and comforted her. Whatever foolish things she might have done in the past, falling in love with him had not been one of them.

He gave a rueful shrug. "I can't even promise I'll become some kind of paragon once you and I are together. Though I reckon it won't be so hard. Have ye ever noticed how much easier it is to be a better person when ye're happy and content with yer own life?"

"And you think you could be happy and content…with me?"

"Aye. Don't sound so doubtful about it. I reckon I could make ye happy and content with me, too, if ye'll give me a few more weeks to court ye proper."

"I will…on one condition."

Ewan raised one full emphatic brow. "And what might that be?"

"Call off this ridiculous duel with Spencer?" Claire clutched his hand tighter. She could not take the chance of something so needless and foolish destroying the happiness that was finally within her grasp. "Apologize to him or whatever you have to do to make him withdraw the challenge!"

She could tell, even before she finished speaking, that her plea was falling on deaf ears.

Ewan's forceful features clenched in a stubborn frown. "The challenge has already been thrown down and accepted. If either of us withdraws now, it means dishonor. Ye heard what names the man called me, Claire. I can't just let that kind of thing pass. It's a matter of—"

"I know! I know!" She jumped up and strode toward the window. "Your cursed pride. You said you have more of it than is good for you. Can't you swallow it just this once—for me?"

She shouldn't risk setting conditions, a part of her warned. Not when she stood on the verge of a whole new life and the kind of happiness she'd scarcely allowed herself to dream of. With a man—perhaps the one man in the world—who did not consider her too clever, too wealthy and too plain to love. The only man in the world she had ever wanted.

Ewan had already proved himself more forbearing than she deserved. She should not take any chance of frightening him off. But Ewan had also been the man who'd begun to convince her she deserved love and happiness. Even if she wasn't perfect. Even if they disagreed or quarreled.

"Think what could happen." Was she reminding Ewan—or herself? "If you hurt Spencer, or worse, you could go to prison. Not to mention what a catastrophe the whole thing could be for Brancasters!"

"Ah, that's what it really all comes down to, isn't it, Claire?" The harshness of his tone stung her. "In a choice between my pride and yer company, there's no real contest, is there?"

She whirled about to face him. "What if it were *my* pride and *your* company? Would you throw away something you worked so hard to build, just to satisfy some dangerous whim of mine?"

"It's more than a whim. Can ye not see that?"

She remembered the ring of pride in his voice when he'd told her about his ancestors and the history of Eilean Tioran. She recalled also the bitterness with which he'd told her of the clansmen being forced from their lands.

"I *want* to understand, Ewan—truly. It's just…" Claire struggled to find words that might sway him.

He crossed the room and took her hands in his. "Will ye just trust me…please? It'll be all right."

"You're certain?"

"I swear."

Steeling herself, Claire clutched his hands tight and spoke the most difficult words she'd ever uttered to a man. "Do what you must, then. I trust you."

* * *

"A duel!" grumbled Fergus Gowrie in the early hours of the next morning as he cleaned and polished an old pistol that had once belonged to Claire's father. "What's this place coming to, eh? Grown men wasting bullets on each other when there's game in the hills that needs culled."

In a corner of the keeper's workshop, Ewan tried to ignore the dour litany as he practiced his grip on another pistol that Fergus had finished cleaning. He raised and lowered the weapon several times, getting his hand accustomed to its weight. Then he practiced taking aim at an imaginary target.

Finally, he sought out an uncluttered strip of floor, where he rehearsed the whole sequence of movements. So many paces, followed by a smooth turn while raising the pistol. Then aim and pretend to shoot.

"Lairds' business, this," Fergus muttered as he tamped a bit of oiled rag down the barrel of the pistol he was cleaning. "Ye reckon ye're one of them, now, do ye?"

"I reckon I'm the same fellow who left here ten years ago, only with a sight more brass to his name." Ewan lowered his pistol and turned to face the gamekeeper. "This duel wasn't my idea, Fergus. I'd far rather shoot a grouse. Do ye think I should have backed down when the

Englishman challenged me? When he called me a scoundrel and a blackguard?"

Fergus made a vague rumbling noise deep in his throat. His scowl darkened further as he polished the pistol with fierce energy.

"It wasn't my choice to leave Strathandrew ten years ago, either." Ewan returned to his practicing...pace, stop, turn, aim, fire. All the while he continued speaking, as if to himself. "It was forced on me because I didn't have the power to stand up to them. Now that I do, I won't give it up."

"Humph!" Fergus held out the second pistol to Ewan. "See which balance ye like the best. And mind how ye hold the thing when ye fire. It'll buck like a bad-tempered pony."

"It wasn't my choice to go," Ewan repeated. "But I'm not sorry I went, and I'm not sorry I made something of myself."

The gamekeeper gave no sign he'd heard...or cared. But while Ewan compared the two pistols for balance and grip, he muttered, "I reckon ye'll need somebody to see that this duel business is all done proper?"

"Aye. I hadn't thought of that. A *second* it's called. Are ye willing to be mine?"

Fergus gave a curt nod. "If ye'll have me."

"Oh, aye." Ewan set down the pistols and extended his hand to the gamekeeper. "If I'm still here next week, do ye reckon we could scare up some grouse?"

Fergus mulled over the question, then nodded again.

A few hours later, on a level bit of ground overlooking the loch, Ewan faced Spencer Stanton, while the Talbot women watched from a distance.

Lady Lydiard looked altogether shocked and offended by the whole proceedings, for which she clearly blamed Ewan. Tessa appeared stirred by the drama of it all, with little regard for the possibility that one or both men might be injured. Pale and hollow-eyed, Claire looked worried enough for both of them.

"It'll be all right." Ewan nudged her cheek with his knuckle, trying to coax a smile from her. "Ye'll see."

"I know. I trust you." She spoke in a flat tone, as if reciting a difficult passage of scripture she'd taken great pains to memorize.

Suddenly she lunged toward him, pressing her lips to his in a fierce kiss. "But *do* be careful!"

Was he daft? Ewan asked himself as he and Stanton met in the middle of the field to choose their weapons. Risking everything he'd worked so hard to build, as well as something precious that had come to him by good fortune? All over a few words spoken in anger by a man he had wronged? Was there no way to satisfy honor without spilling blood?

Perhaps...but did he dare risk it?

The pistol was in his hand as he stood back-to-back with the Englishman. Captain Mac-Leod gave the signal to begin, then counted their paces.

...Eight...nine...ten.

Ewan stopped. He turned. He took aim. Then he raised the barrel of his pistol toward the sky and fired. Honor would be satisfied and conscience, too.

His shot rang out, echoed by another. Then a burst of pain knocked him to the ground. The next thing he knew, Claire was hovering over him, the moist warmth of her tears anointing his cheek and her slender fingers trembling as they caressed his face.

"Ewan, can you hear me? Please don't die, dearest! I've never loved any man but you and I can't bear to lose you again! If you live, I promise I'll marry you or do anything you want. Only please, please don't leave me!"

He knew how frightened she must be, and how desperately she must love him, to abandon the cultivated restraint of a lifetime and make such reckless promises.

"Hush, now, I'm not going to die." He forced the words through teeth clenched against the pain as he pulled Claire into a reassuring embrace. "Stanton only nicked me in the leg."

"Ye were a lucky young fool," muttered Fergus, pressing a flask into Ewan's hand. "It's bleeding some, but that's about all. Hold still while I wrap it."

As Claire clung to him, her tears mixed with frenzied laughter, Ewan choked down several swigs from Fergus's flask. By the time they'd carried him back to the house and settled him in bed, the pain in his leg felt dull and distant.

He gave a befuddled chuckle when Claire tried to wrestle him out of his coat. "Why, Miss Talbot, are ye taking my clothes off?"

"I am." She sounded like her brisk, capable self again, but her swollen eyes betrayed her recent anguish. "You're in no condition to do it, and you need to be comfortable to rest."

"Are ye going to ravish me?" He tried to mimic the innocent tone in which she'd asked him that question, not so long ago.

"I am not." She tried to look severe, but he could tell she was fighting to keep from laughing. "You don't deserve it, after the scare you gave me just now. Besides, don't you want to save yourself for our wedding night?"

Wedding? Her tearful pleas and promise came back to him.

"Hang on a minute, lass." There was something he needed to say, while he still had a few of his wits about him. He patted the bed beside him. "Sit down and let's talk."

"Very well." She perched beside him and began to untie his neckcloth. "What do you want to talk about? The wedding? You know Tessa is trying to persuade Spencer to marry her before we leave Scotland. After he chased her the length of England, then challenged you to a duel, she saw that his feelings for her were more passionate than she'd ever guessed."

"Aye, well, that's nice." Ewan struggled to marshal his skittish thoughts. "But about ye and me—I'm not going to hold ye to a promise ye made in the heat of the moment. Marriage is an important, lifelong enterprise. I want ye to consider it as long and as carefully as ye would any business decision. There are a lot of factors against us, ye know."

He started to list them off, but Claire leaned forward to hush him with a kiss. By the time she drew back, his head was spinning…and not just from the whiskey.

"We are two strong, determined people," she reminded him, gazing deep into his eyes. "We have thrived on challenges all our lives. Think what a brilliantly successful marriage we can forge, if we pool our forces in the enterprise of love."

"Since ye put it like that…" Ewan puckered his lips, inviting another kiss. "Are ye sure I can't change yer mind about ravishing me?"

Epilogue

"Are they ready for us, Mr. Catchpole?" Claire glanced up from adjusting the tartan sash Tessa wore over her wedding gown.

With their holiday at Strathandrew coming to a close, the sisters had decided upon a double wedding in Scotland. Lady Lydiard's brother would escort Tessa down the aisle, but since Claire had no near male relations, she'd wired Brancasters' head office, summoning her secretary to do the honors.

Now, Mr. Catchpole consulted his pocket watch, then cast a wary glance at the sky. "The last of the guests has just been ferried across from the estate, miss. I believe Mr. Geddes and the Honorable Mr. Stanton are anxious to begin…while the weather holds."

Claire rolled her eyes at her sister. "I still say

we should have held the wedding at the village kirk. Then we wouldn't be fretting over every cloud and breeze."

"But the ruins of a Highland castle make a far more romantic setting for a wedding." Tessa adjusted the circlet of late summer flowers in her sister's hair. "And there wasn't room in the poor little kirk to hold all the guests for one wedding, let alone *two*."

Under her breath, Claire muttered, "There might have been if your mother hadn't invited half the peerage."

Tessa picked up their bridal nosegays from a tumbled bit of castle wall and handed Claire hers. "As Mama says, at this time of year, half the peers of the realm are in the Highlands."

Catchpole removed his pince-nez, then immediately replaced it, as he was apt to do when flustered. The presence of so many titled wedding guests had taxed his composure to the limit.

Despite her show of impatience with Lady Lydiard's elaborate wedding plans, Claire was secretly delighted with the arrangements. In addition to thrilling Tessa's romantic heart, a ceremony held on Eilean Tioran also celebrated Ewan's Highland ancestry and demonstrated how proud Claire was to become his wife.

"Let's not keep everyone waiting, then," she said. "I can smell the wedding feast Mrs. Mc-

Murdo and Monsieur Anton have prepared for us. I expect our guests are anxious to sample it."

She took Mr. Catchpole's arm and thanked him once again for coming all the way to Strathandrew to give her away.

"It is an honor, Miss Brancaster Talbot. Your Mr. Geddes is a very lucky man to acquire such a bride. I told him so at the bachelor dinner last evening and he was quick to agree with me."

Claire chuckled. "I'm glad you approve of him."

The two men had immediately taken one another's measure upon Mr. Catchpole's arrival. Their obvious mutual respect had pleased Claire very much.

"And I suppose that's the last time you'll call me by those names. In a very short while I shall be Mrs. Geddes."

As the two fell in step behind Tessa and her uncle, Claire juggled her nosegay for a moment to smooth down her skirts. Lady Lydiard had been appalled when she'd announced her resolute intention not to wear a corset beneath her wedding gown. Claire could only imagine how scandalized her ladyship would be if informed of Ewan's threat regarding any future corset wearing.

A grin tugged at Claire's lips as she thought of it. But when the bridal party entered a large open area that must once have been the castle courtyard, and a distant piper began to play a stirring, majestic march, her eyes misted with tears of sweet, hopeful happiness.

In front of a great vaulted archway, Ewan and Spencer stood waiting with the minister—both wearing splendid dress kilts. In the past weeks the two had become better friends than Claire had ever thought possible for men who had faced one another on a field of honor. Perhaps the fact that they had *both* emerged victorious, each in his own way, contributed to their mutual respect.

The ceremony was short and simple, but very proper and dignified. And when Ewan fixed her with an adoring gaze and repeated his vows, Claire knew with wondrous certainty that in spite of her plain features, flat figure and tart tongue, she was his ideal of beauty.

After the wedding, the bridal couples were aboard the first boats heading back to Strathandrew for a gillie's ball to celebrate their nuptials.

"Toss your flowers!" a clutch of debutantes called to the Talbot sisters.

Tessa's nosegay sailed in a high arc, followed by Claire's.

Cries of disappointment rose from the young ladies when one bouquet landed in the hands of Glenna McMurdo, while the other came to roost upon Lady Lydiard's very elaborate hat!

As Jock McMurdo rowed them back across the loch, Ewan slipped his arms around his bride and whispered in her ear, "I stocked up on plenty of hard cider for the ball tonight. If all these lairds and ladies enjoy it as much as ye did, they'll be crying for it in London when the Season starts."

"Why, Mr. Geddes," cried Claire, throwing her arms around his neck, "you are a born businessman!"

He chuckled and pointed to the water. "I reckon it's not so different from being a gillie. Ye bait yer hook and keep casting it until ye land yer catch."

"Love is a little like that, too, isn't it?" Claire relished the warmth and constancy of his embrace. "It takes patience...and strength...and perhaps a little luck?"

"Aye." Ewan's eyes shone with affection and pride in her. "And I reckon I've made a fine catch, Mrs. Geddes!"

In the instant before he kissed her, Claire whispered, "I would say we both have...*muirneach*."

* * * * *

Have Your Say

ou've just finished your book.

o what did you think?

e'd love to hear your thoughts on our
ave your say' online panel
ww.millsandboon.co.uk/haveyoursay

Easy to use

Short questionnaire

Chance to win Mills & Boon®
goodies

The World of Mills & Boon®

There's a Mills & Boon® series that's perfec
for you. We publish ten series and, with ne
titles every month, you never have to wait
long for your favourite to come along.

Blaze.

Scorching hot, sexy reads
4 new stories every month

By Request

*Relive the romance with
the best of the best*
9 new stories every month

Cherish

*Romance to melt the
heart every time*
12 new stories every montl

Desire

*Passionate and dramatic
love stories*
8 new stories every month

What will you treat yourself to next?

Ignite your imagination,
step into the past...
6 new stories every month

NTRIGUE...

Breathtaking romantic suspense
Up to 8 new stories every month

Captivating medical drama –
with heart
6 new stories every month

ODERN

International affairs,
seduction & passion guaranteed
9 new stories every month

octurne

Deliciously wicked
paranormal romance
Up to 4 new stories every month

RIVA

Live life to the full –
give in to temptation
3 new stories every month available
exclusively via our Book Club